D1008984

... ...cious wit
—*Booklist*

"Candice Hern will make you laugh and cry . . . and then go back for more." —Sabrina Jeffries

"Ms. Hern brings historical details and witty characters to life. Pure fun!" —Judith Ivory

"Charming and emotional, with a story that drives straight to the heart, this is a winner, and Hern an author to cherish." —*Romantic Times*

"A must read! An uplifting affirmation of the healing power of love." —Mary Balogh

"Writing that sparkles! Candice Hern is a gem!" —Julia Quinn

"Hern has done a masterly job. . . . Charming and especially memorable." —*Library Journal*

In the Thrill of the Night

Candice Hern

A SIGNET ECLIPSE BOOK

SIGNET ECLIPSE
Published by New American Library, a division of
Penguin Group (USA) Inc., 375 Hudson Street,
New York, New York 10014, USA
Penguin Group (Canada), 90 Eglinton Avenue East, Suite 700, Toronto,
Ontario M4P 2Y3, Canada (a division of Pearson Penguin Canada Inc.)
Penguin Books Ltd., 80 Strand, London WC2R 0RL, England
Penguin Ireland, 25 St. Stephen's Green, Dublin 2,
Ireland (a division of Penguin Books Ltd.)
Penguin Group (Australia), 250 Camberwell Road, Camberwell, Victoria 3124,
Australia (a division of Pearson Australia Group Pty. Ltd.)
Penguin Books India Pvt. Ltd., 11 Community Centre, Panchsheel Park,
New Delhi - 110 017, India
Penguin Group (NZ), cnr Airborne and Rosedale Roads, Albany,
Auckland 1310, New Zealand (a division of Pearson New Zealand Ltd.)
Penguin Books (South Africa) (Pty.) Ltd., 24 Sturdee Avenue,
Rosebank, Johannesburg 2196, South Africa

Penguin Books Ltd., Registered Offices:
80 Strand, London WC2R 0RL, England

First published by Signet Eclipse, an imprint of New American Library,
a division of Penguin Group (USA) Inc.

First Printing, February 2006
10 9 8 7 6 5 4 3 2 1

Dedicated with love to my mother, who, though she may not realize it, provided the last key I needed to unlock this story.

ACKNOWLEDGMENTS

This book could not have come together without the help of my brainstorming partners, the Fog City Divas (www.fogcitydivas.com). Their help has been invaluable throughout. Thanks, ladies! And of course Greg, as always, contributed a brilliant insight or two, not to mention supporting me so I can write full-time. Thanks also to Ellen Edwards for her keen editorial eye and for helping to make this a better book. And to Annelise Robey, agent extraordinaire, whose support has been unflinching and much appreciated. And finally, I'd like to express my gratitude to Emily Cotler and her excellent team at Waxcreative Design, who continue to make www.candicehern.com a gorgeous and very cool Web site.

Chapter 1

London, March 1813

"How did I occupy my time during the winter?" Lady Gosforth spoke with a twinkle in her bright blue eyes as she addressed the other ladies in the room. "Delightfully, I assure you. I took a lover."

A collective gasp was followed by stunned silence. The Season's first meeting of the trustees of the Benevolent Widows Fund came to a dead halt.

Grace Marlowe, hostess of the gathering and chair of the Fund, spilled the tea she'd been pouring and her high-boned cheeks turned a horrified shade of pink. She quickly replaced the teapot on its stand, with a decided clatter, and covered her mouth with her hand. Lady Somerfield, a striking redhead in her midthirties, grew round-eyed and did not bother to hide a mouth that hung open in astonishment. She gripped the silver tongs in her hand so tightly that the lump of sugar they held was crushed into bits. The Duchess of Hertford, a handsome woman of indeterminate age with bright golden hair that might, or might not, have owed its brilliance to nature, chewed on her lower lip in an obvious attempt not to smile.

Mrs. Marianne Nesbitt, the youngest of the trustees at nine-and-twenty, simply stared. She could have been knocked over with a feather, the bald announcement had so surprised her. It was not the sort of thing one discussed calmly over tea. Or at any other time, in Marianne's experience. And it was certainly not to be expected from a group of respectable widows who ran a charitable organization.

The trustees were widows of means and traveled in the highest levels of Society, where they were all, or almost all, recognized as pattern cards of dignity and respectability. Before they got down to the business of planning their annual series of charity balls, their first meeting had begun with lively conversation as they caught up on news and gossip. They had talked of house parties and family gatherings, of holiday celebrations and hunt meets, of children and mutual friends. But not lovers.

Lady Gosforth, a pretty woman of about thirty with a halo of chestnut curls, rolled her eyes and clucked her tongue. "Oh, don't all of you look so shocked. You would think I'd committed a murder, for heaven's sake. It is not a crime to take a lover, you know."

Marianne was the first to recover her wits enough to speak. "Of course not, Penelope. You just surprised us, that's all."

"It is a private matter," Grace said in a tremulous whisper as she wiped up the spilled tea. "We should not speak of such things."

"Among friends?" Penelope frowned and the twinkle in her eyes faded into disappointment. "It is not news I want bantered about town, to be sure, but I thought at least I could share my happiness with all of you. I have been almost bursting with the news."

Marianne felt pity for her friend. She reached across the tea table and patted Penelope's hand. "Then you must tell us all about him. He must be a very special gentleman for you to be willing to give up your independence."

Penelope's brow furrowed. "My independence? What are you talking about?"

"We all agreed," Marianne said, "did we not, that the financial independence we enjoy as widows was to be treasured? And none of us—least of all you, Penelope—was anxious to relinquish her purse strings to another husband. But of course, none of that matters, I suppose, when one falls in love."

"Who said anything about a husband?" Penelope asked. "Or falling in love?"

"Oh!" Marianne said. "I just assumed . . ."

"Just because I take a man to my bed does not mean I'm going to marry him. Or that I'm in love."

Grace groaned and her elegant face scrunched up into a mask of flustered unease. "Penelope, please."

Marianne could not help but smile at Grace's discomposure. As the widow of a prominent bishop, Grace Marlowe was an exemplar of chaste propriety. The mention of a man and a bed in the same sentence must have been beyond mortifying for her.

Penelope clucked her tongue again. "Don't be such a prude, Grace. Women *do* take lovers now and then."

"Other women," Grace said. "Not us."

Marianne felt the same as she studied the other women seated comfortably around the tea table in Grace's elegant drawing room. Each of them was respected and admired, with an unblemished reputation. And then her gaze fell upon the duchess, who caught her eye. Marianne's cheeks flushed and she looked away.

The duchess cleared her throat. "Some of us do," she said.

Grace uttered a little squeak of distress. "I'm sorry, Wilhelmina. I did not mean—"

"You do not consider me as one of 'us.' I understand perfectly, my dear."

"Oh, no, that is not at all what I meant. *Of course* you are one of us. I just . . . forgot. Penelope's talk of . . . of such things has me all flustered. Forgive me. I meant no offense."

The Duchess of Hertford was the only trustee of the Benevolent Widows Fund who was not entirely respectable. Marianne knew, as all of Society did, that Wilhelmina had begun life as plain Wilma Jepp, daughter of a blacksmith. She was plain only in name and circumstance, however, and she set about to change both. Her incredible beauty had taken her far, eventually to a number of protectors that had included some of the highest-ranking members of the aristocracy, including, it was rumored, the Prince of Wales.

Her last and most loyal protector, the Duke of Hertford, had genuinely loved her. When his wife died, he married Wilhelmina, much to the shock and outrage of Society. If the Duke of Devonshire could marry his longtime mistress after the duchess died, then Hertford felt free to do the same. Or so Wilhelmina had once told Marianne. Hertford was dead now, but Wilhelmina still held the title and the fortune that came with it. She was reluctantly accepted at most *ton* events, though certain doors, as well as the court, were forever barred to her.

When Grace Marlowe had devised the plan for the Benevolent Widows Fund the year before, when the battlefields of the Peninsula had produced so many widows left destitute, she had shown remarkable openmindedness in inviting the very rich dowager duchess to become a trustee. Marianne and all the others had welcomed Wilhelmina warmly, not only for her vast fortune, but because they sincerely liked her. The wit and kindness of the duchess charmed them all, and her worldliness fascinated Marianne.

"It is quite all right, Grace," the duchess said. "No offense was taken."

"Grace is right, though," Lady Somerfield said, brushing bits of crumbled sugar onto a plate. "Taking lovers is not the sort of thing we do. At least I don't think we do." She looked up. "Do we?"

Grace shook her head vehemently. Marianne did

the same. Frankly, it had never occurred to her to seek out a lover. Once she had overcome the paralyzing grief of David's death just over two years ago, she had settled into a reasonably contented widowhood. She had never once entertained the idea of another marriage, and never would. It wasn't only about the independence she and her friends enjoyed. David had been the one great love of her life. He could never be replaced, in her heart or in her life, so a second husband was out of the question. It was important to Marianne to retain his name as a symbol of all he meant to her. But a lover? She had certainly never imagined sharing her bed with another man.

"We have our reputations to consider," Grace said. "And that of the Fund."

"For heaven's sake, Grace, no one beyond the four of you need ever know of my little indiscretion. He is not someone likely to show up at one of our balls."

"Who was he?" the duchess asked.

Penelope's face softened into a wistful smile. "He was the son of one of the guests at a house party in Dumfries. A perfectly gorgeous young man with a mane of golden red hair and a voice dripping in ripe vowels tinged with a delicious burr. I was lost the moment I set eyes on him. No, I did not fall in love, Marianne. It was pure . . . lust."

Grace sucked in a sharp breath. "Oh, my."

"And I haven't felt so alive in years," Penelope said, "not since the early days of my marriage to Gosforth. That young man was like a tonic to me." She gave a little laugh. "The dear boy was built like a stallion. What he could do with his hands, and his tongue, and his . . . my friends, it was positively sinful. I never had such powerful climaxes in all my life."

His tongue? Climaxes? Marianne felt a blush color her cheeks, and she suddenly felt as prudish as Grace. She had never heard anyone speak so frankly about the intimate details of sexual relations. It embarrassed her, but also excited her interest. Her experience with David, the man she'd loved more than life, was nothing like what Penelope seemed to imply.

"I had almost forgotten," Penelope continued, "what it was like to be loved, physically loved, by a man. But I tell you, ladies, we should never forget. Yes, we all decided we would not allow ourselves to be bullied by our families or friends to marry again. None of us wants to sacrifice our financial freedom. But does that mean we must sacrifice everything else? Must we also forsake physical pleasure for the rest of our lives?"

"But our reputations," Grace said, "are our most precious possessions and should never be sacrificed."

Penelope rolled her eyes heavenward. "That was true when we were younger, to be sure, when our virtue was a requirement of marriage. But we are widows, not virgins. The expectations are not at all the same. And there is such a thing as discretion. I'd be willing to wager no one at the Dumfries house party knew about Alistair and me. We were exceedingly careful to keep our affair private. Though I suspect some of the guests may have wondered about that extra spring in my step, that special glow about me. I certainly felt as if I was lit from within. So to speak."

"You *are* looking rather radiant, my dear," the duchess said, and then laughed aloud. The others joined her. Even Grace stifled a giggle.

It was true. Marianne had never seen Penelope in such good looks. There was a luminous quality about her—her eyes, her skin, even her hair, seemed to shine with happiness. Had a love affair really done that, made that much of a change in her?

"Thank you, Wilhelmina," Penelope said, smiling again. "I do indeed feel radiant. Young. Alive. It was such a marvelous thing, you see, that I wanted to share it with all of you, with my closest friends, and to encourage each of you to do the same."

"What?" Lady Somerfield exclaimed, laughter coloring her voice. "You want all of us to take lovers, too?"

Impossible, Marianne thought. Penelope could not be serious. Could she?

"Of course," Penelope said. "Why not? We talk of relishing our independence, our freedom." She looked at Lady Somerfield. "You most especially, Beatrice. You were the one, after all, who encouraged our little agreement to stand together against social and family pressures to marry again. None of us wanted to lose the freedom we'd gained as widows. Yet we have not allowed ourselves to be free in every respect." Feverish excitement brightened Penelope's eyes as she spoke. "We've become too steeped in propriety, too wrapped up in our mantles of respectable widowhood. Our husbands may be dead, but *we* are not. We are alive, with many long years ahead of us, God willing. Why should the rest of our lives be empty of pleasure just because we've lost our husbands? Must we yoke ourselves to new husbands in order to experience sexual fulfillment again? Or must we sacrifice sexual pleasure for the financial independence we all enjoy? No, I say. No! We can have both. We can have everything!"

No one responded to this extraordinary speech. Marianne wondered if they were all, like her, intrigued, even a little titillated, by Penelope's suggestion. Could they really enjoy that sort of freedom?

"Besides," Penelope continued, smiling, "it would do each of you a world of good. I guarantee it. Am I not correct, Wilhelmina? You know what I'm talking about."

The duchess chuckled and shook her head. "I do not think I should comment, if you please." Instead, she reached for a sweetmeat and took a bite.

"And what about you, Marianne?" Penelope asked. "David was a remarkably handsome man and I have no doubt he treated you well. Don't you miss him? In that way, I mean. Don't you miss having a man's arms around you at night?''

Marianne missed David in every possible way. Theirs had been an extraordinarily happy marriage, even though it had been arranged when they were both children. David had been the best of men, the best of husbands. But after she had suffered a series of miscarriages, he had feared for Marianne's health and had allowed their sexual relations, which had always been more tender than passionate, to dwindle into the occasional cautious coupling.

Having little or no hope of children—Marianne was quite sure she was unable to carry a child to term— was one more reason a second marriage had never been a consideration. Most men wanted an heir. David had, but when she could not provide one, he'd loved her anyway. One could not expect such compassion, such unconditional love, twice in a lifetime.

But to take a lover? Frankly, she did not see the point. Though she had enjoyed physical intimacy with David—for the most part, anyway—it was not the sort of thing she wished to repeat with someone else, just for the sake of doing so.

Not wishing to reveal the nature of her relations with David, Marianne simply shrugged in response to Penelope's question. She lifted the teacup to her lips, took a dainty swallow of tepid Bohea, and prayed Penelope would not press her on the matter.

"And what about you, Grace?" Penelope said, blessedly turning her attention away from Marianne. "Though the bishop was so much older than you, and ever so proper, he may have been a randy old goat in the bedroom, for all we know."

Grace gave a little shriek and her blush deepened to a dangerous shade of purple. It was too much. The image of the late, great Bishop Marlowe, orator extraordinaire, champion of the oppressed, frolicking in the bedroom with his young wife sent Marianne into whoops of laughter. The other ladies were equally amused, and poor Grace had to contend with several minutes of uncontrolled merriment.

Finally, wiping her eyes, Penelope looked to Lady Somerfield. "And you, Beatrice. You cannot tell me Somerfield did not teach you the pleasures of the bedroom. He was a notorious libertine in his youth. Surely you must miss his lovemaking."

Beatrice took a deep breath and her countenance sobered. "Not that it is any of your business, Penelope, but I do miss it. I miss *him*. I do not miss having a man rule my life, to be sure. But when he wasn't making me want to throttle him, I was quite fond of Somerfield and I will confess that I often miss the closeness we shared, the intimacy, the warmth. It simply never occurred to me to . . ." She shrugged and shook her head.

"It never occurred to any of you," Penelope said. "Wise Wilhelmina excepted. Frankly, it never occurred to me, either. Until Dumfries. And I tell you, ladies, we have been fools to ignore that aspect of our lives. We can keep our financial independence as widows and still find fulfillment as women. I stand before you as proof that it can be done. I've never felt better in my life, and I can promise you that I will no longer be so quick to rebuff a gentleman's advances. If it's the right gentleman. And because you are my friends and I wish for your happiness as well as my own, I must encourage you to follow my example."

"You want us all to take lovers just because you did?" Beatrice scowled as she stared at the cup of tea she seemed to have forgotten about, and retrieved the silver tongs again to reach for the sugar. "Will it perhaps make you feel better about what you've done if we all do the same?"

Penelope lifted her chin. "I assure you that I have no guilt to assuage, and harbor no regrets, if that is what you are suggesting. I am only encouraging you to find a lover because I know it will make you happy. It will rejuvenate you, invigorate you, make you feel like a girl again. Don't you want to feel desirable? Don't you want a man to make you feel beautiful again? Yes, of course, all of you are very beautiful women, but what good does it do you to hear it from me? How much more satisfying to hear it whispered in your ear while a man's hands caress every beautiful part of you?"

"Penelope!" Marianne said, more intrigued than outraged. "You are incorrigible."

"Am I? Or am I just speaking out loud the thoughts every one of you has entertained at one time or another? Ladies, we are all friends, and as friends, we should be able to speak frankly with one another, even about such private matters. To be honest, I have been burning with the need to talk with someone about my affair. I cannot keep such excitement bottled up inside me. So here I am, confessing my little transgression without the least remorse, and with every hope that I can repeat it again soon. And hoping the same for all of you." She clapped her hands together with glee. "We must find lovers for each of us. Even Grace. Especially Grace."

"I could never do that," Grace said, busying herself with a mote spoon as she cleaned the teapot spout. "Never."

"Don't be so sure," the duchess said. "If the right man came along . . ."

Grace shuddered visibly. "Never." She kept her eyes down, not looking at any of them, as she refilled the pot with hot water from the silver urn at her side.

"Poor Grace," Penelope said. "That shudder of yours speaks volumes. The old bishop wasn't so randy after all, was he? A bit of skillful lovemaking from a handsome young man would do you a world of good. But I see you are not yet ready to loosen those tight stays of yours, even for a moment, so I will not press you. What of the rest of you? Marianne? Beatrice?"

"What, exactly, are you asking of us, Penelope?" Beatrice asked. "That we each make a promise to seek out a lover?"

"Yes!" Penelope bounced with enthusiasm and clapped her hands together. "A pact! A real pact this time. A secret pact, just among the five of us."

A secret pact? To take a lover? The notion both disturbed and excited Marianne. Could she ever agree to such a thing? Did she want to?

"Not me," Grace said. "Do not expect me to become party to some sort of improper agreement."

"Yes, my girl," Penelope said, wagging a finger, "even you. Our pact shall be that we give ourselves permission to break out of those self-imposed restrictions of respectable widowhood and truly live as independent women, in control of every aspect of our lives. And that means if an attractive man catches our eye, we are free to act on that attraction. We will, of course, be discreet. In public. But among ourselves, we should feel free to be as indiscreet as we want. In fact, I believe each of you shall be required to share every delicious experience, as I have done. No detail will be considered too intimate."

They looked at one another, all save Wilhelmina apparently as stunned, and fascinated, as Marianne at what was being suggested. Could they really do it? Could they be that candid about things most people never discussed at all? Assuming they actually found lovers. Marianne felt a rush of anxiety, as though she was about to be initiated into a secret society she had no desire to join.

"We once made another sort of pact," Penelope continued, "to lend our support to one another if our families attempted to pressure us into an unwanted marriage. Let us simply extend that pact with a promise not to judge or censure and scold one another

about our lovers, but to offer good, solid female understanding and encouragement. Among friends. What
do you say?"

Marianne's uneasiness lifted. She could do this. No
one was making her promise to find a lover, which
she could not imagine doing. "You are only asking us
to be open-minded, then. I am willing to do that. Grace,
even you could promise as much."

"I suppose so," Grace said, though a skeptical
frown marked her elegant brow as she poured fresh
tea for everyone.

"So long as we keep it to ourselves," Beatrice said,
"*strictly to ourselves,* then you have my promise as
well."

"And mine, of course," the duchess said with a
wicked smile. "This should be interesting."

Penelope beamed at the group. "Wonderful. But I
challenge you all to take our pact a step further. I say
we should each *actively* seek out a lover."

"What?" Beatrice exclaimed.

Marianne shook her head.

"You go too far," Grace said.

"Oh, do not worry, Grace. I am pleased enough to
have your promise not to scold the rest of us as we
dip our toes in sensual waters. Though it would delight
me if you did, I do not expect *you* to take a lover.
Beatrice, what about you? Are you ready to accept
the challenge? To make a true effort to find a lover?"

Beatrice laughed. "It will be a challenge, indeed.
Chaperoning my niece, Emily, in her first Season, is a
time-consuming enterprise. I swear we must have every
evening booked for the next three months. That girl
is determined to land a husband before summer. And
my two girls are forever underfoot, impatient for their
own Seasons. I cannot imagine how I could squeeze
an affair into my schedule."

"But you will keep an open mind?" Penelope
prompted. "And an open eye?"

"I promise to do my best," Beatrice said, and gave a wistful sigh. "All that talk of stallions and hands and such does indeed remind me of my dear Somerfield and what I've missed since he's been gone. It would be nice to . . . well, it would be nice."

"Excellent. And you, Marianne?"

Oh, Lord. What could she say? Stallions and such certainly did not remind her of David. The marriages of Penelope and Beatrice had obviously been quite different from her own. It was a bit of a revelation to Marianne that perhaps the physical intimacy she'd shared with her husband was not as fulfilling as it might have been. Had she in fact missed something essential, something wonderful?

She gave herself a silent scold for such a disloyal thought.

"I am willing to support the rest of you," she said, "if you decide to take lovers. I am not so sure I am ready for that step just yet. It seems . . . I don't know. A betrayal of David's memory, I suppose."

"Did you sleep with other men while he was alive?"

Marianne uttered a gasp of outrage. "Of course not."

"Then you have not betrayed him," Penelope said. "Listen to me, Marianne. We all loved our husbands and would never have been unfaithful to them while they lived. But they are gone. We are no longer bound to them. I certainly do not feel I have besmirched the memory of Gosforth by taking a lover three years after his death. And I do not believe David would have wanted you to pine away in cold solitude for the rest of your life."

"You are too young for that," the duchess said.

Despite Penelope's logic, Marianne was not entirely sold on the idea. For one thing, she did indeed still feel bound to David. She always would. But she had never intended for her own life to be a shrine to his memory. She missed him, she grieved for him, but she enjoyed being alive. She had a rich and contented life filled with friends and charity work and Society events. But she was willing to admit it might not be as full a life as it could be. She gazed at Penelope's radiant face.

"I suppose you are right," she said. "I just never thought about it before. It's all so new. You must give me a little time to consider the matter. Besides, I am not at all sure how I would go about it."

The duchess smiled at her. "You must find the right man."

"Easier said than done," Beatrice said.

"Well, it should not be just anyone," the duchess said, her green eyes flashing with amusement. "Pay closer attention to the gentlemen at our balls, for example. When you see an attractive man, look him straight in the eye. If he looks back in a way that makes your toes curl up inside your slippers, he is a likely candidate."

"Oh, my," Grace said.

"The most obvious candidates," Penelope said, "are those men well-known for their amorous adventures, the most notorious seducers. Cazenove and Rochdale." Her eyes brightened with gleeful excitement. "Which of us shall have them?"

Adam Cazenove? Oh, no. Not Adam. He was Marianne's dearest friend in the world. Though he'd had a string of lovers over the years, it seemed odd and unsettling to imagine him with Penelope or Beatrice.

"Have a care, my dear," the duchess said. "Lord Rochdale is a bit too public with his seductions for my taste and not always honorable, I'm told, though it is true he is said to be quite skillful in the bedroom."

Marianne would not be surprised to learn that Wilhelmina had firsthand experience with Rochdale's bedroom skills.

"Cazenove is a much more attractive subject, in my opinion," the duchess continued.

Good heavens. Had Wilhelmina been with Adam,

as well? An image of his beautiful hands on the duchess, of her beringed fingers in his long hair, sent a shudder across Marianne's shoulders.

"He should be a convenient candidate for you, Marianne," the duchess said. "That is, of course, should you decide you want to get into the game after all."

Marianne laughed aloud at the very idea. "Yes, he is conveniently situated in the house next door to mine, but he is also a very close friend. I would never dream of violating that friendship. Neither would he."

Adam Cazenove and David had been the best of friends, more like brothers, in fact. They had bought the adjacent town houses on Bruton Street at the same time, shortly after David's marriage to Marianne. The second-floor balconies adjoined, and the two men had made a game of leaping back and forth over the balcony railings whenever they wanted to share a bottle and a bird, or a game of cards, or simply good conversation.

Adam had become as good a friend to Marianne over the years, and remained so since David's death. In fact, he still climbed over that second-floor balcony railing to visit her in her private sitting room. It was as though that boyish prank somehow kept David's memory alive for him. She could not remember the last time Adam had used the front door.

But to take him as a lover? Impossible. He was an exceedingly attractive man and she had a great deal of affection for him, but she had listened to enough tales of his love affairs to know that she was the last sort of woman he would find desirable. Not to mention that he thought of her as a sort of sister. No, he was too good a friend ever to be considered as a lover.

"Well, if you are not interested in him," Penelope said with a grin, "I'm sure he would do very nicely for one of the rest of us. He is certainly the sort of man who could make a woman's toes curl."

Good Lord. It would be beyond awkward if one of

the Benevolent Widows was to take Adam to her bed. Marianne had no desire to hear from one of them the intimate details of Adam's lovemaking.

"But if you change your mind," Penelope said, "and decide that friends make the best lovers, then you must tell us. We cannot poach on another woman's territory. That should be one of our rules."

"Absolutely," Beatrice said. "No poaching. But there are lots of other available men besides Adam Cazenove and Lord Rochdale."

"Sir Neville Kenyon, for example."

"Or Lord Hopwood."

"Harry Shackleford."

"Lord Peter Bentham."

"Sir Arthur Denney."

"Trevor Fitzwilliam."

"Lord Aldershot."

That last suggestion had come from Grace. When all eyes turned in her direction, her cheeks flamed and she gave a sheepish little smile. "I can get into the spirit of the game, can I not, without actually participating?"

The ladies stared at her in astonishment for a moment. Then one after the other they burst into laughter.

"Of course you can!" Penelope said, and reached across the tea table to squeeze Grace's hand. Turning her attention to the rest of the group, she said, "You see? I knew this was a good idea. Why should men have all the fun? We shall be just as merry as they. In fact, that's what we shall be: the Merry Widows."

Penelope stood and held up her cup of tea, and the others joined her, Grace included. "To the Merry Widows," she said. Marianne and the others tapped their delicate porcelain cups together in toast.

"The Merry Widows," she responded.

And so it began.

Chapter 2

Adam Cazenove leaned against the black iron railing of his second-floor balcony. Light shone from Marianne's sitting room window next door, but he hesitated before hoisting himself over the railing and onto her balcony. He had done it a hundred times before. It had been something of a running joke between him and David Nesbitt. Why walk down two flights of stairs, across the few steps between one front door and the next, then up another two flights of stairs when their two sitting rooms were virtually side by side? It was so much simpler to climb over the railing.

But not for Marianne, of course. And since her company had become as dear to him as David's, Adam had most often been the one to do the climbing. And he continued to do so, even after David was gone.

Yet tonight he hesitated. He had been away for several months and wanted nothing more than to see Marianne's face again, and yet it was not a visit he anticipated with the usual excitement. He had news, important news, to tell her. But once he had done so, things would be forever changed between them, and so he stalled.

He leaned against the railing and watched the flickering candle in her window. He remembered all the times the three of them had spent together in that room, laughing over Adam's amorous adventures, talking until dawn about art or music or politics or Society gossip, crying over their failures to have a child. And he remembered the times after David's sudden death when he and Marianne had clung together in grief, and all the times since, as she'd valiantly put her life back together. His late friend's memory still loomed large between them, but Adam treasured his friendship with Marianne for its own sake.

But he suspected they would never be as close again. Not after he told her.

The air was growing damp. If he dawdled any longer, he'd be soaked. He looked up and down the street to ensure no passersby would witness him sneaking into Marianne's house. He glanced at the windows of the houses across the street, looking for peering eyes behind curtains. He never saw any, but would not be surprised to learn his comings and goings over the years had not gone unnoticed.

He hooked a bootheel on the lowest crossbar of the iron railing and swung himself up and over onto the adjacent balcony, taking care to avoid the spearlike finials on the upright bars.

He saw her at once. Marianne sat in her usual chair by the fireside, wrapped in a large paisley shawl. She had a book in her hand but was not looking at it. She had obviously not heard his approach, for she did not stir.

Glossy brown hair, dark as Turkish coffee, was pulled back into a loose knot at the nape of her neck. Her face stood in profile, showing to advantage the straight nose, the sharp line of her jaw, and the high angle of her cheekbones. She wore a wistful expression as she gazed into the fire.

Adam straightened his coat and rapped on the window glass.

Marianne turned and smiled, revealing the dimples he admired, so unexpected in such an elegantly modeled face. Leaving the shawl behind, she rose and opened the balcony doors.

"Adam!"

She stretched out both hands and he took them, bringing each to his lips, then placed a chaste kiss upon her upturned cheek.

"I am so glad you are back," she said. "I have missed you."

"And I you. How are you, my dear?"

"I am fine, Adam. Do come in and sit down. We have much to catch up on. And I've just bought a small Varley landscape I wish to show you."

"Which Varley brother?"

"Cornelius. I haven't even hung it yet. Pour yourself a glass of claret while I go get it."

He placed a hand on her arm. "I'll see it later, if you please. There is something more important to discuss."

Her eyes grew wide. "Indeed?"

"Yes. I have news, my dear."

"Then you must tell me at once." She gazed at him quizzically for a moment, then smiled. "Should I be seated for this?"

"Perhaps you should. It is rather big news, I fear."

Her brows lifted in interest. Then she returned to her chair beside the fire and wrapped the shawl about her shoulders. "I am positively agog, Adam. Tell all, if you please. What is this big news?"

He took a deep breath and plunged ahead. "I have quit the field, my dear. I have just come from two weeks in Wiltshire, where my future was settled. Wish me happy, Marianne. I am officially betrothed to Miss Clarissa Leighton-Blair."

Marianne stared at him, making a supreme effort to keep her jaw from dropping open in a stunned gape. She should not be so shocked. She had known it was going to happen eventually.

But the Leighton-Blair chit? Had he gone mad?

"Well, well. I confess you have shocked me to the core, Adam."

"Have I?"

She shook her head in disbelief. "I had no idea you were seriously pursuing Miss Leighton-Blair. You never mentioned any plans to visit her family in Wiltshire."

She wondered why he'd neglected to mention it. Had he known she would disapprove? Of course he had. How could he have expected otherwise? Marianne did not know the girl well, but had seen enough of her last Season to know she was exactly the wrong sort of wife for Adam. Clarissa was a beautiful young girl, but the thing that most came to mind was her giggle. Every other word was punctuated with that annoying titter. And the words in between did not exactly sparkle with wit and intelligence.

What was he thinking? Adam was a man who thrived on lively conversation, even debate and argument. It was difficult to imagine him with a giggler.

"Her father invited me to a house party," he said, "and the motive was obvious. But since I had decided to take the plunge anyway, and since Clarissa is really quite lovely and sweet, I allowed myself to be swept along by their expectations."

"Allowed yourself?" Marianne pressed a hand to her forehead in exasperation. "I cannot believe that. You would never give over such a momentous decision to someone else. Is there something you're not telling me? Did you get the girl with child, Adam?"

"No!" He ran agitated fingers through his hair. "Good God, Marianne, you know I don't dally with innocent young women. How could you imagine such a thing?"

"It is the only reason I can possibly imagine for you getting betrothed to such a girl."

He frowned. "The *only* reason? Don't be naive,

Marianne. And what do you mean, 'such a girl'? She's extraordinarily beautiful."

"And without two thoughts to rub together. She will bore you to death within a month. Blast it all, Adam, I never expected you to put beauty above all else. I simply cannot believe it."

His frown deepened and he looked away to gaze into the fire. His sandy brown hair fell, as it always did, into a deep wave over one eye, giving him a rakish, almost piratical air. Adam made a show of trying to tame his thick hair, ruthlessly combing it straight back from his forehead, but to no avail. He might have cut it shorter, of course, but Marianne secretly believed he rather enjoyed the inevitable parting of the waves, that he knew quite well it made him more attractive. The poet's hair, along with the heavy-lidded, slumberous green eyes, lent him an air of seductiveness that many women found irresistible. Many, many women.

He could have had anyone.

He turned those eyes on her once again, and they were filled with consternation. "I had thought you'd be pleased for me, settling down at last. And you're being unfair. She is not as empty-headed as you suggest. Clarissa is very sweet-natured. She will make a fine, dutiful wife to me and mother to our children."

The intense look in his eyes seemed to implore her to agree with him, as if her approval was important. She understood that. If she had become betrothed, she would want Adam's approval. He was the same age David would have been, four-and-thirty. It was time he settled down.

But with Clarissa Leighton-Blair?

The recent discussions with her fellow Fund trustees, the Merry Widows, still rang loudly in Marianne's head. All that joyful talk about the pleasures of the marriage bed brought to mind unsettling images of Adam eliciting such joy from young Clarissa.

When Penelope and Wilhelmina had mentioned him, she had not wanted to entertain such images of Adam with one of them. But at least they were intelligent, interesting women. This new image of the beautiful, silly Clarissa—would the girl giggle in bed?—was almost too much to bear.

When the Merry Widows had made their pact, there had been the merest twinge of an idea—not even an idea, just a tiny whiff of a notion, a fleeting fantasy so brief she'd not even acknowledged it—that the only man she would ever consider as a lover was Adam Cazenove. It was foolishness, of course. Even if she were interested in a love affair, which she was not, Marianne knew she was not his sort of woman. Adam's taste ran to the exotic, the voluptuous, the openly sensual—as different as they could possibly be from Marianne's slender frame, ordinary English face, and conventional reserve.

And yet, Clarissa Leighton-Blair was not his usual type, either.

"I am sure she is very sweet," Marianne said, "but she is not the sort of woman I expected you to marry. She is not at all like your . . . your other women."

"A man looks for something different in a wife."

"Why? Why would you not want someone who excites you, who challenges you, who makes you a better person?"

"Dammit, Marianne, what makes you think Clarissa will not be all those things to me?"

She snorted. "Please. I've watched the girl. I've heard that giggle. I am sorry to be so negative. I know I should be pleased for you. But you are my dearest friend, Adam, and I want you to be happy. I want you to have what David and I had."

"You are too romantic, my dear. Not all marriages are as perfect as yours was. You and David were companions as well as lovers. Friends and equal partners. It is a rare marriage that is so fortunate."

"And you are being cynical. Surely you at least hope for that sort of marriage."

"This is not a love match, Marianne, but I am quite fond of Clarissa and I am certain affection will deepen over time. But she is not . . ."

"What? She is not what?"

"Like you." He smiled. "A termagant who does not know when to curb her tongue."

She should not have spoken in so unguarded a manner to him. She ought to have kept her thoughts to herself. She managed a smile. "Then you are to be congratulated, my friend, on a brilliant match. Making off with the prettiest girl of the Season will certainly make every other gentleman green with envy." She tried to keep sarcasm out of her voice. She really tried. "Bravo, Adam. Well done. We must toast your happiness."

She rose from her chair and walked to a small table upon which a decanter and glasses were set out. She poured the wine, and turned to find him standing close behind her. She gave a little start as her arm brushed against his chest. An unexpected tingle danced up her shoulder and down her back.

What was wrong with her? Just because, for the tiniest instant, she had imagined him as a lover, she was now very much aware of him in a physical way. Damn the Merry Widows for planting that seed in her brain. She should be grateful he was soon to be married. It would put an end to any further fanciful imaginings.

She gave him a glass, then held up her own in toast. "To Adam and Clarissa. May you have a happy life together."

"Even though I know it pains you to have said it, I thank you for the good wishes." He clinked his glass against hers, then swallowed the contents in a single gulp.

Marianne, who'd taken a more dainty swallow, chuckled and said, "Bridegroom nerves? Already?"

He held out his glass as she refilled it. "Nerves? Me? Nothing of the kind. Merely a bit of fortification as I enter this new phase of my life."

Marianne smiled at his attempt to appear cavalier. Adam often donned a mask of fashionable ennui when he wanted to hide his true feelings. She wondered what he was thinking now. Was he hoping he'd made the right decision? Had he acted too fast? Was Clarissa the right woman? Could he make her happy? Would she make him miserable? Poor Adam. His mind must be in turmoil over such a momentous change in his life.

Her own thoughts were racing, as well. Everything was going to change between them. He would move Clarissa into the house next door and would never climb over the balcony again. No wife would stand for her husband's climbing into another woman's boudoir. Would Clarissa allow their friendship to continue at all? Or was Marianne about to lose her closest friend?

She took the decanter and placed it on the candlestand beside his chair. Let him get roaring drunk if that's what he needed. Any man about to marry the giggling Miss Leighton-Blair would need fortification. Perhaps she would join him. It might help assuage the unexpected pang of sadness that threatened to overcome her.

Adam helped her move the pair of wing chairs so that the candlestand and its wine stood between them, within easy reach. She curled up in the big chair with her feet tucked to one side. He settled into the other chair and crossed one leg languidly over the other. It was the way they often sat here together, cozy and comfortable by the fire, once three of them, now only two. Would Clarissa make it three again? Marianne doubted it. She took a hearty swallow of claret.

"I must confess I am still a bit overwhelmed by this turn of events," she said. "I really had no idea you were seriously interested in Miss Leighton-Blair."

"I wasn't certain about it myself," he said. "She caught my eye last Season, to be sure, but when I spent more time with her in Wiltshire, my interest was definitely piqued."

"How did that trip come about?"

"You have listened to me complain for years now about having to endure my father's constant pleas for grandchildren. At Christmastime, he claimed to be at death's door, declaring loudly that his heart could go at any time. He said he wanted to die content in the knowledge that his name would continue through the sons he hoped I would sire."

"Poor man. Is he quite ill, then?"

Adam chuckled. "The man's heart is sound as a bell. He has the strength of a plow horse, the old devil. He was only trying to force my hand, and I decided it was time to stop fighting him and give him what he wanted. Besides, I have never intended to remain a bachelor my whole life. It was time I got serious about settling down."

"I would think the selection of a bride would be an equally serious business."

Adam gave a frustrated sigh. "It was. It is. I began to ponder who might be considered as a prospective bride when, quite serendipitously, I received the invitation to visit the Leighton-Blairs in Wiltshire."

"Her mother, no doubt, noted your interest last Season."

"Yes, I'm sure she did. And there is no need for that contemptuous tone of voice. Mrs. Leighton-Blair is no different from any other hopeful mama trying to secure a suitable match for her daughter. I was wide-awake to her intentions. I was not entrapped, no matter what you may wish to believe. I was . . . am, in fact, very much attracted to Clarissa, so I accepted the invitation, knowing full well what it implied. But I went to Wiltshire thinking she just might serve my purposes very nicely, and I discovered that to be true.

She may not be clever or witty or given to elevated conversation, but she is very gentle and warm and amiable. She suits me, Marianne. I like her. She will make a fine wife, even if it is not a love match."

Did he really believe that? Was he so infatuated he could not see how it would end? Marianne feared he would not realize he'd made a profound mistake until it was too late. Perhaps it was already too late. A gentleman could not honorably break off a betrothal. It was one of the few advantages Society allowed women over men: the right to change one's mind.

It would do no good, therefore, to try and talk him out of it. The deed was done. Marianne would have to learn to live with it.

She frowned. "Even if it is not a love match, I hope you will at least try to love her, try to make a true partnership of this marriage. I cannot believe you would be happy without love and companionship."

He smiled. "I will visit you whenever I require sensible companionship."

But would his young wife allow him to do so?

She almost spoke her concern aloud, but kept her tongue between her teeth. She'd said enough already. If she continued to express her disapproval, it would only make things unpleasant between them. That was something she did not want to do, not when this might be one of the last times they would share a cozy evening together by the fire in her sitting room.

"What are your plans?" she asked, in as cheerful a tone as she could muster. "When is the big day?"

"We haven't yet discussed a date for the wedding. Clarissa wants to enjoy the Season first."

"You will be the busy escort, then."

He groaned. "I suppose so. But it is her right to enjoy one last carefree Season before settling down. Things will be different for her after the marriage."

Things would be different for all of them.

*   *   *

"You're not wearing your brooch today." Lavinia Nesbitt's brows knit together in a deep frown. Then she returned her attention to the needlework in her lap.

Marianne silently cursed herself for forgetting the mourning brooch with David's golden hair woven in an intricate pattern beneath the glass. She always tried to wear it when visiting his mother. Damn. She ought to have remembered. Relations with her mother-in-law had been strained at best since David's death, which was a source of great sadness for Marianne, who had no other family of her own. She had no siblings and both her parents were dead. Lavinia Nesbitt had taken Marianne into her home after Marianne's father had died, and had provided a welcome haven of warmth and comfort. She would always be grateful for that.

There was no warmth or comfort anymore, however. Lavinia would never be convinced that Marianne was not somehow to blame for David's death. She believed that if Marianne had notified her more quickly of his illness, she could have rushed up to town from the estate in Kent and nursed him back to health. But it had happened too fast and there was nothing anyone could have done to save him. The putrid sore throat had brought on a debilitating fever, and he was gone within days. But Lavinia truly believed her presence would have made a difference, and no one could disabuse her of that notion.

"I'm sorry, Lavinia, but the brooch did not suit this particular dress, so I left it off today."

Lavinia let out a disdainful little huff. "If you still wore mourning instead of bright colors, it would suit well enough."

"Oh, for heaven's sake, Mother." Evelina Woodall, David's sister, was seated beside Marianne on the settee, and she reached over and gave her arm a reassuring pat. She was a few years older than Marianne and had the same fair good looks as her late brother. "It's been over two years. Marianne is far too young to swathe herself in black for the rest of her days."

Lavinia looked up and scowled at her daughter. The words "like you" hung unspoken in the air between them. William Nesbitt had left Lavinia a widow fourteen years ago, and she still dressed in the unrelieved black of full mourning. Marianne had felt the force of her mother-in-law's disapproval when she had changed to half-mourning a year after David's death. When she had retired her black gloves entirely after another six months, Lavinia had never forgiven her. She saw it as a betrayal of David's memory. The notion of betrayal, combined with her belief that Marianne was at least partially to blame for his death, along with her disappointment that Marianne had failed to produce a child to carry on David's blood, meant the two women who had once been close would never be so again.

"Besides," Evelina said, interrupting Marianne's reverie, "I would hardly call that lovely blue spencer a bright color. It's a fetching style, Marianne. Do you have a new modiste?"

"No, this is Mrs. Gill's design." She sent her sister-in-law a grateful look for changing the subject. "She still suits me, so I have seen no reason to seek out another dressmaker."

They spoke for several minutes on the latest fashions and fabrics, but Lavinia broke in, as she always did, to steer the conversation to a topic that involved David. She was determined that Marianne's weekly visits would remind her of her duty to David's memory.

"I trust," she said, "that David's gallery is making progress in locating paintings for the summer exhibition. I have sent orders for the Reynolds to be brought up from Kent. It was his favorite painting, you know. I think he would be pleased to have it displayed in his gallery."

Evelina laughed. "It is not David's gallery, Mother. It belongs to the British Institution."

"Of which he was a governor."

"Yes, along with several other connoisseurs. It was not his alone."

"But you are right, Lavinia," Marianne said. "He would be very pleased. He thought more highly of Reynolds than almost any other British painter, and always felt he was important enough to warrant a retrospective exhibition. And to have his favorite painting included will be a fine tribute. I have also been able to convince several other friends to send portraits from their country estates. It will be a wonderful exhibit."

"How unfortunate, then, that he did not live long enough to see it," Lavinia said, casting Marianne a withering look. "And I have no doubt that wretched Cazenove fellow spoke against the exhibit. Thank goodness the other governors are more of David's mind on such matters."

Marianne winced. David's mother had always disapproved of his friendship with Adam. Lavinia never understood the bond between them, never understood how someone so unlike David could have become his closest friend. And the fact that Adam had been with him when he died, and his own mother had not, only made her dislike him more.

"Adam has his own taste in art," Marianne said. "It is not the same as David's, to be sure, but it is a connoisseur's taste just the same." Adam was a passionate collector of modern art and a patron of several artists. His taste in art reflected the way he'd lived his life: impulsive, intuitive, slightly reckless. He loved the wild, frenzied paintings of Fuseli, and the restless movement of light and color in Turner's work. David's taste had been more conventional and analytic, just as his life had been more cautious and conservative. Poussin and Claude were his models of perfection; Benjamin West was his favorite contemporary artist. But each of the two friends had appreciated the other's eye for a good painting.

Marianne had become caught up in their passion for art and over the years had developed her own preferences. She had a partiality for the brushwork of Thomas Lawrence, but preferred watercolor paintings most of all. David had encouraged her interest by patronizing the best painters in watercolor and presenting her with frequent presents of their work. Though the public rooms of the Bruton Street house were adorned with the classical works David preferred, the walls of their private sitting room were filled with the watercolors of Payne and Girtin and Cotman and the Varley brothers.

"And remember," Marianne said, trying to improve her mother-in-law's perception of David's best friend, "that Adam endowed the Nesbitt Prize in David's honor. We must surely be grateful for that."

"It was a magnificent gesture," Evelina said. "Nothing could have been more appropriate."

David and Adam, both art-mad when they returned from a tour of the Continent during the brief peace of 1802, were among the founders of the British Institution, which had its own gallery in Pall Mall and hosted two major exhibitions of paintings each year. The spring exhibition provided a facility for living artists to display and sell their work. This was Adam's purview. The summer exhibition displayed old masters, David's passion, and students and amateurs were provided with an opportunity to study and make copies. The governors devised a series of prizes based on an idea once suggested by Reynolds—instead of painting laborious copies of old-master works, each student was asked to paint a companion piece. Prizes had been awarded since 1807, and last year the first Nesbitt Prize was added to the list.

Adam could not have better honored his friend.

"In any case," Lavinia said, "I look forward to the Reynolds exhibit, even though it will break my heart that David cannot be there to see it. When it opens, I trust you will lend me your arm, Marianne, so that we can both enjoy the legacy of David's gallery, and be reminded of his generosity and vision."

Evelina caught Marianne's eye and then lifted her own gaze to the ceiling in silent exasperation. "I must be off," she said, and rose from the settee. "I need to stop by the lending library and return a book. Will you walk with me, Marianne? I'd appreciate the company."

"Of course."

Marianne stood and shook out her skirts, grateful for an excuse to leave. While Evelina sought out a footman to retrieve their bonnets and shawls, Marianne bent over Lavinia and kissed her raised cheek. After a few parting words, she walked out the front door with her sister-in-law.

"I'm sorry Mother is still being so difficult," Evelina said as they walked along St. James's Square.

Marianne shrugged. "I have grown accustomed to her behavior."

"But it still hurts?"

Marianne sighed. "Yes, it does. I just wish she did not expect me to be a martyr to David's memory." For some reason, her mother-in-law's attitude was particularly aggravating today. It made her feel constrained and stifled, jittery and on edge. Marianne had the irrational desire to burst out of those constraints and do something reckless. Something rash.

Like acting on the Merry Widows' pact. She had not been able to get it out of her mind for the last few days. She still was not sure she could ever do such a thing as take a lover, or even if she wanted to do so. But the notion had grabbed hold of her and would not let go. Marianne smiled to consider what Lavinia would think if she acted on that silly pact.

"What else can you expect," Evelina said, "from a woman who's worn widow's weeds for fourteen years? Don't take her too much to heart, Marianne. No one else blames you for casting off your black dresses after a year. Any other widow would do the same."

"David often spoke with sadness, and even a bit of frustration, about your mother's inability to move on with her life. I like to believe he would not have wanted me to wear my widowhood like a shroud, as Lavinia has done."

"Of course he would not. You're a young woman, Marianne. You must get on with your life. Live for today and for tomorrow. Do not waste time pining after yesterday. It will only make you bitter and lonely, like Mother. You are too young and too lovely not to live life to the fullest. Have you thought of marrying again?"

"Good heavens, no. I cannot imagine ever being married to anyone else."

"Perhaps it is too soon. But I expect you will change your mind one day. You will want to find happiness again."

"I doubt I will change my mind, Evelina. And there are many other ways to find happiness."

Evelina stopped and stared at her, then flashed a broad smile. "Indeed there are."

Oh, dear. Marianne knew exactly what she was thinking, and it wasn't what she had meant at all. "I have the Benevolent Widows Fund, for example, which gives me a great deal of pleasure and satisfaction."

Evelina chuckled and said, "Yes, there is pleasure and satisfaction in that, *too,* of course."

Marianne felt a blush color her cheeks. Evelina was beginning to sound just like Penelope. Or was it simply that blasted pact again that made her imagine sexual undercurrents in every conversation?

"Please do not worry about me," she said. "I promise you I am not lonely or unhappy. At least, not very often. I am quite busy most of the time."

"I am glad to hear it. But you cannot blame me for wanting to see you have more. Someone to love. Children, perhaps."

As they walked through Green Park, she went on to speak of her own children and some of their recent antics, while Marianne's mind wandered back to the pact and the conversation with her friends. Until that day, she had never given much thought to physical relations with a man. She'd had a good marriage, but the physical aspect was never the most important part of it. Yet, since listening to her friends talk about the joys of the bedroom, she had become more and more convinced that she'd missed something, that David, who'd been the love of her life and the perfect husband, may not have been the perfect lover.

They walked past a man and two women who stood beside the gravel path in conversation. Marianne noticed the man surreptitiously touch one of the women on her lower back. It was a fleeting touch, but the woman straightened ever so slightly, and brushed a hand against his hip. There was an air of intimacy about those brief touches that Marianne would never have noticed before the Merry Widows had altered her perception.

As they walked past the threesome, they came upon a man on horseback in polite conversation with a woman whose maid stood a few steps behind her on the path. As they neared, Marianne could hear they were speaking of a new pantomime at Drury Lane, but their eyes seemed to hold a different conversation altogether. The woman had the same sort of incandescent glow they'd all noticed about Penelope. Was the horseman her lover?

What nonsense. She was being foolish, seeing lovers everywhere these days. It was all Penelope's fault,

blast the woman. But it seemed a great many people
were living a fuller life than Marianne. Evelina with
her devoted husband and children. Penelope with her
young lover. Even Adam, whose life was about to become more full with his ninny of a fiancée and doubt-
less the onslaught of children.

Marianne really had nothing to complain about.
She'd had a great love, even if it was cut short, and
would never marry again. But did that mean she had
to end up like her mother-in-law, her life a sad memo-
rial to her late husband?

No, by God, it did not.

"Marianne? Have you heard a word I've said?"

She had not, in fact. She shot Evelina a sheepish
look. "I'm sorry. My mind was wandering."

Evelina smiled. "In an interesting direction, I trust."

"I was just thinking about something we discussed
a few days ago at a meeting of the trustees of the
Benevolent Widows Fund."

Thinking hard about it, in fact. Marianne began to
wonder if the Merry Widows' pact was not such a bad
idea after all.

Chapter 3

Adam watched as Marianne paced the sitting room. This wasn't going as he'd expected. She was clearly distracted. Something other than his betrothal was on her mind.

He'd climbed the balcony again tonight to talk this out once more with her. He hated that she was so upset about his engagement to Clarissa. He'd given a lot of thought to her reaction to the news. He'd been angry that she'd been so quick to judge. Yes, Clarissa's conversation was less than brilliant and her education was limited to the usual feminine accomplishments. But he liked her, dammit. She was sweet and quiet and very innocent. That innocence—something of a novelty for him—was one of her attractions. She was a beautiful girl and he had visions of all that white skin laid bare for the first time just for him.

He wanted to make Marianne understand his decision. He disliked being at odds with her. But she barely paid him any attention.

"What is it, Marianne? What is troubling you?"

She stopped pacing and looked at him. "Nothing is troubling me. It is just . . . there is something I want to tell you and I don't know how."

"You may tell me anything, my dear, as you well know. Has something happened?"

She gave an odd, sheepish little grin. "Not yet."

"Tell me, then. What is it?"

Marianne chewed on her lower lip for a moment
and furrowed her brow, as though measuring the
words before speaking. Her fine brown eyes sparkled
with suppressed excitement, and he realized that whatever she had to tell him, it was not something dreadful. She had the air of a child with a rousing good
secret, and looked much younger than a woman approaching thirty. It had been a long time since he'd
seen this side of her—not since David's death, in
fact—and Adam was utterly charmed as he watched
her.

She walked back to her favorite wing chair, retrieved the ubiquitous paisley shawl, and wrapped it
around her shoulders as though girding herself for bat-
tle. Standing tall, she looked Adam square in the eye
and said, "I am going to take a lover."

Adam stood stunned and silent for a long moment.
A lover? David's wife was going to take a lover? It
was the very last thing he might have expected her
to say.

"You are shocked," she said. "I suppose I should
not have blurted it out like that. Perhaps you should
sit down." She took her seat by the fireside and nodded toward the matching wing chair on the other side
of the hearth that had been "his chair" for as long as
he could remember.

"Yes, perhaps I should." He took the chair and sat
rather stiffly, too tense for his usual comfortable sprawl.
A small knot of anger tightened in his gut. "This is
rather big news, is it not?"

"Are you disappointed?"

It was something of an understatement, though he
was not sure why this news should affect him so
strongly. He supposed it was that he'd always thought
of her as David's woman. To imagine her in another
man's arms was almost blasphemous.

"Do you think less of me for wanting to take a lover?"

"My dear Marianne, I think the world of you, as you know, and nothing could ever make me think any less of you."

"You do not believe it to be a betrayal of David's memory?"

Adam fell silent. It was precisely what he thought, but it seemed churlish to say so. Especially since he knew it to be an irrational, emotional reaction. David was dead, after all.

"You *do* believe it." Her hand balled up into a fist and pounded the arm of the chair. "Blast it all, Adam, I thought you, at least, would understand. You are acting just like Lavinia Nesbitt."

"Good God. Do not tell me you made a similar bold announcement to David's mother."

She snorted in disgust and glared at him. "Of course not. I am not *that* stupid. But apparently you want me to spend the rest of my life as a martyr to David's memory, just like she does."

Did he? Adam did not want to think so. What had he expected? That she would remain alone, and possibly lonely, for the next forty or fifty years? As he looked at her, he realized how ridiculous a notion it was. Marianne was a strikingly beautiful woman. Naturally other men would want her. Hadn't he always harbored a twinge of attraction for her himself? But she'd been David's woman, and always would be.

"No, I don't want that for you," he said. "I am sorry, but it is difficult for me to imagine. . . ."

A blush colored her cheeks. "You don't want to think of me with any man but David."

Adam shook his head. "It's a difficult notion to get my brain around, that's all. The two of you are inextricably linked in my mind. It's hard to think of you without him."

"But he's gone, Adam. It's not as though I'm planning to be unfaithful to a living husband. You know I would never have done that. But David is dead. I wish everyone would stop thinking that I am, too."

"I've never thought of you as dead, Marianne. And I don't want you to be a martyr to David's memory. Frankly, I'd assumed you would marry again one day. You're still a young woman, after all."

"I have told you I have no intention of marrying again."

"So you have said. But I must tell you that this business of a lover is likely to be a mistake. It will lead to nothing but heartache for you."

She frowned. "How can you say such a thing? You cannot know that, and it is very presumptuous of you to make such a statement."

"Do you remember what David said to me just before he died?"

Her shoulders hunched inward, cringing at his words. "I find it difficult to remember anything of that day."

"He told me to look after you. And that's what I'm doing. He would not want you to plunge into a potentially disastrous love affair."

Her chin lifted a notch and her eyes narrowed. "But recollect what he said to me. This I *do* remember. He told me to be happy. I couldn't imagine it at the time. My heart was breaking and I could not conceive a happy future without him. But when he knew he was dying, he told me not to waste my life in grief, as his mother had done. 'Be happy,' he said. Well, that's what I'm doing. Taking a lover will make me happy."

"No, it won't. Trust me in this, Marianne. I have much more experience in these matters. You are not the kind of woman to casually give her body to a man. You could never be content with a mere love affair, or a brief dalliance. You will always want more, need more, of a man than that."

"You presume to know what would make me content?"

"I know you."

"I wonder. Do you?"

Adam stared at her in astonishment. Did he? Had he never really known her as well as he'd thought? He could recite her opinions on art and literature and politics. He knew she had a passion for lemon ices and that she preferred her tea with milk and no sugar. He knew where she banked and what investments she held. But did he know her heart?

He thought he did. He knew how much she'd loved David, and how devastating his death had been for her. He knew the efforts she'd made to come to terms with it and make a life on her own. But he did not know what she felt when she lay alone in her bed at night.

He reached out and touched her hand. "Listen, Marianne. I know you are missing David. You had a warm body curled up beside you every night for eight years. You are missing that perhaps most of all. But if you take a lover, he will only get dressed and leave you alone in your bed again. Why not look for a new husband instead? David would understand that better than a lover."

"I don't want another husband. David was the one true love of my life. He can never be replaced in that way for me. Besides, it is likely I can never bear a child, and a husband will want an heir."

"A man who loved you would not care about that."

"But I do. And besides, if you know me so well, then you would know that I am quite serious. I've decided to take a lover, and that is the end of it."

One thing he did know about her was that once she made up her mind about something, it was difficult to shake her determination.

"Then we will both have to accept each other's decisions, will we not? I will take a wife and you will take a lover. Though we both seem to think the other is making a mistake, let's try to move on. Our lives are changing, but I hope we can still remain friends."

She reached across and laid her hand over his. "Of course we can. I have already decided I was too quick to judge Miss Leighton-Blair. I have determined to become her friend, too."

Adam turned his hand over and grasped hers, then brought it to his lips. "Bless you, my dear."

She gave an odd little shiver and gently pulled her hand away. Another blush colored her cheeks. How very interesting. Having spent years seducing women, Adam knew the signs well. But Marianne had never reacted to him physically before now. It must be all the talk about lovers.

"So tell me," he said, "how did all this come about? This business of taking a lover." It was really the last thing he wanted to know, but he could sense she was fairly bursting to tell him and so he offered an encouraging smile.

She gave a little shrug and suddenly looked bashful. "I'm not sure I can explain," she said. "You know I am not interested in marrying again. But that doesn't mean I . . . that I shouldn't . . . that I don't . . . oh, blast, you know what I mean, Adam."

He did indeed. She missed having a man. She missed sex. Of course she did. How could he have been so stupid not to have realized she still had desires—desires that were not being fulfilled?

"I believe I understand," he said, and flashed a teasing grin. "But you really ought to have mentioned it sooner. I would have been happy to oblige, you know." More than happy, if he'd ever thought for a moment she would have considered it. Or if he could have done it without feeling he'd betrayed his best friend. "It is too late now, unfortunately, for me to do so. Now that I am betrothed to Clarissa."

She returned the grin. "Yes, what a pity."

"And who, may I ask, is the lucky fellow?"

"I have no idea."

What?

"You don't know?" He shook his head to jiggle loose anything that might have blocked his hearing. "Forgive me, Marianne, but I am afraid I don't understand."

"It is simple, really." She adjusted her position in the chair and wrapped the shawl about her knees, looking like a young girl full of life, not a dried-up widow. Of course she wanted to experience physical pleasure again. She was too vibrant to ignore it. "I have realized there is no reason to sacrifice that aspect of my life," she said, "just because I do not wish to marry again. So I have decided it would be nice to have a lover. I just haven't yet decided who he will be."

Adam understood her needs, and reluctantly applauded her open-minded attitude. Even so, he experienced a tiny glimmer of hope that since no man had been chosen, the whole idea could be squashed before it became a reality. It was a selfish notion, to be sure, but he did not believe he could bear the thought of her in another man's arms. In his mind, she still belonged to David, the finest man Adam had ever known. Marianne had loved him, and he'd been thoroughly besotted with her. Adam had been secretly jealous of their happiness together, the joy they found in each other.

As a witness to that joy, he found this idea of an unknown lover problematic at best.

"Remember," she said, "when I told you that all of us in the Benevolent Widows Fund had agreed we were content to remain widows? How we enjoyed our independence and were not looking for marriage again?"

"Yes, I remember."

How could he forget? It had been made very clear to him that she would never consider a second marriage. At the time, he thought she must have believed he might make her an offer. Perhaps she imagined that he felt she needed someone to take David's place, and who better than himself? Her announcement about never wanting to marry again had seemed aimed directly at him, to preempt any awkward, and apparently unwanted, declarations.

Adam had never, in fact, considered offering for her. No, that was not entirely true. When he told his father that he was going to seriously consider marriage, Marianne was the first woman to come to mind. But only for an instant. Yes, he had a great deal of affection, even love, for her. But as a friend. She was David's wife to him, and always would be.

Besides, even if Adam thought for one moment that she would entertain an offer from him, he was not sure he wanted it. She had known a great love with David, and would spend the rest of her days grieving for him. Adam was sensible enough to realize that marriage to her would be a constant and unbearable heartbreak, as he knew he could never fill that hole in her life. And even if she allowed him to try, it would always seem a sort of betrayal of David. Like stealing his best friend's wife. Silly, of course, since the man was dead, but there it was.

"Anyway," Marianne continued, "just because I don't wish to marry again shouldn't mean I have to give up . . . everything. Should it?" She dropped her gaze and flushed a delightful shade of pink. "I only want a bit of pleasure."

Of course she did. Damn him for a fool for not realizing it sooner. He might not be able to replace David in her life, but he could have offered this. If he were not betrothed to Clarissa, would Marianne have considered him for the part? Would he have offered?

"I do wish you had decided upon this course sooner,"

he said with a seductive smile as he refilled both their glasses. "What a pity you waited until I had betrothed myself to another woman. Otherwise, I would have been happy to provide you with all the pleasure you could possibly imagine." He gave her a slow wink. "I know a thing or two about pleasing a woman."

She pulled a face and turned away, and he realized that she did indeed know that about him, knew of his history with women.

He'd been very candid over the years in her presence, trusting her with the same confidences he'd shared with David. He was very much afraid, unfortunately, that she had sometimes heard rather ungentlemanly, even coarse, remarks about the women in his life. He'd had a shocking number of lovers, but he had never had a serious relationship, or one that lasted very long. Most of his liaisons were highly charged sexual encounters that burned out quickly when he became bored. No woman kept his interest for long. In fact, his friendship with Marianne was the longest and most satisfying relationship he'd ever had with a woman.

But to imagine he could take that friendship further was absurd. He was surely the last person she would have considered as a provider of sexual pleasure. He was a fool even to tease her about it. But joking about it was the only possible way to get through this awkward discussion.

That, and more wine. He took another swallow.

Marianne looked up at last and smiled. "I am very much aware of your expertise," she said, dimples twinkling at him, charming him, "which is why I feel bold enough to admit my plan to you. I would like your advice."

He stifled a groan. "Advice?"

"Who better to help me find the right man to show me the full pleasures of physical love?"

Dear God.

"And who better to instruct me in the most effective way to entice such a man . . . into my bed?"

It was too much. He emptied the decanter into his glass and tossed back the wine in a single swallow.

"Who better," she continued, "than a man of the world? A man of vast experience in such matters. A man like you."

Who indeed?

"You want me to help you find a lover?"

Put so bluntly, it did sound rather ridiculous. Marianne suddenly felt very foolish for even mentioning the idea. What had possessed her to do such a thing? She still could hardly believe she'd decided on this course. But in her mind's eye she had seen Penelope's glowing face on one side and Lavinia's dark martyrdom on the other. There was no question about which of the two faces she wanted to wear.

"Forgive me, Adam. I should not have asked. I just thought . . ."

What had she thought? That he'd do exactly what he teased her about? That he would step in and do the job, providing her with "all the pleasure you could possibly imagine"? She was quite sure he could have followed through on such a promise. One had only to look in those green eyes to know it. She was almost glad his betrothal precluded such an arrangement. He knew her well enough to realize she would never seek intimacy with another woman's man.

"You thought I was your friend," he said, "and would help you, as friends do. So, how can I help you?"

She was not entirely sure. But since the last meeting of the Fund trustees, she realized she was not as experienced in the bedroom as she had thought. She did not even know what she did not know. And that was what excited her about this whole business. What would it be like to be physically intimate with a man again, intimate in ways she could not even imagine? It sometimes thrilled her to think of it, but just as often frightened her.

"Well," she said, "David is the only man I . . . well, you know. I never . . ." She felt her cheeks flame with embarrassment. She could not believe she was having this conversation. "Oh, Adam, I just don't know how to go about this. I don't know who would be a good . . . who would know how . . . damn it all, I don't know anything. I don't know how to find the right man."

Adam shook his head. "If you expect me to tell you which man would make the best lover, then you're out, Marianne. I'm sorry, but that is asking too much. How should I know something like that? You'd be better off asking another woman." He grinned. "The duchess, for example."

She had thought about talking to Wilhelmina, but became too tongue-tied to do so. And yet here she was, having just such a conversation with Adam.

"You are right," she said. "I shouldn't be bothering you. It's just . . . well, it's not all about what a man does in the bedroom."

He arched a brow. "Is it not? I thought that was the whole point."

"Yes, but I also need a man who will be discreet. I don't want my name bandied about at the clubs or, God forbid, mentioned in the betting books. I would like my privacy respected."

"A gentleman of honor, then," he said. "I would expect nothing less. And what else?"

"I do not want a man with an eye to marriage, or an eye on my fortune. It must be someone willing to accept me on my own terms."

"A physical relationship only?"

"For the most part. No entanglements."

"A man of the world, one who covets your body but not your fortune." His hooded gaze followed the line of her hips and thighs, sending a sudden flush of heat through her veins. "That should not be difficult. And what else?"

Damn the man for looking at her like that. She had become much more aware lately of the words and looks and touches that passed between men and women. She had known Adam most of her life, knew him to be a seducer of women, but he had never turned those bedroom eyes on her in such a provocative way. Or had she just never noticed?

She gathered her composure and smiled at his feigned insolence. "Well, it would be nice if he was handsome, of course."

He laughed. "Of course. A handsome gentleman of honor with some skill between the sheets who is content with an uncomplicated affair. The field narrows. And what else? A man of fashion?"

"I do not think that is important. He should be presentable and clean, naturally, but I doubt a man overly concerned with his wardrobe would be an appropriate candidate."

"Quite right. No pinks of the *ton*. Too absorbed in themselves to do right by a woman. What about fortune?"

"That should not be a consideration," she said.

"And age?"

"Hmm. I had not thought of it. I suppose it would not serve the purpose for him to be in his dotage."

"Certainly not. The fellow must be able to perform, after all. And an old roué would not suit you." He gave an exaggerated shudder. "So, we are looking for a gentleman who is handsome, discreet, and not given to dandified ways, who offers no entanglements, and is still vigorous enough to satisfy a woman's needs. Have I got it right so far?"

She grinned and realized that he had put her entirely at ease by making a game of the whole business.

"Yes," she said, "that sounds about right to me. And also—"

"Egad, there's more? My dear, if you become too particular in your tastes, you risk narrowing the field to the point where there is no man left standing."

"But, Adam, this hypothetical man and I will spend a great deal of time together, and not just in the bedroom. There ought to be more than just . . . *that,* shouldn't there? I would like a man I can talk to, a man who has a way with women, a man I can enjoy being with."

A man like you.

"A gentleman with both conversation and charm," he said.

"Yes, that's it."

"A tall order, my dear. And, of course, none of it matters if the chap is not also a skillful lovemaker. Correct?"

"Yes, I suppose that's true. Oh, Adam, I know it sounds foolish and you are merely teasing me, but I just want . . ."

She could not admit it aloud, not to Adam, but she wanted that excitement and passion Penelope talked about. She wanted what her friends had experienced. Just once in her life.

Adam knew what she wanted, probably better than she did. And yet, out of sheer perversity, he seemed determined she should not have it. What man could possibly be worthy of her? And how could any man hope to measure up to David Nesbitt, who was no doubt as talented and skillful in the bedroom as he was at everything else he did?

Poor Marianne was doomed to disappointment.

Adam did not lack confidence in his own sexual prowess, and thought he just might be able to best the memory of David in that particular arena. Now that it was impossible to put that confidence to the test, he was strangely loath to see any other man make the attempt.

"All teasing aside," she said, "would you be willing to advise me on whether certain men would . . . meet my needs?"

"You have someone in mind?"

"Actually, I have a list."

"Good God, a list? Damnation, Marianne, this will require more wine. Do you by chance have another bottle at hand?"

"You know where to find it."

He did indeed. She still kept it in the deep bottom drawer of the kneehole desk in the corner, where David had always kept a ready supply. Adam retrieved a bottle and uncorked it. Without bothering to decant it—this business of a list of potential lovers could not wait for such niceties—he carried the bottle with him and set it on the candlestand between them. He topped off her glass before refilling his own.

After taking a restorative swallow of claret, he said, "You have a list."

She reached for the book she'd tucked beside the seat cushion and retrieved a folded sheet of paper from between the pages. "I jotted down a few names. What do you think of Lord Peter Bentham?"

Devil take it, he was going to have to think fast. "Bentham? Younger son of Worthing? Big, strapping chap with yellow hair?"

"Yes, that's him."

"I would steer clear of that one if I were you."

"Why?"

"I've heard the fellow has a hot temper and a violent streak."

"Lord Peter? I can hardly believe it. He seems like such a kind gentleman."

"Appearances can be deceiving. Most fellows are on their best behavior in public, especially around females. But one hears talk in the clubs. I would be uneasy if I thought you were involved with a man like Bentham. For my peace of mind, may we cross him off the list?"

"All right." Her voice was tinged with disappointment. Had she really been attracted to that great hulking oaf?

"Who's next?"

"Sir Dudley Wainfleet."

He chuckled softly. "You'll have no success there, my dear."

"Why not?"

"Just between you and me, the man is not particularly interested in women."

Her eyes widened. "You mean . . ."

"Precisely. Cross him off. Who's next?"

"Robert Plimsoll."

He shook his head and laughed. "It is a good thing you sought my advice on this list of yours."

She lifted her chin at a challenging angle. "Is there some objection to Mr. Plimsoll?"

"Only that he keeps a mistress and their five children in a house in Hampstead."

She gave a little gasp of surprise. "You're joking? I never heard such a thing about him."

"Women never do. Sometimes not even wives know about their husbands' second families. Trust me, my dear. Every man of the *ton* knows about that house in Hampstead."

"Oh, dear. How very frustrating. It is indeed fortunate that I asked your advice." She sighed and took a sip of wine as she looked down at her list. "Harry Shackleford?"

Adam frowned, but said nothing. This exercise was becoming more distasteful. The thought of any of these men with Marianne was intolerable.

"What? Is there something wrong about him, too?"

He shrugged. "Nothing specific. Just a gut feeling."

"And what does your gut say?"

"It may sound odd, but I don't like the way the man treats his horses."

A puzzled frown marked her brow. "His horses?"

"Yes. He shows no care at all for them, and is a tad too free with the whip and the spur. He is downright cruel to the poor beasts, running them until they're lame. And I have observed that a man who mistreats his cattle often shows the same disregard for his women. I don't trust him."

A suspicious glint lit her eyes. "You think I should cross him off the list?"

"It is entirely up to you, my dear. I am only offering an observation."

"Hmm. All right, then. Lord Rochdale."

Adam almost choked on his wine. "Rochdale?" he sputtered. The fellow was one of his closest friends and a notorious libertine. The very idea of Marianne and Rochdale together was simply not to be borne. The man would use her and toss her aside without a second thought. Surely she knew that. "You're not serious?"

She smiled. "No, I'm not."

He heaved a sigh of relief. *Thank God.*

"I only wanted to get back at you for objecting to every other man on my list."

"Wretch! You almost gave me an apoplexy."

"Serves you right."

Her dimples flashed and she looked adorable, all curled up and cozy in her shawl with her feet tucked underneath her like a girl. Funny. He'd never noticed what dainty feet she had. Despite Adam's best efforts, it seemed some lucky fellow was going to tuck those pretty feet in a very different posture and wrap himself around her better than any shawl. Damn.

"Now," she said, "shall we continue?"

"There's more?"

"Lots more. It's quite an extensive list, you see."

She held up the paper and it did indeed look like there were twenty or more names on it. Adam poured another glass of wine. It was going to be a long night.

The tiny candlestand was crowded with empty wine bottles by the time Marianne's list had been narrowed to a small handful of unobjectionable gentlemen. She was a bit the worse for drink and not clearheaded enough to trust her perceptions, but she would swear that Adam was not at all happy that even so few men remained on the list. She had the distinct impression that he would have preferred to cross off every single name, leaving her with no options. And no hope.

Perhaps he was merely acting the role of an older brother, one who thought no man was good enough for his sister. Or perhaps he simply took his promise to David to look after her too much to heart. Either way, some of his excuses grew thin after a while. A man was either too tall or too short, too stout or too spare. His eyes were too narrow, his ears too big, his nose too long.

"Your idiotic objections have become quite tiresome," she said. "I am keeping Lord Aldershot on the list despite his big feet."

He gave a groan. "If you must. But have a care when dancing with the man. One false step and those dainty toes of yours could be crushed to bits."

Marianne giggled. "You are being foolish, Adam. Too much wine has made you silly."

"And you, my goose, are giggling."

They looked at each other and dissolved into sloppy, uncontrolled laughter, as they had done more frequently as the night wore on, and the wine flowed freely. What a sight they must have made. If any of their friends could see them together in such a state, they would very likely be scandalized. Marianne's shawl had fallen away, and she had long ago kicked off her slippers and propped her feet on the grate.

Adam's coat had gone missing, his waistcoat hung open, and his neckcloth was untied. Shards of a broken wineglass littered the hearth. One empty bottle had rolled beneath Adam's chair.

"Stop laughing," she said, not quite stopping herself. "We still have serious business to consider."

"Thought we were quite finished with your wretched list. Please do not tell me there is another sheet tucked inside that book."

"No more lists, I promise you."

"Thank God. M'brain is all used up. You've no idea." He picked up his glass, found it empty, and groaned. "Devil take it, that was the last of it."

"There are no more bottles in the desk? We drank them all?"

"So it would seem."

"Good heavens. I may never be able to stand up again. You, sir, are a bad influence."

"At least your bed is just through that door. I still have to crawl over that bloody balcony."

"You can stay here if you like. I could round up a pillow and blanket."

"No. Bad idea. I'll be fine."

When David was alive, Adam had often spent the night in the sitting room when he'd drunk too much to attempt the balcony. But he'd never done so since she'd been alone. He was always cautious about her reputation. He didn't seem to consider that simply being here with her, drinking together like two men, could have the same effect on her reputation whether he stayed the night or not.

But he was right. Considering the topic of conversation, inviting him to stay the night had been a stupid idea.

"You'll be careful?" she said. "I don't want to find your broken body splattered to bits on the street in the morning."

"Egad, what a gruesome imagination you have. You almost tempt me to use the front door."

She chuckled. "Never say so!"

"Don't worry, it hasn't come down to that. There's life in the old boy yet. I promise to be careful."

Neither of them made a move to leave. Marianne, at least, was content to remain where she was. She suspected Adam was trying to summon up a modicum of sobriety before climbing back over the balcony.

She gazed at him fondly, wondering if she would ever feel as comfortable with any of those men on her list. It really was a shame he was not available. She wondered how he would assess his own qualifications if his name had been listed. But his name had not been there. She had been too sensible to include it.

"Despite the descent into silliness," she said, "you have been exceedingly helpful, Adam. I do appreciate it. You have saved me a great deal of time."

"Wouldn't want you to seduce the wrong sort of chap, would we?"

"No, indeed. And that brings me to the next problem."

"Ah, yes. You did say there was still serious business to consider. Now that we are out of wine, I suppose there is nothing for it but to get serious. What is it, m'dear?"

"Adam, I have no idea how to seduce anyone. You must teach me."

He shot her a sharp look. "Egad, woman, you go too far."

"But I do not have a clue how to begin. It's been years since I even knew how to flirt with a man. And the match with David had been arranged for so long, there was never any need to hone my feminine wiles to win him. I don't know how to seduce a man, Adam. What do I do?"

He ran a hand through his hair, pushing it off his

forehead—it fell right back, of course—and he looked at her with a plaintive expression in his eyes. "Please, Marianne. I don't want to teach you how to entice a man into your bed. Don't ask me that."

"But, Adam, I really and truly need your help. You know how ignorant I am in such matters. But you are not. You are a man of the world. How would I entice *you*?"

He groaned as though in pain. "Don't. I beg you."

"Please, Adam."

"This is your game, m'dear. You decided what you want. It is up to you to figure out how to get it."

"A fine friend you are," she said in disgust. "Who else can I ask? I was counting on your help."

"Ask one of those other damned charity ball widows," he said in an angry tone, waving a hand in the air. "Ask anyone else. Ask the duchess. Just don't ask me."

"I will ask her, you may depend upon it. But I was hoping for a man's opinion, as well. Only you can give me that, Adam. How, for example, will I know if a man is interested?"

"Do not play coy with me, Marianne. You can't tell me you don't know when a man finds you attractive. A beautiful woman like you must've had chaps sniffing about your skirts since you was a girl."

She flashed a grin. "I thought I could tell, but I never knew *you* found me beautiful. That's a lovely surprise. But then, you're well and truly foxed, so I suppose it doesn't count."

"Hmph. Of course you knew it, you silly woman. How could you not?"

"It just goes to show you how dense I am about these things. Anyway, I wasn't talking about knowing when a man thinks I look pretty. How will I know if he wants to take me to bed?"

"They all want to take you to bed. Your job is to let the right one know that he can."

"And how do I do that? How do women let you know that you can?"

"They just do, that's all."

"But how?"

He gave a deep sigh and sank lower in his chair. "Arrange it so that he drives you home. Then invite him in for a brandy. That's as clear a signal as you could give."

"And then what? Do we discuss it? Do I invite him upstairs?"

"Leave it to him. The lucky fellow will know what to do, damn his eyes."

Marianne smiled at his drunken distress. "You don't like this idea at all, do you? This business of me taking a lover?"

"As a matter of fact, I do not."

"Don't you want me to be happy?"

"Ah, m'dear. Of course I do."

He reached out to touch her, lost his balance, and almost overturned the chair. Trying again, he finally made contact with her hand and gave it a reassuring squeeze. He allowed his fingers to skim lazily over her knee before he fell back against the chair cushions.

It must have been the wine, for Marianne could still feel the warm imprint of his touch.

"Of course I do," he repeated. "Want nothing more, in fact. It's just . . . awkward, you know."

"I know."

"And I suppose I can no longer blithely leap over the balcony to visit you unexpectedly. I might run into your unknown swain, which would be embarrassing at best."

"I had not considered that. But I don't want you to stop visiting, Adam."

"Then perhaps we need a signal."

"What sort of signal?"

"Let's see." He looked around the room. "How about that orchid plant?" He gestured toward an exotic plant in a French cachepot. "Put that out on the balcony when you are willing to have me visit. If I do not see the orchid, I will not intrude."

"All right. If that will make you feel more comfortable."

"Nothing about this situation makes me comfortable."

"I just wish you would stop acting like an older brother protecting his charge and think of me as a woman for once."

Adam stared at her openmouthed for a long moment, then burst into laughter. When he could manage to speak again, he said, "I promise you, m'dear, to make an effort to curb my protective instincts."

And then his lazy green eyes took on an intense expression she could not read in the dwindling light of the dying fire, but that look held her captive so that she almost forgot to breathe.

"I also promise," he said in a voice thick and soft as butter, "never, ever to think of you in a brotherly manner. You shall always and forever be a woman to me."

Good heavens, the man's voice sent a shiver dancing down her spine. Adam did not often turn his seductive charm on her, but when he did, it was potent. If just one of those men remaining on her list could make her feel like that, perhaps she would finally discover what Penelope had been talking about.

She looked down at the remains of her list. Which one would it be?

Chapter 4

"I tell you, it was more than a man should have to endure, listening to that long list of potential lovers. I had to get drunk just to get through it."

Adam sat with Lord Rochdale in a dark corner of the Raven Coffee House. Their cups had twice been refilled and the remains of ham sandwiches littered a platter between them. It was an old-fashioned establishment on Fetter Lane, one of the few old coffeehouses that had not been converted into a private club or a tavern. A broad central stairway led up to rooms where business of all sorts—most of it legitimate—was transacted, just as it had been for over one hundred years. Rochdale preferred it to any of the gentlemen's clubs in Mayfair or St. James, since they were unlikely to run into familiar faces, particularly those belonging to angry husbands or others connected to the women in his life. They could sit and converse in one of the old churchlike box pews with relative anonymity. Adam had grown fond of the old place, as well. The low ceiling with its heavy beams made it dark inside even at midday, and the air was thick with tobacco and the smoke of oil lamps. Best of all, though, was the coffee, which Adam preferred to tea. Still an expensive indulgence at fivepence per cup, it was worth it for the dark, rich brew that suited his mood today.

"You may laugh," he said, scowling at his friend,

"but if I hadn't armored myself with drink, I could not have faced that damned list. And the lowest cut of all was that my name was conspicuously missing."

"Does that surprise you?" Rochdale asked.

"Unfortunately, no. She knows me too well, knows my history with women too well. No, I would not expect to see my name on such a list, but it was no less painful to see all those other names. I tell you, there must have been twenty or twenty-five of them. It was pure agony."

The dim light of a sputtering candle carved harsh shadows in the hollows of Rochdale's cheeks, making the grin he flashed appear all the more wicked. Clearly he was enjoying Adam's distress. "I sincerely hope my name was there," he said. "I would be more than happy to accommodate her."

Adam glared at him across the narrow table, darkened and scarred with a century of wear. "Your name came up."

His lordship's brows lifted in surprise. "Did it? Well, then, I have underestimated your Marianne. I trust you supported my candidacy?"

"Though I would have done no such thing, it was not necessary. She mentioned you only in jest."

"Ah, so I have become a joke among respectable ladies. How mortifying." His grin held not a hint of mortification, however. Adam sometimes believed Rochdale enjoyed his unsavory reputation. He certainly cultivated it.

"She only wanted to tease me," Adam said. "Though I cannot imagine you would have been interested. She is not your usual type."

"I would have made an exception in order to bed the lovely Marianne."

Adam leaned forward to ensure his words would be heard clearly above the hubbub of a dozen lively conversations, the clatter of cups and dishes, and the constant rumble of carriages and carts passing outside. "Over. My. Dead. Body."

Rochdale narrowed his eyes and glared indignantly at Adam. "Cazenove, you are a fool. Just because you cannot have her, no other man is to be allowed that pleasure?"

"That's not it at all. She is too much an innocent for someone like you."

"And for someone like you?"

. Adam shrugged. "And for me, too. Even were I free."

"Well, you're not anymore, so why such a fuss over Marianne Nesbitt?" Rochdale leaned back and sipped his coffee. "The woman's been widowed more than two years. You've had ample opportunity to make a move if you were so inclined. And since you have never done so, one can only assume the inclination is not there."

He paused and lifted a quizzical brow, as though waiting for Adam to contradict him, but Adam only shook his head in response. Of course he had not made a move.

Rochdale shrugged. "So I can't see you have any cause to complain if she wants to seek out another man for her bed."

His friend was right. Adam had no right to interfere. It was just that he did not think any of the men they'd discussed would satisfy her. And he truly did believe she would have her heart broken in the end. She would discover he was right, that a sexual relationship would never be enough for her.

"Leave her to her own devices," Rochdale said. "What she does is none of your business."

"You're right, of course. But damn it all, I just can't seem to reconcile myself to the idea of her in another man's arms."

"Instead of *your* arms?"

"No! Nesbitt's."

"The man is dead, for God's sake."

"I know. But she will always be his woman to me."

"She'll be in some other man's arms soon enough. Which should be of no consequence to you, as your arms will be full of the beautiful Clarissa."

"Touché."

Adam emptied his own cup and looked about for Alfred, the headwaiter. He found him serving a group of older men seated nearest the hearth. Wearing old-fashioned bob wigs and buckles on their shoes, the men looked like a scene out of his father's time. They passed around several long-handled clay pipes, and one of them toasted a muffin on a stick held over the fire. Adam would not have been surprised to learn these same old chaps had been holding down that spot in the Raven for forty years or more.

He caught Alfred's eye and nodded, then turned back to Rochdale, whose brows were lifted in amusement.

"I do wish you didn't find this business so damned entertaining," Adam said, but couldn't hold back a smile. "It was tough going, I tell you, dealing with that list."

"You're in love with the woman. Always have been."

Adam snorted. "What rot. She was my best friend's wife, for God's sake. I admire her more than any other woman I know, but I am not in love with her."

"You don't want any other man in her bed, then, because you admire her so much?"

"I worry that she'll be hurt, that's all."

"I think you want her for yourself, and now that you can't have her—because, I remind you again, you have the lovely and innocent Clarissa—then you don't want any other man to have her. Sounds suspiciously close to being in love with her, if you ask me."

"Well, I don't ask you, and I am not in love with

her. I'm just watching out for her best interests, as Nesbitt asked me to do. I promised to look after her."

"I still say you should stay out of it. And certainly stop talking to her about it. Whoever heard of a woman having such a discussion with a man, anyway?"

"We've always been candid together. We're friends."
Rochdale snorted. "For now."

"What do you mean, 'for now'?"

"If you think Clarissa is going to allow you to continue in close friendship with a beautiful woman like Marianne, then you'd better think again. That tie is going to be cut, whether you like it or not."

"Damnation. I hope you're wrong. That would be . . ." *Impossible to imagine.*

"You know, old chap, it might be the best thing of all if Marianne became linked with another man. It might stave off any bridal jealousies."

"Perhaps. Marianne is bound and determined on this course in any case."

Alfred approached with a steaming pot of coffee and refilled their cups. In an Oxbridge voice, he asked if they wished for anything more to eat. Rochdale declined and sent him away. Adam watched the tall, straight-backed figure as he retreated, and marveled that he managed to keep such a pristine appearance in a bustling coffeehouse. The man was always well dressed in a smart black coat, knee breeches, black silk hose, and a spotless white cravat.

"What do you suppose is his story?" he asked.

"Rumor is," Rochdale said, "that he was once a gentleman, but lost his fortune on the Exchange."

"Really? Poor old sod. Well, I suppose it is better here than debtors' prison."

"Indeed." He shot Adam a speaking glance. "We must all make hard choices from time to time."

Adam looked at his friend and nodded. "Yes, we do. And yes, I have made mine."

Rochdale raised his cup in salute. "Good man." After taking a drink of the hot brew, he said, "What do you think set Marianne off? Why this sudden resolution to find a lover? Why now?"

"I don't know," Adam said, "but I have a sneaking suspicion it has something to do with the other women in the Benevolent Widows Fund. She told me once how they all decided to remain widows rather than seek remarriage. I'm wondering if they have perhaps all decided to seek lovers instead."

"Egad, you don't suppose the rest of them are on the hunt as well, do you?"

"It's quite possible. I can't help but believe Marianne did not come up with this idea on her own. I would not be surprised to learn that it was a group decision of some kind, and Marianne got swept up in it."

"Good Lord. All those Benevolent Widows on the loose." Rochdale rolled his eyes to the ceiling. "Spare me."

Adam grinned. "Willing young widows looking for pleasure? How could you resist such temptation?"

"With the greatest ease, I assure you. Ladies given to good works make me nervous." He shuddered visibly. "They never really want a quick shag, you know. They always want more."

"Perhaps not, if all the preaching about independence I've heard from Marianne is any indication." Though Adam sincerely hoped it would not be so crass in her case. She deserved more than "a quick shag."

"Trust me, Cazenove. None of those women are the type given to an uncomplicated tussle between the sheets. They will wheedle and cajole until they have turned a simple affair into something more serious."

"That is precisely what I tried to tell Marianne. She is not the sort for a casual affair. She will want more than that."

"As will all those Benevolent Widows. It's in their blood. I wouldn't go near any one of them."

Adam smiled. "Come on, old boy. Attractive women out for a bit of pleasure—what could be easier game?"

"Sorry," Rochdale said, shaking his head. "Not interested."

"Not at all?" Adam did not believe his lordship for a single moment and flashed a grin that told him so. "The lovely Countess Somerfield?"

"Very attractive, but not my type. A bit on the cool side."

"Lady Gosforth?"

Rochdale shrugged. "I might consider it, in a pinch. I have to admit, she does have a perfectly luscious bosom. Though I cannot say I admire those cropped curls of hers. I prefer a long, thick mass of hair that I can get my hands in."

"Then Mrs. Marlowe should do quite nicely," Adam said, his grin widening. "All that golden hair. I'd be willing to bet it falls to her waist."

"I'd be willing to bet she never allows it to do so. Too prim and proper, that one. A bishop's widow, for God's sake. Old Marlowe's ghost would probably be watching."

Adam let out a bark of laughter, and several patrons turned their heads. He lowered his voice. "Well, then, there's always the duchess."

Rochdale smiled. "Willie's a dear creature, and a bit of a frolic with her would always be welcome, but I doubt she'd be interested. She generally does not look backward once she has moved on. No, I will keep my distance from the Benevolent Widows, if you don't mind."

Adam did not mind at all. In fact, the farther away Rochdale kept from Marianne, the better. At least for his own peace of mind. The fellow was a good friend, but Adam did not trust him where women were concerned.

But there were still all those other gentlemen on that blasted list. What was he to do about them?

*   *   *

"Ladies, please!" Grace Marlowe wrung her hands in frustration, clearly annoyed that she had lost control of the meeting. Again. "We have work to do."

She gestured toward the sheets of paper, checklists, ledgers, and account books on the small French writing desk in front of her. The other ladies were arranged in chairs and a settee in the cheerful morning room. Sun streamed in the large windows overlooking Portland Place, giving a gleaming brightness to the white moldings and plasterwork ceiling, and picking out glints of gold on picture frames, porcelain figures, and a fine garniture on the mantel. A fire burned low in the grate, though it was not needed, and the soft aroma of early roses filled the air.

The duchess smiled and said, "My dear Grace, I believe you must allow us a moment to be merry before we become benevolent. The work will get done."

"Of course it will," Marianne added. "But we did agree, after all, to allow discussion of these matters among ourselves." She was very anxious to hear if anyone was making progress in the quest for a lover. Despite Adam's advice, she still felt awkward about the whole business and would welcome any details the others had to offer.

Grace gave an unladylike snort and crossed her arms over her chest. "Ten minutes," she said. "No more. Then we really must review the final details for the ball at Yarmouth House, and then get busy planning the next one. Ten minutes."

The duchess, ensconced in a gilded armchair with her skirts arranged about her in studied negligence, nodded in agreement and turned her attention to Penelope. "And so, it is to be Mr. Tolliver?"

Penelope positively beamed and wriggled her shoulders with excitement. "Yes! Is that not delicious? He is *so* handsome. Such shoulders!"

"This all happened rather fast," Marianne said.

"What did you do, exactly?" She flushed slightly, embarrassed to be asking such a question, so blatantly demonstrating her ignorance. But if she was going to do this, she needed a few helpful hints.

"He has been rather attentive for years," Penelope said. "When I saw him at a card party last week, I made sure he knew I welcomed his interest. We haven't actually done the deed yet, but he is sure to be at our ball, and I'm hoping that will be the night." She bounced on her chair with girlish glee. "I can hardly wait!"

Marianne frowned. She had hoped for more details of precisely *how* Penelope signaled her interest. Everyone seemed to think it came naturally, and maybe that was true and she was being overly anxious. Still, she would have welcomed a few pointers.

"What's troubling you, Marianne?" Beatrice, sitting beside her on a settee, touched her arm gently. "You look so glum. Had you perhaps thought of Mr. Tolliver for yourself?"

"Oh!" Marianne lifted a hand to her breast, mortified that she might be seen as jealous, which was ridiculous. The man had not even been on her original list. "No, no, I assure you, I had not set my sights on Mr. Tolliver. I hardly know him."

"I think," the duchess said, "that Marianne was hoping you would be a bit more forthcoming, Penelope, regarding the tactics you employed to let Mr. Tolliver know of your interest." She looked at Marianne with very indulgent and very kind eyes. "Am I right?"

Marianne nodded sheepishly. Bless Wilhelmina for being so perceptive.

"We did promise details," the duchess said.

"And you can be sure that when I have any interesting details," Penelope said, "I will report them. The actual flirtation is not important."

"But not everyone has experience with flirtation."

Wilhelmina turned to Marianne. "Your marriage was arranged, was it not?"

"Yes, when I was still a girl. I never had the need to flirt. I always had David." She looked down at the hands in her lap. "I am so afraid of making a cake of myself."

"Don't think of it as flirting," Beatrice said. "Just think of it as conversation. Ask a gentleman about himself, show an interest in his interests, and that's all there is to it."

"Precisely," Wilhelmina said with a nod of acknowledgment to Beatrice. "Excellent advice. If you think too much about it, you will become unnerved. Just act naturally. Be yourself. You are a charming and beautiful woman. You need only smile, look him straight in the eye, and let the gentleman do the talking. He'll be entranced."

"You make it sound so easy," Marianne said.

"It is easy," Penelope said. "It is just talking, as Beatrice said. It is not a prescribed set of tricks and charades. Whatever you do, do not flutter your eyelashes or sigh wistfully or giggle. Leave that to the ingenues. As older, experienced women, we do not need to resort to such tactics." She leaned forward and smiled. "Do you have someone in mind, Marianne?"

"There are a few gentlemen I am considering. If they're interested." She looked at each woman around the room. "You promise not to repeat it if I tell you who they are?"

"That was part of our agreement," Beatrice said. "At least that is what I understood and what I expect. What is said here stays here."

"Of course," Penelope said.

The duchess nodded, and everyone turned to Grace. She had uncrossed her arms but still did not look entirely comfortable. "I have not yet become accustomed to hearing such talk here in my own morning room, so you can be sure I will not repeat it elsewhere."

"All right, then," Marianne said, "just between us. I had considered Sir Arthur Denney, Sidney Gilchrist, and Lord Aldershot."

The duchess nodded. "All three will do, in my opinion."

"All three?" Grace said, her voice rising to a squeak as she leaned forward over the desk. "Are you suggesting Marianne should take all three of them as lovers? Good heavens."

Marianne laughed and the rest joined in. "I am not sure I'm ready for one lover, much less three! These gentlemen are just three possibilities, that is all."

"Forgive me," the duchess said, grinning broadly. "I ought to have said any *one* of the three would do. Each is attractive, charming, and unattached. If I may be so bold as to suggest it, you might also consider Lord Julian Sherwood. I believe I noted an interest on his part last Season."

"An interest in me?" Marianne asked with some surprise. She had barely paid attention to the young man, except to note his good looks and fine manners. "He is quite young, is he not?"

"And what does that signify?" Penelope asked. "Personally, I prefer a younger man. They are delightfully energetic, and much less likely to want a more serious involvement. And Lord Julian is not all that young. What is he, twenty-five or twenty-six? He would be a splendid diversion for any of us. Not only is he extraordinarily handsome, but he is a very good dancer." Amusement lit her blue eyes. "If a man moves well on the dance floor, it suggests he might also move well in other more intimate situations."

All the ladies—except Grace, who looked thoroughly embarrassed—burst into laughter.

"Penelope is quite right," the duchess said. "I have found dancing to be a very good indication of other skills. Watch your three gentlemen at our next ball, Marianne. If any of them looks stiff and awkward, or has no sense of music or timing, you might want to reconsider."

Marianne tried to bring to mind a memory of any of the three men dancing, but came up short. The only image she could conjure up was of gliding gracefully down a line with Adam, who always danced beautifully. And since he never seemed to be in want of a woman, she would be willing to bet Wilhelmina's theory, in his case, was absolutely true.

"Oh, dear," Beatrice said with a grimace. "I am picturing the somewhat cloddish moves of George Abernathy dancing with Emily at her come-out ball last week. If she develops a tendre for the young man, I suppose I shall have to have a little talk with her." When the rest of them laughed, she added, "I am only thinking of my niece's happiness, after all."

"And what of yours, Beatrice?" Penelope asked. "Have you made any progress in our collective quest for a particularly *merry* Season?"

"Good Lord, no. Have you any idea how much effort is involved in chaperoning a girl through her first Season? I have not had a free moment, I assure you, to even notice if a man shows an interest in me. I am much too preoccupied with assessing the merits of any young men who show an interest in Emily. It's a daunting task. And her mother would have my head if I allowed the girl to be courted by someone unsuitable. But before you ask, yes, I will keep an open mind should an opportunity present itself."

"Our first ball should provide excellent opportunities," Penelope said. "That's one advantage to controlling the invitation list. We can make sure all the attractive, available men are invited."

"All of the men Marianne mentioned received invitations," Grace said, pointing to a list on the desk in front of her. She hoped, no doubt, to steer the conversation back to business.

"Excellent," the duchess said. "It should be the perfect venue for testing the waters, Marianne. If the weather holds, the gardens at Yarmouth House are quite lovely at night.''

Grace frowned. ''As patronesses, we really should remain in the ballroom throughout the evening.''

''Bosh!'' Penelope exclaimed. ''Once we've done our duty in the receiving line, there is nothing more required of us but to mingle and enjoy the evening. You may be sure I intend to take advantage of the gardens with Eustace Tolliver. It would do you no harm, Grace, to find a handsome gentleman and do the same.''

Grace uttered a little hiss of impatience and cast a glance at the ormolu clock on the mantel as it struck the quarter hour.

''I don't know about the gardens,'' Marianne said before Grace had a chance to mention their ten minutes was up, ''but I am ready to begin my woeful attempts at flirtation. At least I think I am. I have a lovely new dress—yards of mulberry crepe with the prettiest beadwork you ever saw.''

''It sounds delightful,'' the duchess said, ''and will no doubt put us all in the shade. There is nothing like a pretty dress to give one confidence. You'll be smashing, my girl. Have no fear.''

''I hope you're right.''

''You always look gorgeous,'' Beatrice said, nudging Marianne gently in the ribs. ''I have long envied your coloring, which goes so well with most anything. With this blasted red hair, I can't wear half the shades you do. It is a constant trial. Can you imagine me in mulberry? But I do have a new apple blossom sarsnet dress made up by Mrs. Osgood that I am planning to wear to Yarmouth House. I am quite pleased with how it came out.''

''And you, Grace?'' the duchess asked. ''What will you be wearing?''

Grace smiled for the first time that afternoon. Mari-

anne knew that all the talk about gentlemen and flirting and dancing—not to mention those more intimate
skills Penelope hinted at—was horribly discomfiting
for Grace. But she was still young and so elegantly
beautiful that it might do her good to be a Merry Widow
for a change rather than the oh-so-proper bishop's
widow.

"I have a new Pomona green silk dress with lovely
embroidered trim," Grace said. "I think—I hope—it
is quite pretty."

"I am sure it is," the duchess replied. "I cannot wait
to see it. Green is a good color for you, my dear.
And Penelope?"

"I'll be in Sardinian blue crepe. Eustace Tolliver
tells me I look best in blue."

"And I shall be in printed India muslin," Wilhelmina said. "What a colorful group we shall make. Now
that I know who is wearing what, I have a little something for each of you." She reached for a large reticule
beneath her chair and retrieved four slim boxes. She
rose with the stack of boxes in her hand. "A small
celebratory token, in honor of our first ball of the
Season."

As she walked about the room, she checked a tiny
painted flower on the lids before handing a box to
each lady.

"Oh, Wilhelmina!" Beatrice said as she opened
hers. "How marvelous."

Each box held a delicate brisé fan of pierced ivory
in the new smaller size that had lately become so fashionable. Each fan was intricately pierced in a different
pattern, and each was painted with a different flower.
Marianne's fan was strung with a dark pink ribbon
and painted with tiny clusters of deep purple pansies.
It was one of the prettiest fans she'd ever seen.

"What a lovely idea," Penelope said. "They shall
be our badges of honor as patronesses of the ball.

Thank you ever so much." She tugged Wilhelmina down for a kiss on the cheek.

Grace seemed overcome with the kindness of the gesture and merely laid a hand on the duchess's arm as she passed the desk.

"Wilhelmina," Marianne said, "they are lovely. How very thoughtful of you."

The duchess fluttered a hand in a dismissive gesture and returned to her chair, arranging her skirts carefully about her. "It was nothing. Merely a small token. Actually, Marianne, it was you who inspired me with the idea of fans."

"Me?"

"Yes. I was pondering your situation, knowing this business of seeking a lover was confounding you a bit. I knew of your arranged marriage and guessed you were somewhat inexperienced in the fine art of flirtation."

Marianne gave a little snort. "You guessed correctly."

"Well, then, it is time for a bit of practice. Ladies, we are going to review the secret language of the fan. Not so secret, after all, since every man on the town knows every signal. Let us begin with the most important signal of all." She opened her own fan and rested it gently on her right cheek. "This means 'yes.' "

Chapter 5

"It worked! Oh, dear."

Marianne watched as Lord Hopwood smiled and made his way across the room. She had touched the edge of her fan with one finger, indicating she wished to speak to him.

"I do not recall you mentioning Lord Hopwood," Grace whispered. "Why did you signal him?"

"It was an impulse," Marianne said, and bit back a smile. "I thought I would practice on someone else first."

His lordship approached and sketched a bow. He was tall and dark-haired, with intriguing sweeps of gray at his temples. "Mrs. Nesbitt. Mrs. Marlowe. You are both looking lovely this evening."

"Thank you, my lord," Marianne said. "You are most kind."

"You have arranged yet another magnificent evening," he said, his glance taking in the elegant drawing room—one of many rooms stripped of furniture for the ball. "I always look forward to the Benevolent Widows' balls." He glanced at Marianne and smiled. "The company is more congenial than at any other."

"We are much obliged to the duke and duchess," Grace said, "for opening Yarmouth House to us. We appreciate your attendance, my lord, and your generous contribution. We have collected a record amount this evening. It is most gratifying."

"You are to be commended on your efforts," he said, "to help those women less fortunate than yourselves."

"It is the least we can do," Grace said, "when considering our own circumstances. Though each of us knows the grief of losing a husband, none of us has suffered financially. But there are far too many who've lost husbands in the Peninsula and are left with nothing. It seemed not only a Christian but also a patriotic duty to offer what help we can. And to encourage others like you to do the same. You may be certain, my lord, that your contribution will go to a worthy cause."

"I have no doubt of it," he said.

"Now, if you will excuse me," Grace said, "I see a few late arrivals who must be welcomed."

Thank goodness. Marianne had feared Grace would launch into a lengthy sermon on the necessity of good works and drive Lord Hopwood away. His lordship bowed as she left, then turned to Marianne and lifted an interested brow.

"May I procure you something to drink, Mrs. Nesbitt? Or would you perhaps prefer to join the set in progress?"

"Oh, do let us join the dancing, if you please. I like nothing better than a lively Scotch reel."

"I am honored," he said, and offered his arm.

He danced quite well, which made Marianne recollect Wilhelmina's words. Lord Hopwood was a very attractive man. She wondered why she had failed to include him on her list. While they danced, she kept in mind the advice of her friends and did not make a deliberate effort to flirt. Instead she simply tried to be as pleasant and charming as possible. If the increased attentions of Lord Hopwood were any indication, it was a good tactic. He asked if he could call upon her the next day and take her driving in the park.

Her next three partners, Sir Arthur Denney, Sidney Gilchrist, and Trevor Fitzwilliam, were equally attentive. All were good dancers. Suddenly, the world seemed full of possibilities and Marianne had to rein in an almost giddy excitement.

Most of the gentlemen in attendance had been known to her for years. At some time or another, she had talked with them, or danced with them, played cards with them, or even dined with them. But never before had she been so conscious of them as men. Now almost every man she encountered might be considered as a potential lover, and that changed everything. Every word took on nuance; every glance seemed infused with new meaning; every dance step suggested more intimate moves. Had Society gatherings always been so sexually charged, and she simply too naive to notice?

Mr. Fitzwilliam led her off the dance floor, bowed over her hand with florid words of appreciation, and took his leave. Marianne turned to find Adam approaching with Clarissa on his arm. She had caught a glimpse of them dancing in one of the other lines. A tiny pang of emotion—regret? wistfulness? inevitability?—gripped her heart for an instant at the sight of them together. She would have to become accustomed to it. From now on, she would be more likely to see Adam with Clarissa than without her.

She put on her best smile and held out her hand in welcome. "Adam, it is good to see you."

"Marianne." He took her hand and kissed it. Even through the fabric of her gloves she felt the heat of his lips. How very disconcerting to be so damnably aware of such things. How had she managed to be so insulated from sexual feelings all her life?

Adam relinquished her hand in order to bring Clarissa forward. "I believe you have met Miss Leighton-Blair."

"Yes, of course." She smiled at the girl, whose eyes held a mixture of triumph and nervousness. She was no doubt proud to be paraded about on the arm of her betrothed, eager to flaunt her good fortune to one and all. But she was also very young and very innocent, which tempered any pride with an appealing freshness. No wonder Adam wanted her. She really was quite lovely.

"I am so glad you came," Marianne said. "It gives me a chance to offer my best wishes on your betrothal."

"Thank you, Mrs. Nesbitt." Her voice was girlishly high and slightly breathy. "For your good wishes and for sending an invitation. The Benevolent Widows Fund balls are always much talked about. It is indeed a pleasure to have the opportunity to attend one."

"Your future husband is a good friend and neighbor to one of the trustees," Marianne said with a sly wink, "so you can be assured of invitations to all our balls from now on."

"Oh! How kind of you." Her blue eyes grew large with excitement. "Thank you ever so much."

"Think nothing of it," Marianne said, smiling at such youthful enthusiasm. "These are charity balls, after all. We extort a great deal of money from Mr. Cazenove in exchange for invitations."

"Oh." Clarissa looked at Adam with confused distress. "I hadn't realized—"

"Mrs. Nesbitt is joking," Adam said as he patted the hand resting on his arm. "She does not extort money from me. I give it willingly to a worthy cause. As does everyone else in attendance."

"How silly of me." Clarissa blushed prettily and giggled. "I had forgotten about that aspect of the balls. They are so popular, and invitations so treasured, that it is easy to forget their true purpose."

"The balls are our biggest fund-raising activity," Marianne said. "Their success has been quite gratifying. But enough of that. I hope you will enjoy the ball. And I hope you and I can become friends, Miss Leighton-Blair. We shall be neighbors soon, after all. You and your mother must call on me. I am at home on Tuesdays."

"Thank you, Mrs. Nesbitt. I would like that."

"Miss Leighton-Blair? I believe it is our dance."

The gentleman's voice came from behind Marianne, so she turned to acknowledge him. It was Lord Julian Sherwood, dressed all in blue and silver and looking very dashing. No wonder Wilhelmina had recommended him. He was a very handsome young man.

"Cazenove, Mrs. Nesbitt," he said as he offered his arm to Clarissa.

Marianne caught his eye and smiled. He returned her smile and a discreet flicker of interest lit his eyes, reminding her of Wilhelmina's words. She moved her fan to her left hand, opened it, and held it in front of her face.

Lord Julian arched a brow. "Mrs. Nesbitt, are you perhaps free for the set after this one?"

"I am indeed."

"I would be honored if you would save it for me."

"I am happy to do so. Thank you, my lord."

He flashed a brilliant smile, then turned to lead Clarissa to the lines forming for the next set.

"Shameless hussy!" Adam whispered, his voice full of amusement. "And you said you did not know how to attract a man's attention. What are you up to? Lord Julian wasn't even on that damned list."

"It is a woman's prerogative to be spontaneous about these things." She closed her fan and rapped him with it playfully on the arm. "And it is none of your business, anyway."

"I believe, Mrs. Nesbitt, that too much dancing has had a dizzying effect on you, making rational thought an effort. Here, take my arm. I was going to invite you to join the set but I think a slow turn around the room would be better for your health."

Marianne laughed and placed her hand on his sleeve. "What a charming invitation. No wonder so many women find you irresistible."

"Everyone but you, my dear coquette."

"Because I know you too well. Besides," she teased, "you are no longer available."

"Unfortunate, but true. Once again I must express my regret for the timing of this quest of yours. A bit earlier and I might have saved you the effort of all that fan waving and offered up my poor self to your cause."

"So generous of you."

"What are friends for?"

He led them away from the crowds lining the walls and toward a large pair of doors opening onto the garden terrace. So they were not going to walk about the room after all. He opened the doors and they stepped out into the cool night air. Several couples strolled about the terrace and down the steps into the garden. Adam led her to one of several stone benches that skirted the terrace balustrade. Marianne took a seat and arranged her skirts with care for the delicate beadwork. Adam did not sit, but leaned against the railing instead.

"Thank you," he said, "for being so kind to Clarissa. That was very gracious of you to offer your friendship. I am sure she appreciated it."

"She is marrying my dearest friend, and so she must be my friend as well."

"I am pleased you feel that way, especially considering your initial reaction to our betrothal."

Marianne wrinkled her nose. "Do not remind me of my impertinence. I was exceedingly rude to you that night. I trust we can forget about it? We have agreed, have we not, to accept each other's plans without further debate? I will accept your young bride and try to be her friend, and you will stop teasing me about my . . . quest."

His mouth curved into a roguish grin. "I never agreed to stop teasing you. It gives me too much pleasure to do so and puts such a lovely pink in your cheeks. I am only doing you a favor, my dear, by making you even more attractive to all those chaps on your list."

"You, sir, are a scoundrel."

"Guilty. But seriously, Marianne, I am very grateful for your efforts to befriend Clarissa. I know she is young, but perhaps you will find something in common once you get to know her."

And you, Adam? What do you have in common with her?

"She and I both want you to be happy," Marianne said, "so we have that in common already. And soon enough, we will have a balcony in common."

"Actually, I've been thinking of selling the house."

Marianne was momentarily stunned into silence. It seemed there would be changes she had not anticipated. She could not even imagine life without Adam close at hand. She took several steadying breaths before speaking. "You are moving away?"

"I am thinking of buying a larger house here in town. The Bruton Street house is fine enough for me, but I thought perhaps something a bit more spacious would be in order. Especially if there are children."

"Of course," she managed. "Clarissa will be pleased."

"I hope so. I have spoken with my solicitor about selling the house in Dorset. I seldom go down there and have never much enjoyed country life. Never could see myself as a country squire. Despise rusticating. I thought to use the capital to buy a larger house in town, where we could live year-round."

"We are of like minds on that subject, as you know," she said. "I never understood the attraction of the country. I despise a country house party. While you men go out shooting and fishing and racing about, there is never anything for ladies to do but read and stitch and sketch, all of which I can do just as well here in town, while at the same time having good shops and theaters and galleries at my fingertips."

"I remember," he said, "how you hated when David felt obliged to visit the estate in Kent."

Marianne groaned. "I was never more bored in my life than during those long months in the country. You cannot imagine how pleased I am that the place was entailed to his brother, George, and that I seldom, if ever, have to set foot in it again. If he had left it to me, I do not know what I'd have done with it. Sell it, I suppose, as you are doing. Is Clarissa amenable to living in town all year?"

"I haven't spoken to her about it yet. But she does seem to prefer it here in town. She positively glows whenever I escort her someplace new."

Because she was so young and still agog with *ton* life. But would she really be happy living in London all year round? Or would she be miserable during the winter months when company was thin and everyone had retired to the country?

"I have given this a great deal of thought," he said. "I remember as a boy being so restless in the country. When I finally got to Oxford, I was completely entranced by town life, and wondered why I had been forced to waste so many years with nothing but a small village at my disposal. People always talk about the benefits of raising children in the country, but look how much London has to offer a child. Museums and menageries and parks. Medieval towers and royal palaces. Troops of soldiers on review and docks bursting with ships of every kind. I would have loved all that as a boy."

"Yes," she said, "I see what you mean." His normally hooded eyes had grown round with a sort of

wonder. Adam was still a boy at heart who loved all
those things. But would the girl he was marrying agree
with him?

"I am hoping Clarissa will approve," he said, as
though reading her thoughts. "She will no doubt enjoy
furnishing and decorating a new, larger house. She has
excellent taste, in fashion, at least."

"That is certainly a very pretty dress she is wearing tonight."

"It is indeed. Clarissa is one of those girls, though,
who would look pretty in a feed sack."

"She is indeed lovely, Adam. She will make a beautiful bride."

"Yes, she is lovely, but you, my dear, outshine every
other woman tonight. You look stunning in that dress.
The color suits you."

Marianne looked down at the mulberry crepe, its
faint sheen picked up by the moonlight. "Do you
think so? You do not think it too bold?"

"For such a brazen flirt? No, it is perfect."

Marianne laughed. "I confess I am feeling a bit brazen tonight."

"So I noticed. How many other gentlemen have
fallen victim to that fan?"

She shrugged and smiled. "Only a few."

He gave a snort and looked away. "I never before
knew you to employ a fan. Is this something new?"

"Wilhelmina gave us a refresher course in the language of the fan, and I have come to find it quite
useful."

"Us?"

Oh, dear. She could not tell him about the Merry
Widows. It was a secret pact, and she had almost let
it slip. "The trustees. We got a bit silly at one of our
meetings, that's all. I had quite forgotten all those sig-
nals one could send with a fan."

"It seems to have come back to you easily enough."

Marianne hunched a shoulder. "It has certainly

made things easier for me. I am still feeling awkward and uncertain when it comes to attracting a man with words. I've never known how to flirt properly, so all I've done is talk with them. It seems to be working."

"My dear, you underestimate your powers. You don't need to make a special effort to attract a man."

He reached out and ran the back of a finger gently along her cheek. She caught her breath. He noticed, of course, and his lazy green eyes twinkled.

"All you need to do," he continued, "is smile and look up at him with those big brown eyes and he will be lost to you." He gave a rueful little laugh. "I guarantee it."

"Thank you, Adam." Her skin still tingled where he'd touched her. "I appreciate your advice, even though I know you do not approve of what I'm doing."

"I do not disapprove, my dear. If I said anything to the contrary the other night, you must blame it on the drink. You are entitled to your pleasure. But you must permit me to be provoked that I cannot be the one to share it with you." He flashed a wicked grin.

He was teasing, of course—he was always teasing—but she wished he would not. It only encouraged impossible fantasies.

"So, have you made your way through the list yet?"

"Almost," she said. "I have not yet seen Lord Aldershot this evening, but Sir Arthur and Mr. Gilchrist have been most attentive. Not to mention Lord Hopwood."

"Hopwood? I don't recall discussing him."

"We didn't. It was an impulse."

"Hmph. He is too old for you."

"Nonsense. Oh, and there was Mr. Fitzwilliam, as well."

"Fitzwilliam? Egad, another impulse?"

"Yes, as a matter of fact. Just because I didn't think to put a man's name on my list does not mean I cannot consider him if I so choose."

"Fitzwilliam is too dreamy. The man always has his head in the clouds."

Marianne laughed. "Adam, you are hopeless. You think no one is suitable."

He leaned down and placed his lips so close to her ear she could feel his breath. "No one is good enough for you, my dear."

His breath and his words sent a shiver down her arms. Lord, how on earth did people survive in such a charged atmosphere? How had she lived almost thirty years without recognizing it all around her? This new self-conscious sexual tension she'd felt all evening with every man who danced with her was even stronger around Adam. Had it been there all along, the whole time she'd known him, and she'd been too self-absorbed to notice?

"Got caught in the parson's mousetrap, eh, Cazenove?"

Lord Ombersley guffawed loudly and slapped Adam on the back. If Adam heard that old chestnut one more time he'd be driven to violence. But it seemed every man at White's had to comment upon his betrothal.

"Pretty little thing, though," Ombersley said. "Should make a sweet armful, eh, what? No hardship in that duty, I'll wager."

His bawdy laughter was picked up by other gentlemen in the cardroom, and Adam was forced to endure more commiseration and backslapping as he made his way through. Clarissa's youth and beauty were much remarked upon, as though those were the only qualities that mattered in a wife. Of course, they had been his primary reasons for choosing her, so he should not be offended by that attitude. He was no different from the rest. He did have hopes, though, that there would eventually be a deeper connection between them. She was very young and their betrothal was still new, but

Adam hoped the skittishness he often noted whenever he tried to kiss her or touch her would melt over time.

He finally extricated himself from the general bonhomie and made his way across the room. Before he reached the door and his escape, the words "Mrs. Nesbitt" rang in the air, followed by laughter. Adam turned to find Lord Aldershot among a group of men standing near the window. A genial, good-looking man, he was one of the few candidates whose name remained on Marianne's list. If the fellow was making sport of Marianne's name in public, by God, Adam would be sure he was struck from that list.

Adam accepted a glass of wine from a waiter and wandered casually toward the group.

"Ah, Cazenove," Sir Neville Kenyon said. "I understand we are to wish you happy. Miss Leighton-Blair, is it?"

"Yes, she has done me the honor of accepting my offer of marriage."

"Very pretty girl. Good family. Well-done, old man."

After more talk of his betrothal, conversation moved on to an upcoming race at Newmarket. Adam managed to ease Lord Aldershot slightly away from the central group.

"Did I hear you mention Mrs. Nesbitt earlier?" he said, keeping his tone indifferent, as though the matter were of no real consequence. "An attractive woman, is she not?"

"I should say so," Aldershot replied with enthusiasm. "Danced with her last night at Yarmouth House. Thinking of calling on her. Keep in her good graces and all that."

"Ah. So you have an interest in that quarter?"

"Possibly. Pretty woman, Mrs. Nesbitt. Was just saying to these chaps that she never seemed approachable before, but last night there was something about her. The way she smiled. Something, I don't know. Thought perhaps she was finally through being the grieving widow. Oh, I say. You were a friend to Nesbitt, were you not?"

"Indeed, he was my closest friend. His widow is still my friend."

"Then tell me, is she on the lookout for a new husband this Season? Is that why she seemed so amiable? For if she is, then I'll think twice about paying a call. Don't mind telling you that I ain't looking for leg shackle just yet. But if it's just a bit of company she's after," he said with a grin and a poke in Adam's ribs, "then I'm her man."

Adam controlled the instinct to plant the fellow a facer, and decided to take advantage of his candid request. "Mrs. Nesbitt is a highly respectable widow, Aldershot, and not the sort of woman interested in a bit of dalliance. But it has been over two years since Nesbitt's death, and I believe she might be ready to consider another marriage. In fact, when I told her of my own betrothal, she mentioned how she hoped she could make a similar announcement by the end of the Season."

"Did she, by Jove? Then it was prodigious good luck I ran into you, Cazenove. That bit of intelligence will save me a great deal of awkwardness. Much obliged, old chap." He took Adam's hand and pumped it vigorously. "Much obliged."

Adam took his leave of the cardroom, feeling rather smug. It had been the easiest thing in the world to dissuade Aldershot from pursuing Marianne, even if it did involve the tiniest bit of prevarication. And she need never know why his lordship flew out of her orbit. He'd only done it, of course, because the man's attitude was disrespectful. Adam was willing to allow Marianne her quest, but he would be damned before he'd allow some vulgar nincompoop to get past her bedroom door. If only he could do the same with every other unworthy gentleman who'd shown an interest, he would feel he'd done a good day's work in upholding his promise to David to look after her.

When he went downstairs and passed through the morning room, more gentlemen came over to offer congratulations on his upcoming nuptials. Even the bow window set strolled over to pay their respects.

"Fortunate fellow," Lord Worcester said. "You've made off with the prettiest girl on the Marriage Mart. Quite a coup, Cazenove, you dog."

"She'll keep you nice and warm at night," Lord Alvanley said. "Lucky devil. Hey, Fitzwilliam. Did you not once pen a sonnet to Miss Leighton-Blair's eyes?"

Trevor Fitzwilliam strolled languidly from his seat in the window to join them. Another of Marianne's candidates. The damned place was teeming with them.

"That was last Season," Fitzwilliam said in a drawl dripping with fashionable ennui. "A lifetime ago. The lovely Clarissa was fair game then. Not to worry, Cazenove. I do not carry a torch. I'll be sending my poor scribblings to someone else this Season."

"I am glad to hear it," Adam said. "Anyone we know?"

"As a matter of fact, I believe she is well-known to you. The beautiful Marianne Nesbitt."

"Mrs. Nesbitt?" Alvanley said. "One of the patronesses of those charity balls? Never knew you went for respectable widows, Fitz. Would have thought her a bit too tight-laced for your taste."

"Her laces were not so tight when I danced with her last night," Fitzwilliam said. "Her smile was so warm I almost broke out in an embarrassing sweat. And she moves like an angel on the dance floor."

"You sound besotted," Lord Worcester said.

"Merely intrigued," Fitzwilliam replied. "But I intend to test the waters a bit with a modest floral offering."

It was the opening Adam had waited for. He would

send this idiot packing, just as he had done with Aldershot. "Then be sure to send gardenias," he said. "She positively adores gardenias."

"Are you quite certain?" Fitzwilliam asked. "I had planned to send lilies, which she mentioned as her favorite flower."

"You must have misunderstood," Adam said. "I've known her for years and she has always favored gardenias. Nesbitt would send a bouquet if they'd quarreled or if he wanted to soften her mood, so to speak. Gardenias did the trick every time."

"Is that so?" Fitzwilliam smiled. "Then gardenias it shall be. I appreciate the advice, Cazenove."

"It was nothing, I assure you."

When he finally made his way out the front door and down the steps, Adam was grinning like a fool. Aldershot had left the field and Fitzwilliam would soon be out of the running. It was no doubt wrong of him to interfere with Marianne's life, and worse to feel so gleeful about it. But he had meant it when he'd said no one was good enough for her. Certainly not Aldershot or Fitzwilliam. Or any of the others.

The second lie, to Fitzwilliam, had come as easily as the first. Of course, it was not really the second lie, or even the third. He'd lost track of how many lies he'd told Marianne that night in her sitting room when he'd first been confronted with that damned list. He supposed he was turning into a scoundrel of the first degree. He ought to feel ashamed. He ought to feel remorse. Instead, he felt wildly amused and devilishly pleased with himself.

He suddenly felt the need to run each one of the remaining listees to earth and put a spoke in his wheel. He was so full of high spirits he laughed out loud as he walked down St. James's Street, and decided to visit Gentleman Jackson's boxing saloon to work off some of his excess energy.

And quite miraculously, his luck continued. Soon

after entering the rooms on Bond Street, he stood watching Jackson spar with some young buck Adam did not recognize when Sir Arthur Denney came in. He stood beside Adam and observed the famed pugilist's instructions with keen interest. When the lesson was over, he fell easily into conversation with Adam, who made sure to mention Marianne in passing. Soon enough, Denney was seeking advice from Mrs. Nesbitt's dear friend.

"What topics of conversation are sure to please her? Well," Adam said, "I can tell you that she has always been intrigued by manly pursuits. I never knew a woman who so enjoyed hearing all the details of a mill, or a cockfight."

"You're joking," Denney said as he removed his coat in preparation for his own sparring match. "I cannot believe we are speaking of the same woman."

"I am quite serious. Where other women would swoon, Mrs. Nesbitt relishes every gruesome detail. Just between the two of us, I suspect she secretly finds something seductive about activities so thoroughly masculine."

"Does she, now?"

"I am only guessing, of course. But whenever her late husband and I used to speak of a boxing match, for example, she would insist on hearing every blow described in detail. She was clearly excited by it, and I gathered from Nesbitt that she was always in a passionate mood after such discussions. If you get my meaning."

"Good Lord. I would never have imagined it. How fascinating."

"She does not advertise this passion of hers, of course, and most men would never dream of speaking to her of such things. You might win the day by being the only man who dares to do so."

"By God, I will!"

And just like that, a third name was poised to be

struck from the list. Three men now whose faces
would no longer play a role in the troublesome images
that had begun to plague Adam's thoughts, images of
Marianne making love to another man.

*You see how I look out for her, David, just as I
promised? I won't allow some unworthy nincompoop
to take your place in her bed.*

Marianne would murder him if she ever discovered
his lies and trickery, and he was quite sure he deserved
it. Even so, Adam was unable to stop smiling, for he
could not remember when he'd had such fun.

Chapter 6

All eyes were on the stage and all attention was directed to the beautiful voice of Angelica Catalani as she sang the role of Susanna in *Le Nozze di Figaro*. Adam, however, could not concentrate on the performance. There were too many distractions, most particularly the unsettling sight of Lord Hopwood seated altogether too close to Marianne.

They had not arrived at the theater together. Marianne had come with Lady Somerfield, her niece, and another young woman. But Hopwood had not left Marianne's side and made it clear that for tonight, at least, she belonged to him. Just as Eustace Tolliver had done with Lady Gosforth. Adam would bet a monkey those two were lovers. He did not miss the sly, secret touches and burning glances. Was Marianne engineering a similar situation? Had she already planned an assignation with Hopwood? Perhaps even tonight?

When she had offered seats in the Somerfield box to Adam and Clarissa, he had been pleased at the invitation, pleased that Marianne seemed to want to spend time with Clarissa and get to know her better. He had not expected to be forced to witness a seduction in progress. For even if Marianne had not yet narrowed the field to a single gentleman, Hopwood was most definitely making a play.

Adam had teased that Hopwood was too old for

her, and he still believed it. It wasn't so much a matter of age—the man was only in his early forties—as it was attitude. Hopwood did not demonstrate a vigorous approach to life. He drove carriages cautiously, and when he rode he always kept his mount at a polite canter, seldom breaking into a gallop. He was never seen at sporting venues such as Jackson's boxing saloon or Angelo's Fencing Academy. One had to wonder if he was at all fit. He was likely not fit enough for Marianne's purposes. The way Adam saw it, Hopwood was not worthy of her in any respect.

As Adam watched, the man took Marianne's hand and placed it on top of his arm, then covered it with his other hand. She turned to him and smiled, and left her hand in his for all the world to see, damn her.

It felt odd to see her with another man, to see her hand in another man's hand. He had been so accustomed to seeing her with David, knowing she belonged to David, that it quite simply felt wrong to see her with someone else. It was like an affront to his late friend. Adam had an irrational desire to lift up Hopwood by the scruff of his collar, plant his foot firmly on the man's backside, and send him careening over the edge of the box and into the pit below—all on David's behalf. But his friend was dead and Marianne belonged to no one. Not even the man who held her hand.

Adam scowled, and reached over for Clarissa's hand. She gave a little start, but did not pull away. He breathed a sigh of frustration. Why could she not be at least as accommodating as Marianne? Especially since he had a better right to take possession of her hand than Hopwood did of Marianne's. Throughout the week, Adam had been squiring his fiancée about town and she had yet to demonstrate any degree of warmth toward him. She smiled prettily and responded pleasantly to his attempts at conversation. But she seldom initiated conversation on her own.

He'd expected her shyness would have begun to fade a bit by now.

The betrothal had been a typical arrangement. Everything had been discussed and approved with her father before Clarissa was even consulted. They had never been together unchaperoned until the few minutes Adam was given with her to make his offer. Her acceptance had been sweetly given, and he did not believe she was displeased with the match, even if her parents had encouraged it. Yet every time he touched her he could feel the tension in her. And every time he tried to kiss her she presented tight, unyielding lips and pulled away quickly.

It was a troubling situation. Adam had been successfully wooing ladies for years, and yet he did not seem able to woo his own affianced wife. She was very young, of course, but younger women had thrown themselves in his path on occasion, flirted with him openly, invited seduction. He feared it was a matter of innocence rather than youth. He suspected Clarissa was simply very naive about the relations between men and women, and it was up to Adam to teach her.

He studied her profile as she watched the stage. Her pale blond hair was swept up into a riot of soft curls at the back of her head, and a few wisps curled at the nape of her neck. He'd been attracted to that pretty neck, had once wanted to run his tongue up the length of it. He still did.

He looked over at another neck he'd known and admired for much longer. Marianne's dark hair was pulled up higher on her head in a more sophisticated style, threaded with beads and tiny sprigs of flowers. No curls sprang loose at her neck. Her nape was perfectly exposed, as was a good deal more. The dress she wore was cut quite low in the back, revealing the elegant line of shoulders and spine, and a glorious expanse of pale skin as smooth and fine-textured as Chelsea porcelain. And though she sat at an angle that did not allow a view of her bosom, he could not forget that it was as well exposed as her back. She had dressed for seduction, and Hopwood was getting an eyeful of soft, white, womanly curves. And David's emeralds at her throat.

Adam had plenty to keep his own eyes pleasantly occupied. Clarissa had ample charms of her own, even if they were cloaked in youth and innocence. He had been attracted enough by those charms, after all, to pursue a betrothal.

He would drive himself mad if he continued to make comparisons between Clarissa and Marianne. There was no comparison. They were completely different, completely unique, each beautiful in her own way. It was not fair to compare Clarissa with a mature, sophisticated woman who knew more of the world, who had experience with men.

Adam tore his eyes from the sight of Marianne's perfect nape in such close proximity to Hopwood. He would concentrate instead on wooing his betrothed.

His hand still covered hers, and he began to slowly stroke her fingers. He heard a tiny intake of breath, but she kept her eyes on the stage. Adam loosened a button of her glove, placed a finger in the opening, and proceeded to trace little circles on her exposed flesh. At first, she sat so stiff it seemed she did not breathe at all. Gradually, though, he felt her relax, and sent up a silent prayer of thanks. A little patience was all that was needed. He must remember her youth and take time with her. And so he continued to gently fondle her wrist throughout the rest of the first act.

At the interval, Adam rose with the other gentlemen in the box and offered to procure refreshments for the ladies. He was pleased to see Marianne gather the younger women—Lady Somerfield's niece, Miss Thirkill, and her friend Miss Billingsley—around Clarissa. She would likely be more at ease with girls nearer her own age. He sent Marianne a message of thanks with his eyes, and she smiled in acknowledgment.

Just as he turned toward the door of the box, Adam caught a glimpse of Hopwood placing a hand on Marianne's bare back while he leaned down to speak to her. Images of the fellow touching her more intimately caused a knot to twist in Adam's stomach.

He really must get hold of himself. Marianne's private affairs were none of his business. He did not know why this whole question about her taking a lover got under his skin, but it was driving him to distraction.

You're in love with the woman. Always have been.

Rochdale's accusation rang in his head. It was not true, of course. Adam admired her. He respected her. He cared about her a great deal. But Marianne was his best friend's wife. He would never have betrayed David by falling in love with her.

He was, however, willing to admit that he was attracted to her. He might even concede that he'd *always* harbored a glimmer of attraction for her, but for the sake of his friend had buried it so deep it had virtually disappeared over the years. Now, however, as he watched other men look at her with admiration, even lust, that long-buried attraction had inconveniently risen to the surface once again. And because his engagement to Clarissa meant he could not act on it, he was driven to do stupid things to ensure that none of those other men did, either. He was fairly certain, in fact, that he was about to do one more stupid thing.

He turned away and left the box with Tolliver. Hopwood followed close behind.

"I say, Hopwood," Adam said as they made their way along the crowded corridor, "you have an estate in Suffolk, do you not?"

*   *   *

"I am so pleased to see you out . . . and about." Evelina Woodall, who'd left her own box to call upon a few others, darted a glance in the direction of Lord Hopwood's empty chair. "You look stunning tonight, and have the attentions of a very attractive man. I'm proud of you, my dear."

"Are you? You don't think I'm being . . . disloyal?"

"To David? Nonsense. He would want you to enjoy yourself. I have no doubt he would approve. And so do I."

Marianne took her sister-in-law's hand and squeezed it. "Thank you, Evelina. It pleases me to know that at least some members of David's family do not think me heartless."

"None of us think that of you, my dear."

"Not even your mother?"

Evelina lifted a shoulder. "She will come around one day. Give her time."

Marianne did not believe David's mother would ever come around, but she kept quiet. Evelina spoke briefly of the opera, then said her farewells as she left to visit other boxes. Marianne went to stand beside Beatrice and Penelope.

"So?" Penelope whispered. "Is it to be Lord Hopwood?"

"Hush," Marianne said, and glanced toward Clarissa and the other two young women standing nearby. "The girls might overhear."

"They are much too busy discussing bonnets and lace trimmings," Beatrice said, looking over her shoulder at the trio. "They are not the least interested in what we older women have to say. They are bound to assume three dried-up widows have nothing more interesting to discuss than tisane recipes or the best way to relieve the pain in our aching joints."

"If they only knew," Penelope said with a laugh, then glanced at the girls. "I confess I am surprised that Cazenove offered for the Leighton-Blair chit. What a shame to waste all that glorious masculinity on such a ninny of a girl. That giggle!"

The infamous titter rose up, as if on cue. Marianne stifled a groan.

"I confess I feel the same," she said. "But Adam seems to be infatuated with her. She is very sweet. And very shy, I think."

Penelope shrugged. "Still, it seems a shame. But I want to hear all about Lord Hopwood before he comes back. So tell us, Marianne."

"There is nothing to tell." Marianne kept her voice low so that the other two women had to lean in very close to hear. "Lord Hopwood has been very attentive. But other than a brief drive in the park, this is the first time we have spent much time together. I do like him, though."

"He is extremely attractive," Beatrice said.

"I think he will do very nicely," Penelope said. "Has he kissed you yet?"

"No."

"Then you might wait until he does," Penelope said, "before you decide if you want to pursue it further. At least, that is what I would do. I think a man should be a good kisser, don't you?"

"I do agree with that," Beatrice said. "There's more to physical intimacy than just . . . the act. When he wasn't making me want to wring his neck, Somerfield could make my knees weak with his kisses."

"Tolliver is an excellent kisser," Penelope said with a smug grin. "He has a very agile tongue."

"So you are lovers already?" Marianne asked.

"Since the night of our first ball. He measures up quite nicely to my young Scotsman."

"Congratulations," Beatrice said.

"I don't think I could move into an affair that quickly," Marianne said. "I need to know a gentleman a bit more before I could become intimate with him."

"I couldn't agree more," Beatrice said. "Even if the

physical pleasure was extraordinary, it would not be worth it to me if I discovered I could not like the gentleman."

"Bosh," Penelope said. "You are both too fussy. Remember, we are not looking for husbands. Only a bit of fun."

"True," Beatrice said. "But I'd prefer to know a man longer than a few weeks, I think."

"As for me," Marianne said, "I will continue to be fussy, if you don't mind. I have already been disappointed in several of the gentleman I had considered."

"How so?" Beatrice asked. "What happened?"

"Well, first there was Trevor Fitzwilliam."

"Ah, the poet," Penelope said with a wistful sigh. "Perfectly gorgeous man."

"That may be," Marianne said, "but I cannot think much of a man who does not pay the least attention to anything I say. The blackguard sent me a huge bouquet of gardenias after I had specifically mentioned that lilies are my favorite flower."

"To give him the benefit of the doubt," Beatrice said, "he may have decided that every other man would send you lilies and he only meant to be original."

"After I had said that gardenias make me sneeze?" Penelope chuckled. "Oh, dear."

"I think he ignored everything I said when we spoke about flowers, just so he could send me one of his sonnets comparing my skin to the petals of a gardenia."

"That sounds rather charming to me," Beatrice said.

"The point is he was more interested in his poem than in doing something that would truly please me. How could he have ignored the fact that the damned flowers make me ill? No, I cannot be bothered with a man more interested in himself than he is in me."

"A wise decision," Penelope said. "A man like that is likely to ignore your needs altogether and simply race to his own finish."

All three of them laughed, and a few heads turned their way, so they huddled together more closely.

"And then there was Sir Arthur Denney," Marianne said.

"What happened with him?" Penelope asked.

"He took me driving in the park, and spent the entire time telling me about a cockfight he'd attended the day before."

"Ew." Beatrice's face puckered up in distaste.

"Every spur and thrust was related to me. Every ounce of spilled blood and torn feathers was described in excruciating detail. I thought I was going to be sick."

"How perfectly horrid," Penelope said.

"It does not say much for the man's sensitivity," Beatrice said.

"Indeed it does not. You would think he'd have noticed I had turned pale. Or worse. I felt decidedly green around the edges. But that did not stop him. Even when I asked him to change the subject, he laughed and became even more gruesome. I have never jumped down from a carriage so fast in all my life. I could not wait to get away from him."

"I wonder how a man like that treats a woman in bed?" Penelope asked.

"I trust," Marianne said, "that none of us shall ever know."

"And so it is down to Lord Hopwood," Beatrice said.

"There are still a few others I am considering," Marianne said. "Sidney Gilchrist and Lord Julian Sherwood, for example, have done nothing yet to disgust me. I had thought Lord Aldershot had shown an interest, but he seems to be avoiding me lately."

"If things do not work out with Lord Hopwood," Penelope said, "I would recommend Lord Julian. He is certainly the most handsome, and he fills out his breeches very nicely."

"Penelope!"

"Oh, bosh. Do not tell me you haven't noticed. Ah, here is Tolliver." She got up and walked to the doorway of the box, where Eustace Tolliver stood chatting with two other gentlemen.

"I hope Lord Hopwood does not disappoint you, too," Beatrice said.

"So do I." Marianne glanced over at the three younger women, who were chattering together amicably, and nodded her head in their direction. "They seem to be getting along famously."

Beatrice smiled. "Emily never stops talking. And my own two girls are at the chatterbox stage, as well, wanting to hear every detail of every ball. I declare, the three of them quite wear me out sometimes." She paused and watched her niece and the others for a moment. "Miss Leighton-Blair must be three or four years older than Emily, but seems almost as young."

"Yes, she does seem awfully young for her age. I believe she is twenty or twenty-one. I confess, it is difficult to imagine her as Adam's wife."

Beatrice lifted her brows. "I believe you would feel that way about any woman he decided to marry. You have been close friends for too long to be objective."

"You are probably right. But I worry about this match. I find myself feeling angry with him for choosing such a girl, one who cannot possibly offer him more than her youth and beauty."

"Have a care, Marianne. You are making assumptions where you should not. You do not know how things are between them in private."

"But I know Adam, and I cannot imagine him finding contentment with a biddable young girl. Can you? Clarissa is not the sort who will stand up to him, argue with him, speak her own mind with him."

"Just because you behave that way with him does not mean he wants that in the woman he marries. Perhaps he wants a biddable wife. Most men do."

But Marianne did not think that was what Adam wanted. At least, she could not believe it was. He had seen how her marriage with David had been, how they had been equal partners, how they had much in common but could also disagree and argue, how they shared everything, knew each other inside out. That's the sort of marriage he would want. That was what she wanted for him. Yet, deep in her heart, she did not believe he would find that with Clarissa.

"Do you know, Beatrice, I think she is even a little afraid of him."

"What makes you say that?"

"I don't know. She just never seems quite at ease around him."

"In public. Her behavior with him in private may be a different matter altogether. It is with most of us, after all. Do not worry about them, Marianne. They will be fine. And so will you."

"You are right, of course. I am just feeling a bit sad that my long friendship with Adam will never be the same."

Beatrice touched her arm. "It may never be the same, but it doesn't have to end completely. It would do you good to befriend the girl. If you want to keep Adam in your life, you will need to accept Clarissa."

"I know. Perhaps I will go have a little chat with her now."

She rose and walked over to where the three younger women were gathered and pretending not to notice the shouts from young men below trying to get their attention. She moved to stand beside Clarissa.

"Young men never change," she said. "They were shouting from the pit in my day, as well."

Clarissa turned to her and smiled. "They seem very silly to me."

"Oh, they are just full of high spirits. I think they are great fun. But you prefer older men, do you not? Like Mr. Cazenove?"

Clarissa blushed. "I prefer him. It doesn't matter that he's a bit older than me."

Marianne laughed. "A bit older? My dear girl, he is almost six years older than *me.*"

"He is?"

"But that doesn't signify when you're in love. He will make you a fine husband. And he is very lucky to have such a beautiful, young wife."

"Thank you. That is very kind of you to say."

Marianne gave a dismissive little wave of her hand. "Tell me, are you enjoying the Season so far?"

"Oh, yes. We've been to ever so many balls and parties, and Mr. Cazenove has taken me to galleries and museums and such. It has been great fun. And educational."

"Educational?" Marianne smiled. "Things have certainly changed since I was a girl. The last thing we wanted during the Season was something educational. But things are different now, are they not? In my day, girls were looking for younger men, and everyone wanted one with a title. No one would dream of entertaining the addresses of anyone lower than a baronet, unless he had buckets of money." She chuckled softly. "Of course, I was already betrothed when I came to town for my first Season, and didn't worry about such things. I believe modern girls like you don't worry about them, either, do you? Mr. Cazenove is neither titled nor exceedingly wealthy."

Clarissa lifted her chin a notch. "No, I do not worry about Mr. Cazenove's lack of title, though his grandfather *was* an earl. And his fortune was sufficient to satisfy my father."

"Yes, of course. I did not mean to impugn Mr. Cazenove in any way. As you must know, he is one of my dearest friends. I only meant to compliment you on not being as obsessed with titles and fortunes as girls were during my Season, and still are, I daresay. There are plenty of other girls to vie for the attention

of some of those young men in the pit. Lord Ushworth, for example. Or Sir George Lowestoft. Smile,
my dear. They are both staring up at you with their
opera glasses."

Clarissa giggled.

The sound of the gentlemen returning to the box
caused both of them to turn away from the boisterous
crowd below and return to their chairs. Lord Hopwood, looking somewhat frazzled, handed Marianne a
glass of wine and helped her to her seat.

"I am sorry to have been so long," he said, "but I
have had distressing news."

"Oh, dear. What has happened?"

"As you may know, I have an estate near Higham
in Suffolk. I have just learned that the recent rains
have caused the Brett to overflow and the area is
badly flooded. For all I know, my home may be under-
water."

"Good heavens. How dreadful."

"Yes, I am afraid I must leave early tomorrow
morning. I want to get there as soon as possible and
discover the extent of any damage."

"Yes, of course."

"I am afraid that means I will not be able to escort
you to the Missenden rout, after all. I am terribly
sorry. I was looking forward to it."

"So was I, my lord, but I understand perfectly. You
must not be concerned on my account."

"You are too kind. But more than missing the rout
party, I'm afraid I cannot even stay for the end of this
performance. I really must take my leave at once to
begin preparations for the journey. I trust you will
forgive me."

He rose, took her hand, and bowed over it. "Your
servant, madam."

When the box curtains had closed behind him, Marianne gave a frustrated sigh, then caught Penelope's
eye. Her friend raised her brows in question. Mari-

anne shook her head. One more disappointment. Would she ever find the right man? Would she ever truly be a Merry Widow?

As she turned back toward the stage, she happened to catch a glimpse of Adam. He wore a disconcertingly satisfied smile.

Chapter 7

"Look at her, Rochdale." Adam stood against the wall in the glittering grand salon at Ellenborough House, which had been converted into a ballroom for the second Benevolent Widows Fund ball of the Season.

"I am looking," Rochdale said, "and I am suitably impressed. Your bride-to-be is a vision. The prettiest girl at the ball. Every man in London is aware of your good fortune. You need not gloat about it."

Clarissa was being led through the steps of a country dance with Lord Ushworth, and she was positively beaming. "But see how happy she looks. See how easily she laughs. Why can she not be as carefree with me as she is with that young puppy?"

Rochdale cast him an appraising glance. "Good God. Are you acting the jealous bridegroom already?"

"I am not jealous. Not exactly. I just wish she could be more comfortable with me. She has shown more vivacity with every other partner than she did during our set. More than she ever does with me, in fact."

Rochdale arched a brow. "Are you worried she will throw you over?"

"No. Clarissa is too well-bred to do something like that. But I begin to worry if I can make her happy. Am I too old for her?"

His friend groaned. "Not too old, but possibly too

stupid. You both knew what you were getting out of this bargain—you when you offered, she when she accepted. Do not start second-guessing the match now. It is too late for that."

"I am not second-guessing it."

"But you are getting cold feet, I think."

"I'm just feeling old, that's all. Even Marianne is radiant on the arm of a younger man. Look at her out there with Sherwood."

Marianne was in the same line as Clarissa, standing right beside her, in fact. Certain figures of the dance required them to cross one another and switch partners. Both ladies were clearly enjoying themselves. Marianne smiled and laughed with Lord Julian Sherwood just as easily as Clarissa did with Ushworth.

"And that is the real problem, isn't it?" Rochdale said. "You are still vexed over Marianne taking a lover. That smile for her young man is all the more provoking because you know where it could lead, whereas you have no fear of betrayal from Clarissa."

Was he doing that? Was he inventing problems with Clarissa because he was still irritated over the whole business of Marianne with a lover?

There was probably a germ of truth in what Rochdale said. Sherwood was still in the running, and Marianne appeared to favor him. Adam hated the idea, thought it would end badly, though there did not seem to be a damned thing he could do about it.

"Marianne is not my problem," he said.

"Indeed, she is not."

"But Clarissa is. I am hoping she will warm up to me eventually, but I have no experience with innocent virgins."

Rochdale lifted his hands and held them palm out at his shoulders in a gesture of protective dismissal. "Don't look at me," he said. "Innocent girls give me a bellyache. Never go near them. Still a bit twitchy, is she?"

"Yes, for the most part, though very occasionally she will let her guard down a bit. I am learning that when dealing with young innocents, one must move slowly, and with caution."

"Or perhaps not."

Adam turned to Rochdale. "What do you mean?"

"You have something of a reputation with the ladies. It is possible that reputation is intriguing to Clarissa. For all you know, she could be secretly hoping you will pounce, secretly panting to discover if everything said about you is true."

"Pounce?" Adam chuckled. "I suspect if I pounced, poor Clarissa would fall into a dead swoon."

"Are you certain? You might be reading her all wrong."

Adam watched Clarissa glide through the figures with Ushworth, smiling happily. He found it difficult to believe Rochdale's theory. If she wanted him to pounce, she would have at least smiled at Adam like that. "I don't think so, but perhaps I should attempt a bit more aggressiveness just to be sure. Not a full pounce, but more than a chaste salute on the cheek."

He continued to watch his betrothed, wondering what she would do if he really kissed her, thoroughly kissed her. His eyes drifted to Marianne, stepping gracefully through a swing corner, then a double turn. She wore a dress of emerald green in a silky fabric that alternately floated and clung as she moved, providing provocative hints of the body beneath. Once again, she had dressed for seduction, and Sherwood did not bother to hide his appreciation.

"She is a beautiful woman."

Adam turned to find Sidney Gilchrist at his side. Good God. Another man from Marianne's list to plague him.

"Yes, she is," Adam replied.

"Can't keep your eyes off her, can you?" Gilchrist gave a wry chuckle. "Well, you will have her all to yourself soon enough, Cazenove. Stole a march on everyone by managing a betrothal before the Season began, you sneaky devil."

Adam lifted his brows in interest. He should have realized the man would assume he was staring at Clarissa and not Marianne. "Forgive me if I interfered with any plans you may have had involving Miss Leighton-Blair."

Gilchrist gave a bark of laughter. "No such thing, I assure you. I only meant that you spoiled a bit of the Season's sport by removing one of the prettiest girls from the field. Besides," he added with a conspiratorial wink, "I've got my eye on another filly." His gaze traveled to the dance floor and Adam stifled a groan.

"You are hoping, then," he said, "to follow my lead and announce your own betrothal this Season?"

Gilchrist's brows shot up to his hairline. "Good Lord, no." His eyes darted left and then right as he quickly scanned the room. "Please, I beg you, do not even *whisper* such an idea at a gathering like this. Some girl's mama is certain to hear you and decide I am the perfect match for her bracket-faced charge." He gave a horrified shudder.

"Sorry," Adam said, biting back a grin. "I gather you have something else in mind with a certain lady."

"Indeed I do. And it ain't marriage, I can assure you."

"A bit of sport, then."

Gilchrist gave another wink and clicked his tongue. "Just so."

"I wish you good luck in the chase, old boy. And who is the lady, if you don't mind telling?"

Gilchrist leaned in closer and nodded toward the dance floor. "The beautiful Mrs. Nesbitt."

Adam pretended to look shocked. "You're not serious?"

"I know, I know. You will say she is a pattern card of propriety and the least likely woman to engage in a brief frolic. But I tell you, she has changed this Season. I have a very good hunch she is ready to get back in the game."

"Do you think so?" Adam pulled a thoughtful face. "I suppose it is possible she has been too long without Nesbitt and wants to replace him in her bed. I would not be surprised to hear that she misses it. Nesbitt was . . . well, let us just say his replacement will have very big shoes to fill."

Gilchrist's eyes widened. "You mean . . ."

Adam nodded. "He and I were friends since our Oxford days, and I had more than one occasion to observe . . . his assets." He leaned close to Gilchrist and lowered his voice. "The man was hung like a stallion."

Gilchrist paled. "He was?"

"Never saw a man to match him," Adam said in a conspiratorial whisper. "Knew what to do with it, too, I'm told. At Oxford, everyone called him 'the Rod.' Oh, yes, his widow will be missing him, to be sure. It will take the right sort of man to replace him, though, as her expectations are bound to be rather . . . high. You're a better man than I am, Gilchrist, if you mean to even try."

"Well, I, um, haven't yet entirely decided to approach her."

"Oh, I wouldn't worry about it, old chap. She is too refined a lady to remark upon any comparisons. Besides," he said, giving him a friendly pat on the back, "I'm sure you would measure up to the task."

Gilchrist gave an awkward chuckle. "I have no worries on that score, I promise you. But there are other women I have considered. May go after Lady Morpeth instead. Both are beautiful women. Haven't made up my mind."

"I wish you luck with whichever lady you choose," Adam said.

Gilchrist soon made his excuses and beat a speedy retreat to the cardroom.

Lord Rochdale, who'd heard the whole exchange, let out a cackle of laughter. "You blackguard! That was downright cruel, you know. The Rod?"

Adam grinned, feeling rather proud of himself. Another player had left the field. He did not believe his late friend would mind having his assets exaggerated.

I am only looking out for her, David, just as you requested.

"While it is a brilliant maneuver in discouraging interest in the fair Marianne," Rochdale said, "I have to wonder if you have not entirely lost your mind."

"Not at all. I have merely steered away a few gentlemen who are unworthy of Marianne's attention."

"A few? This is not the first man you've bamboozled into abandoning the chase?"

"There were two or three others. None of whom would have suited her."

"And you used the same ploy with each, warning that she might find them unequal to the task?"

Adam smiled. "No, that one was a spur-of-the-moment invention. I did not like the way he ogled her on the dance floor and called her a filly. I employed different tactics for the others."

"It may be amusing to you, but she will not thank you for this." The merriment had faded from Rochdale's eyes. "In fact, I rather imagine she will have your head on a platter if she ever finds out. She will hate you for it, and then where will you be?"

"She will not find out."

"Dammit, Cazenove, this is madness. Do you have any idea how childish your behavior is? And selfish. What gives you the right to interfere in her life like this?" He shook his head in disgust. "You have a bride to see to, for God's sake. Tend to her and leave Marianne Nesbitt to someone else." He turned on his heel and walked away.

Adam's glow of smug triumph dimmed in his friend's wake. Rochdale was right, of course. Adam was being ridiculous and selfish and outrageously presumptuous, and that damned promise to David was merely an excuse. It was his newly acknowledged attraction to Marianne, and the impossibility of acting on it, that was the motivating force behind his idiotic behavior. It wasn't simply a matter of not wanting another man to be Marianne's lover. In the deepest, most secret part of his heart, he knew that if things had been different, if he had not offered for Clarissa, he might have been that lover. *Might* have been. He could not even be certain she would have accepted him, but he was fairly certain now that he would have offered.

For the sake of might-have-beens, he'd escaped into folly, treating the whole business as a lark, as a game. It was not a game. It was her life. If she sought to add a little pleasure to it, he should be happy for her. He should be.

But it was so damned hard.

"Are you as devastated as I?" Adam whispered as he and Marianne stepped through the figures of a country dance. "The smiles of my bride-to-be are turned on your favorite beau. Will they throw us both over, do you think?"

Marianne glanced to the other line where Lord Julian Sherwood danced with Clarissa. They danced well together and the girl did look radiant. But Marianne had often noticed that Clarissa seemed more comfortable with young men closer to her own age.

"Perhaps we will both have our poor hearts broken," she said with a smile when the figure brought them together again.

"Aha. That must mean Sherwood is still in the running, if he has the capacity to break your heart."

"I still have hopes in that direction," she whispered, "but my heart is not involved."

"But certain other parts hope to be?"

Marianne hid an explosion of embarrassed laughter

in a little cough and glared at Adam as he crossed the line in a set-and-change-sides figure. She was unable to look him in the eye during the rest of the dance for fear of dissolving into giggles—unspeakable behavior for one of the patronesses of the ball.

By mutual agreement, they abandoned the dance floor before the last dance in the set commenced, and instead took a turn about the room.

"What a beast you are to tease me so in public," she said. "You will destroy my aura of aristocratic reserve."

"You may be one of the patronesses, but I know you to be neither aristocratic nor reserved, so you must forgive me." He looked toward the dancers still engaged in a longways set and said, "My betrothed is still smiling at Sherwood. Are you jealous?"

"No. Are you?"

He chuckled. "No. But I can see that she might find him attractive. He's a fine-looking chap, is he not?"

Marianne stopped and looked up at him. "Adam? Are you actually singing a man's praises for once instead of finding some ludicrous objection to him?"

Adam shot her an enigmatic look, then tugged her forward again to resume walking. "Sherwood's not a bad fellow."

"High praise, indeed! Let us hope I can fix his interest."

Adam nodded, and Marianne knew that was as close to an endorsement as she would ever receive from him. She was aware that he did not approve of her plan. It was probably difficult for him to think of her with anyone but David, and it was likely he thought she was betraying his friend's memory by considering a lover. His disapproval had been obvious from the start. Marianne often wished she'd never told him about it.

"Ah, and here is Mother," Adam said as Viola Cazenove strolled toward them on the arm of Adam's father. "All my favorite ladies are in attendance this evening."

Marianne removed her arm from his so he could greet his parents. His mother was a handsome woman, still slender and elegant, whose silver hair blended with the natural gold into a beautiful shade the color of pale champagne. Marianne had always envied the way fair-haired women aged. Brunettes like herself were faced with years of salt-and-pepper streaks and finally pure silver—much more aging than champagne gold. She wondered if she would resort to hair dye when her time came.

Adam kissed his mother's cheek and shook his father's hand. "Hullo, Father. Looking hale and hearty as ever, I see," he said with a sly grin.

"Not too bad," Hugh Cazenove said. "Not too bad."

Adam's father did indeed appear to be in fine health. He had thick, white hair—worn a shade too long, just like his son—and bright green eyes that twinkled as he spoke. He was a tall, good-looking man with only a bit of extra weight around his middle, straining against the buttons of his waistcoat.

"And Mrs. Nesbitt," he said, "what a pleasure to see you again. Another very fine ball you ladies have given us."

Marianne offered her hand and he bowed over it. "It is good to see you, too, sir. And you, Mrs. Cazenove."

"You look lovely, as always," Adam's mother said with a friendly smile. "It is nice to see you wearing beautiful colors again, my dear."

"Thank you, ma'am."

Hugh Cazenove's gaze followed Adam's to the dance floor. "Are you not pleased for my son, Mrs. Nesbitt?" he said, beaming with pride. "Is not Miss Leighton-Blair a beautiful girl? Only see how the boy cannot take his eyes off her."

"It's a good match," his wife said, smiling as she watched Clarissa in the dance.

"And about time, too," Adam's father said.

"You cannot rush these things, my love," Mrs. Cazenove said. "Our Adam had to find the right girl. We used to hold you and David Nesbitt up as an example," she said to Marianne. "We so wanted him to find as perfect a partner as David had." Her eyes strayed back to the dancers. "I hope he has done so."

Marianne did not miss the hint of uncertainty in her voice. She looked to Adam only to find his brow creased in a frown as he watched Clarissa.

"Of course he has," his father said. "The girl is a picture. Lovely little thing, is she not?"

"She is very beautiful," Marianne said. "Adam is the envy of every gentleman this Season."

"Ha!" His father clapped him on the back. "I knew it would be so. Well done, my boy. Well done."

"I see Lady Dewsbury across the room," Adam's mother said. "I must have a word with her. Will you excuse us, please?"

After they'd gone, Adam and Marianne resumed their walk. Marianne was tempted to ask about his mother's opinion of the match with Clarissa, but thought better of it. She had said enough on that subject.

They strolled in comfortable silence for a while, watching the dancers. Adam's eyes seemed to be constantly on Clarissa. Marianne wondered if she had been wrong about their betrothal. Was he in fact besotted with the girl? Was his heart involved after all?

He looked down and caught her watching him, then smiled ruefully. "I took her to Somerset House yesterday to see the new paintings."

"Oh?" Marianne had not yet had time to view the new exhibition. She used to look forward to it every year, when she and David and Adam would go together and then have long, animated discussions about all they saw. It was bigger than the annual British Institution exhibitions that both men had sponsored, and was given more importance by the critics because of its association with academicians rather than connoisseurs. It was often the more enjoyable *because* they were not involved financially. They went simply to appreciate the art. Last year Adam had taken her alone, and she had secretly hoped he would do so again this year. She must become accustomed to Adam's giving Clarissa precedence.

"I am looking forward to seeing it," she said. "The new Wilkie is getting a lot of attention in the journals."

"Yes, and not all of it flattering," he said. "But I found the piece charming and full of life. It's a vibrant work, reminiscent of Watteau. You will like it. There is also an intriguing work by Dawe of a child rescued by its mother from an eagle's nest. Very melodramatic. The critics are raving, but you will scoff at its sentimentality. Oh, and there are several new portraits by Lawrence."

"Good ones?"

"Quite good."

"Oh, you are a wretch for telling me. You know my weakness for Lawrence. I must contrive a visit to Somerset House very soon."

"I would be happy to escort you, my dear."

"Thank you, Adam, I would like that."

"And perhaps you would like to accompany Clarissa and me on Thursday when we visit the Institution to view the preparations for the Reynolds exhibit. A majority of the paintings are on site already."

Marianne laughed. "I do not think that is a good idea. Did I tell you Mrs. Leighton-Blair's insinuations when she and Clarissa called on me last week?"

"Insinuations?"

"Well, that is how it sounded to me. She asked a

great many questions about my friendship with you. I believe she has misconstrued our relationship, and I told her so."

Adam groaned.

"She claimed to have no such concerns," Marianne continued, "but I could sense she thought I was some sort of threat to your relationship with Clarissa. With that in mind, I doubt she would be happy to learn that I had been on your other arm while you guided her daughter through the Institution gallery."

"I would claim you to be our chaperone," he said, smiling wickedly.

She laughed. "I hardly think that would suit. I shall find another escort." She cast her eyes meaningfully in the direction of Lord Julian Sherwood.

"I am sorry about Clarissa's mother," Adam said. "Perhaps I should have a reassuring word with her."

"I think that would only encourage her to believe there is more to our friendship than meets the eye. It would probably be best to say nothing at all."

"I suppose she is glaring at us from some dark corner at this very moment," he said.

"Then she will see nothing untoward. We are merely strolling and talking in full view of the entire assembly."

"I could give a surreptitious squeeze to your lovely bottom as we pass by her."

Marianne laughed. "Don't you dare."

"I won't." Adam lowered his voice to a buttery soft and seductive tone that washed over her like warm honey. "But in that clingy dress, you make it *very* tempting."

Marianne's breath came out in a squeaky little sigh and she had to turn away to compose herself. She had thought she was becoming accustomed to the varying degrees of sexual tension that so often charged the air between men and women, that tension of which she'd only recently become aware. But with Adam it was always stronger, always more unsettling, when it ought to be comfortable and playful since he was only teasing. She sincerely wished one of the other gentlemen who showed an interest in her could give her the same tingly feeling Adam so often did.

They walked in silence a while longer until Marianne happened to glance up and catch Adam in a frown. "What is it?" she asked. "What is troubling you? Is it something your mother said?"

"Ah, you caught that, did you? It may please you to know that she has some of the same doubts you expressed about my betrothal."

"It does not please me, Adam. I am sorry if we have made this difficult for you. I have promised to be more hopeful. I can see that you are very fond of the girl. I am sorry I ever said anything against her."

"I would rather you spoke your mind with me, even when it is something I don't wish to hear. Besides, I have been giving a lot of thought to what you and Mother have said, and though I hate to admit it, I am worried."

"Oh, Adam." She squeezed his arm. "I'm so sorry. What worries you in particular?"

"I cannot be sure she is as happy as she could be about our betrothal. She is so reticent with me, so shy. But she is not that way with other men. Look at her with Sherwood. And earlier with Ushworth, she laughed and chattered as she never does with me. And when I touch her . . . well, I worry that she is not happy with me."

Damn. It was beginning to look more and more as if this upcoming marriage was headed for disaster. Though Marianne had never liked the idea of Adam's betrothal to a silly girl like Clarissa, she had finally resigned herself to it, believing he was pleased with the match. It was troubling to learn that he was concerned about it.

"But she spoke very well of you the other night at the opera," she said. "Championed you, in fact."

"Did she? That is surprising." He paused a moment, then said, "So, she has spoken to you about me?"

"Only in the most general way."

"No woman-to-woman confidences?"

"Nothing like that," she said. "Clarissa is polite to me but not overly friendly. She may share her mother's concerns, for all I know. In any case, I believe she sees me as a much older woman, someone of her mother's generation, not someone likely to be a confidante."

"But you are much closer in age to her than her mother. I was hoping . . ."

She tilted her head up to look at him when he did not continue. "What were you hoping? That she and I would become close friends? That the three of us would be like you and David and me?"

That would never happen. She was sure of it.

"My hopes are not that high," he said. "But I was hoping you might talk to her for me, try to get her to open up to you. I want to know her feelings about this marriage, about me. I need to know if she finds me offensive, or if she is afraid of me. I need to know if she is feeling pressured into a betrothal she does not want."

"And you think she will tell me?"

He shrugged. "I don't know. I just hoped she might feel more comfortable talking to another woman."

A deep frown marked his brow. He truly was concerned. And so was Marianne. Maybe she could do something to help put an end to everyone's worries. She squeezed his arm and said, "I will do my best to befriend her, Adam, and hope that she will confide in me."

"Thank you, my dear."

"The set is about to end. Let me see if I can catch her before she is swept away by another partner."

Marianne left Adam and strolled toward the other side of the ballroom. As she neared the line where

Clarissa and Lord Julian danced, she happened to catch sight of Sidney Gilchrist. A handsome gentleman who had been most attentive, he still ranked high on her list of potential lovers. She continued to favor Lord Julian above the rest, but one must keep one's options open. Besides, she really did need to speak with Mr. Gilchrist.

Marianne caught his eye and nodded a greeting. An odd look crossed his face, but he politely awaited her approach and took her proffered hand when she reached him.

"Mrs. Nesbitt," he said, and bowed over her hand. For the first time that she could recall, he did not make a show of kissing the air above her fingers, or even the fingers themselves.

"Mr. Gilchrist, I had not seen you arrive. You must forgive me for not welcoming you properly, as a patroness ought."

"Think nothing of it, ma'am. It is a rare squeeze tonight and you are not expected to tend to each and every attendee, I am sure."

"It is a gratifying turnout, is it not? I believe Fund contributions will reach record amounts this Season. Thank you so much for coming. But I most particularly wished to speak with you, Mr. Gilchrist."

"Oh?"

"Yes. You had very kindly invited me to drive with you in the park the day after tomorrow. I am afraid I am forced to cancel those plans. We have had to reschedule a meeting of the Fund trustees to that same afternoon, and I really must be there. I am terribly sorry."

The tight expression in his face softened slightly and he smiled. "I am disappointed, of course, but understand perfectly."

He did not look the least disappointed, in fact. How very lowering.

"As it happens," he continued, "I have heard of an

opening that afternoon at Angelo's Fencing Academy and will now be able to take advantage of it. Angelo is not as charming as yourself, of course, but I shall muddle through somehow."

"Ah, so you enjoy swordplay, Mr. Gilchrist?"

"I do my best."

"My late husband was an expert swordsman," she said. "A master of the thrust and parry. I always found it thrilling to watch him wield his sword."

The cheerful expression on Mr. Gilchrist's face dissolved and a muscle twitched in his jaw. "Indeed," he said, "I had heard that about Mr. Nesbitt. If you will excuse me, ma'am, there is someone I must speak with. Good evening to you." He sketched a quick bow and walked away.

It almost seemed to Marianne that he had fled. He certainly appeared to be in a terrible hurry to get away. How provoking. It seemed he might not be as interested as she had hoped. Perhaps it was not very tactful to speak so glowingly of one's late husband to a prospective lover. She must remember that in the future.

Chapter 8

"So, tell me, Clarissa, are you getting excited about your upcoming marriage?"

Marianne had been fortunate to find Clarissa without a partner for the next set, and it was no great effort to convince the girl to join her in the tearoom. One of the anterooms at Ellenborough House had been set out with small tables and chairs, and a counter had been placed along one wall, where tea and biscuits were served. Marianne had appropriated an empty table in a corner, slightly removed from the bustle and chatter of the rest of the room.

Clarissa looked up and smiled. "Of course."

"I remember the time before my own wedding very well," Marianne said, hoping she could get more than a few words out of the young woman. "It was a busy time, what with bridal clothes and wedding plans. Not to mention packing up my belongings to move to a new home. I found the idea of leaving my old life behind forever a rather frightening prospect. I suppose you must be feeling much the same."

Clarissa shrugged her slim shoulders. "A little, perhaps."

"You will miss your father's house in Wiltshire, I imagine."

"Yes, I will. I have always loved it there. But I look forward to creating a new life with Mr. Cazenove."

"Then, you are pleased with your betrothal to him?"

She pulled a face. "Of course. Why should I not be?"

"No reason at all," Marianne said. "I was just thinking of my own betrothal. I had known Mr. Nesbitt forever and was very much in love with him. You do not have that advantage, I think. You have not known Mr. Cazenove very long. I would not be at all surprised if you felt some apprehension about entering into a marriage with him."

Clarissa's eye grew wide. "You would be afraid to marry Mr. Cazenove?"

Marianne laughed. "I would not be afraid to marry *him,* because I know him well. But I would be a bit nervous about marrying someone I had not known as long. That is what I meant. There is nothing I know about Mr. Cazenove that should give you alarm, Clarissa. He is a good man." She studied the young woman closely and detected a hint of anxiety in her eyes. "Have *you* heard something about him that gives you alarm? He does have a bit of a reputation with women. Does that worry you?"

Clarissa looked down at her teacup and said nothing.

"Clarissa? Is there something troubling you about him? You may tell me, you know, and I will keep your confidence. I do want us to be friends."

After a long pause, the girl looked up and said, "I am a little nervous, I suppose. He is so much older and has so much experience . . . of the world."

"With other women, you mean?"

"Yes."

"He *is* considered something of a rake."

"I know."

Marianne smiled. "That only makes him all the more exciting, don't you think?"

The girl's cheeks flushed and she averted her eyes. "I suppose so."

"Do you find him exciting?"

Her blush deepened. "Sometimes."

"When he touches you?"

Clarissa did not respond. Perhaps she was embarrassed by such frank speech. The Merry Widows had surely become a bad influence on Marianne, for not so very long ago talking of such private matters would have embarrassed her, as well.

"Don't you like it when he touches you?" she asked.

It was a long moment before the girl spoke. "He seems to like to touch me," she said in a small, timorous voice. "He is always touching me."

Marianne could believe it. Adam was a toucher. He was always reaching for her hand or stroking her arm or touching her cheek. It had always been so with him. Perhaps it was the rake in him, or a sense of playfulness, or just an innate craving for human contact. Touching was so natural with him that he probably wasn't even aware of doing it. It was only lately that his touch had provoked new sensations for Marianne. Clarissa was no doubt experiencing those same sensations.

"But you do not like it?" Marianne repeated.

Clarissa's shoulders hunched inward slightly. "I like it. But it scares me a little, too. The way it makes me feel."

Marianne knew exactly what she was talking about. There was a potent masculinity about Adam that had a strong effect even on a widow like herself. To an innocent like Clarissa, it must be overwhelming.

"That feeling is part of what happens between men and women," she said. "It is nothing to be afraid of."

"I know. Mama told me so. But I never know what to do. I suppose I worry what he will think of me. I sometimes fear he finds me ignorant and gauche. And not just . . . in that way. In other ways, too. I daresay it is silly, but I worry that he thinks me inexperienced and stupid. I am afraid it makes me a bit insecure and shy around him."

Marianne reached out a hand and touched Clarissa's arm. "That is perfectly understandable, you know, especially when there is such a difference in age. But when you get to know him better, you will be less intimidated."

"Yes, I'm sure that's true. It is just that I often feel so tongue-tied round him. I never know what to say. I want to please him, but I feel so stupid and childish. He took me to see some pictures at Somerset House yesterday, and he knew so much about the artists and the subjects. I know he wanted me to appreciate them, but . . ." She gave a little shake of her head.

"You did not enjoy the paintings?"

She shrugged. "They were just pictures. Faces and figures and such, nothing more. They either look pretty or they do not. I could not understand any of what he said about light and color and symbolism. I felt the same way at the opera when he spoke so knowledgeably about Mozart. I am just too unsophisticated, I suppose."

"Or perhaps you simply have other interests. You would likely be more comfortable speaking of things that interest you, things you know about and enjoy. What are your favorite pastimes, Clarissa?"

She looked pensive for a moment, as though the question perplexed her. "Well, I like to take long walks in the countryside. I like flowers, and enjoy gardening. Mama has always scolded me for being so friendly with our gardeners, but I love watching how they tend the plantings from season to season. I embroider quite a lot, mostly floral designs. Oh, and I love festivals and fairs—the Midsummer's Eve bonfires, the harvest festivals, the winter mummings, and spring maypoles."

"You love the country, then. You enjoy the outdoors."

"Mama quite despairs of my complexion because I spend so much time outside. She thinks I will turn brown and give Mr. Cazenove a disgust of me. But I never turn brown. I turn pink." She gave one of her infamous giggles, and a few heads turned in their direction.

Poor Clarissa. She would not appreciate Adam's plan to live in town all year. Marianne was becoming more and more convinced that this marriage would require considerable compromise for both of them.

"You see how easily you speak of things familiar and dear to you?" she said. "If you steer the conversation to those topics, you will likely be much more comfortable in speaking with Mr. Cazenove."

"Perhaps you are right. It would certainly be less awkward than trying to converse about painting and opera. I shall try to introduce topics closer to home."

Marianne assumed that meant home in the country. Would this young woman ever truly be at home in town?

"You obviously love country life," she said. "How would you feel if you had to give it up and live in town?"

Clarissa gave a little moue of distaste. "I do not believe I would like that very much at all, but it is not likely to happen, is it? Mr. Cazenove has an estate in Dorset as well as the house in town."

Unless he'd already sold it. Good Lord, this poor girl was going to be miserably disappointed, and that in turn was bound to make Adam miserable as well.

"I do enjoy London," Clarissa said. "It is exceedingly entertaining, and I am having the most wonderful Season. The Benevolent Widows' balls are the best of it all. I am ever so grateful for your invitations. But I daresay it is a dead bore here in the summer and winter months when everyone is gone."

London was never a dead bore, in Marianne's opinion, at any time of year. She subscribed to Dr. Johnson's opinion: "When a man is tired of London, he is tired of life; for there is in London all that life can afford." Those who came to London only for the Season missed a great deal.

"You must be sure that Mr. Cazenove knows of your preference for the country," she said. And she must tell him before he sold that estate in Dorset.

Poor Adam. He would have to live in the country after all if he wanted to keep his bride happy. She liked harvest festivals and he liked the opera. It was a match, or mismatch, destined to fail.

The best possible solution would be for Clarissa to cry off. It was not a love match. Neither of them would be terribly hurt. Adam would be embarrassed, and perhaps even publicly ridiculed. But the alternative was an unhappy union and she did not want that for him.

It was surely not her place to do so, but Marianne decided she simply had to interfere.

"Clarissa, I hope you will not mind if I speak frankly, but are you quite certain Mr. Cazenove is the right man for you? He is so much older, and his interests are so different—I am wondering if you will be happy with him."

Clarissa looked chagrined. "I am afraid I have given the wrong impression. Yes, he is older and we have different interests, but so do lots of other married couples. I will endeavor to overcome my shyness around him. You can be sure I will do my best to make him happy."

"I have no doubt of it," Marianne said. "It is what is expected of you, is it not? But allow me to give you a word of advice. I had a wonderful marriage, filled with love and happiness. Mr. Nesbitt and I shared everything together because we were kindred souls. We shared ideas and likes and dislikes. We had our disagreements, to be sure, as all couples do. But we survived them because of all we shared. I would like the same sort of happiness for you and Mr. Cazenove, as you are both my friends."

"Thank you, ma'am. I hope that over time, we will be as happy as you were."

"I hope so, too. But just remember, you need not be forced into something you do not truly want. I realize you probably had little say in the betrothal arrangements, but this is not the Middle Ages, after all. No one can force you into a marriage against your will. If you conclude that you cannot be happy in this marriage, then you must not be afraid to say so. Tell Mr. Cazenove and your father. Neither, I am certain, would insist you marry a man with whom you could not be happy. There are, after all, hundreds of other fish in the sea. Just tonight I have watched a dozen young men tripping over themselves for the favor of one of your smiles."

Clarissa frowned. "If you are suggesting I throw over Mr. Cazenove, then I must tell you that will never happen. I don't mind that he is older. I despise all those silly young men tripping over themselves. I prefer a more mature man, someone not so frivolous and care-for-nothing. And we will work out whatever differences we have, I assure you. I am determined upon it."

"An excellent attitude, my dear girl. You put my mind at ease. Now, let us return to the ballroom. You must allow me to introduce you to some of the other guests."

After they left the tearoom, Marianne took on the role of patroness of the ball, introducing Clarissa to a few eligible, handsome young men who would be infinitely more suitable for her than Adam. Young Peregrin Jekyll was thrilled to lead Clarissa into the next set of dancing.

Clarissa might believe she was committed to the betrothal, but Marianne hoped she had not only planted a few seeds of doubt, but also thrown a bit of temptation in her path.

It felt distastefully meddlesome, but she did not care. She had to save Adam from his own foolishness.

"And then we picked wild strawberries," Clarissa said, "and walked all the way back through the eastern wood to the hermitage. We did not return until the sun was down and were roundly scolded for it."

Adam steered the team through the park and marveled at this new gregariousness of Clarissa's. For the first time that he could recall, she had actually initiated conversation, and he'd allowed her to chatter on while he drove. She positively glowed as she spoke, looking so pretty that he could almost forget that she talked of nothing but life in the country.

It appeared he would have to reconsider selling that blasted house in Dorset. His dream of a bigger house in town faded with every anecdote about the spring plantings and harvest home suppers and sheep-shearing festivals. He would have to bite his tongue and become a country squire after all if he wanted his young wife to be as happy as she was at this moment. She looked so deliciously appealing that he wanted to pull the team to a halt and kiss her.

By Jove, that was precisely what he would do. He'd been waiting for just the right moment to try again. Only twice before had he managed a kiss, and both times had been less than memorable. But she was so animated today that she was almost irresistible. Perhaps he would explore Rochdale's notion that she secretly wanted more from him. He would not pounce. Not on a public thoroughfare with a team of horses to control. But that parasol of hers could be used to advantage. He led the team in the direction of a particular stand of trees away from the crowds.

"What is your favorite thing to do when you're at home in the country?" He wanted to stick to her favorite topic in hopes of maintaining that animated glow.

"I like to take long, long walks. I like to sit on a log by the river and watch the ducks and the geese. I like to lie back in the tall grass and stare up at the sky." She gave a sheepish giggle. "I suppose you could say that I like doing nothing."

"Do you never stay indoors, my dear?"

"Yes, of course. Heavens, I have made it sound as though I am completely lazy, have I not? I do enjoy those lazy moments with nothing to do, but you must have no fear that I will not take proper care of your home, sir. I have been well trained in household management and know my duty."

He reached out and patted her gloved hand. "I have no doubt of it. But what do you like to do when all the household work is done and it is raining cats and dogs outside? How do you occupy your time indoors? Do you like to read?"

"Not very much, I fear. I play the pianoforte a little, but mostly I like to embroider. I create my own designs," she said with a proud tilt of her chin.

"Do you? And what sorts of designs are they?" He turned the team into the small grove of trees and pulled back on the reins.

"Flowers, mostly. I love floral borders with twining leaves and vines, and central medallions of individual flowers."

"I shall be pleased to see your work," he said as the team came to a halt.

"Oh! We've stopped." She turned her head in every direction, as though trying to determine where they were, and then up at him inquiringly. "Why have we stopped, sir?"

"Tilt your parasol in that direction, will you?" He

indicated the busier area of the park where they had been driving before. She would be somewhat shielded from view.

She looked a bit startled, but did as he asked. He reached out and took her chin in his hand, tilted her face up so he could dip his head beneath the brim of her bonnet, then kissed her.

He felt her stiffen, so he kept it simple. He moved his mouth over hers, slowly exploring, giving her time to accept him, and ran his tongue along the seam of her lips. They did not part. In fact, they tightened, whether out of fear or modesty he could not tell. It was discouraging enough, though, for him to pull back.

So much for being more aggressive. One touch of his tongue and she'd closed up like an oyster.

He kept his hand on her chin as he looked into her eyes, trying to read her emotions without much success. Was she offended? Embarrassed? Aroused? Frightened? He could not tell.

"Am I moving too fast, my dear?" It was a foolish question. He could hardly move slower.

She flushed a rosy pink and lowered her eyes. "No, sir."

"Do you like it when I kiss you?"

"I suppose."

Not exactly a ringing endorsement. He did not believe she was offended, and she certainly did not seem aroused. Adam decided she was either frightened or embarrassed or both. "Perhaps this is too public a place for kissing," he said.

"Yes."

He released her chin. "Then I must beg you to forgive me. You simply looked too pretty to resist."

She offered a thin smile and turned away. The poke of her bonnet hid her face from view, but her back remained ramrod straight and her hands folded demurely in her lap.

Blast. That had not gone well. He hoped she was

not one of those frigid women who did not enjoy physical intimacy. What kind of a marriage would that be?

Hell and damnation. Life in the tedious countryside
with a cold fish for a wife. What a dismal future.
Should he put a gun to his head now, or wait until
after the wedding?

"And so, it is to be Sherwood?"

Adam sat loose-limbed and languid in the chair beside Marianne's, his long legs stretched out toward the
hearth. It was a chilly night, and they had pulled the
chairs close together to share the warmth of the fire.

Marianne was glad neither of them had engage-
ments that night. She had placed the orchid on the
balcony in hopes he would be home and come over
to visit her. Adam had been busy squiring Clarissa
about town and there had been no time for cozy evenings in her sitting room. She supposed they would
become less frequent as the Season wore on, and finally cease altogether when he married. She would
miss them. She would miss Adam.

She had become too dependent on their friendship.
Clarissa's mother would not be the last person to misunderstand it. If Adam went through with a marriage
to the girl, Marianne would have to learn how to live
without him.

But they had tonight. It was raining and dreary outside and Adam had become soaked on his climb over
the balcony. His coat was hung on the back of a chair
to dry and he sat in his shirtsleeves. His neckcloth,
limp with the damp, had been discarded, as well. Their
close friendship was no secret, but many would be
shocked to know how often he sat in her private sitting room, her boudoir, in a state of such dishabille.
His throat was bared by the loosened collar of his
shirt, which revealed a hint of brown chest hair.

Marianne's recent preoccupation with ideas of sexual intimacy had heightened her awareness of such

things, making that glimpse of bare skin more tantalizing. She had always found Adam extremely attractive, had long harbored a vague sort of infatuation with him, intrigued by his reputation with women. Those suppressed notions had taken on new life of late. All that frank discussion with the Merry Widows continued to have its effect.

He turned his head lazily against the back of the chair and looked at her in question. Marianne realized she'd been woolgathering and had not answered him.

"Lord Julian? Yes, I am hoping he is to be the one. He hasn't said anything, and of course, neither have I. But there is something in the air between us." There was something in the air between Marianne and almost every man she met these days. Her sensibilities were attuned to one thing, and it colored every encounter. But it was strongest with Lord Julian. Almost as strong as it was with Adam.

"No other gentlemen are in the running? It is down to Sherwood?"

"For the moment. You would not believe, Adam, how unsatisfactory some of those men on my list have turned out to be. It has been extremely disappointing."

Adam cleared his throat and turned away to look into the fire. He seemed to have a bit of a cough. She hoped he was not coming down with something.

"Well, then." Adam rolled his head back in her direction and smiled. "Sherwood it is, the lucky devil. He suits all those requirements you listed?"

"I believe so. He is handsome and charming and discreet."

"And he is not after marriage?"

"I doubt he thinks of me in that way. I am an older woman, after all."

"Yes, and such a dried-up old hag. Can't imagine what the man is thinking."

Marianne reached over and poked him playfully in

the ribs. He grabbed her hand, gave her a look of mock apology, and kissed her fingers.

"And he is not after your fortune?" he asked, absently stroking the back of the hand he had not relinquished.

"Lord Julian hardly has need of my fortune," she said, enjoying the warm comfort of his touch. The undercurrent of sexual attraction was still there, but less powerful tonight. Instead, his touch made her feel cozy and snug, relaxed and languorous. "He may be only the younger son of a duke, but you know that he inherited a sizable fortune from his grandmother, including the estate at Ossing Park. No, he is not after my paltry fortune."

"Then he is only after your body. A discerning young man of excellent taste. I salute him."

Marianne laughed.

"I mean it, my dear," he said. "I applaud his good judgment. I hope he shows himself worthy of yours."

"Thank you, Adam. I hope so, too. I appreciate your support. I had begun to think you so strongly disapproved of the plan that you would never accept any man with me who wasn't David."

"It *is* somewhat difficult to imagine. For so long it was always 'David and Marianne,' a single unit. It is hard to uncouple the two of you in my mind, even though he is gone. But he *is* gone, and you must carry on. I do not disapprove, Marianne. Never think that. I just don't want you to be hurt."

He gave her hand a squeeze and she returned it. "Thank you, Adam. And I won't be hurt by Lord Julian, I promise you. I am not in love with him, you know. Only very much attracted to him."

Adam uttered a soft groan, then fell silent again. He continued to absently stroke her hand, and after a few minutes, he said, "There is, however, one thing that still puzzles me. What set you off on this quest in the first place? I have a sneaking suspicion it has something to do with the other trustees of the Benevolent Widows Fund."

Good Lord, had he heard something about the pact? Had one of the Merry Widows revealed their secret? Or was he simply guessing? Marianne would never break their confidence, however, even to Adam. A pact was a pact.

"I just wanted to experience a bit of pleasure, that is all. It has nothing to do with anything or anyone else."

"You miss him. David."

"Of course I do, but this has nothing to do with David."

"Except that you are missing the pleasure he gave you, missing that physical closeness you shared with him. It is understandable, my dear."

The soothing warmth of his hand, the gentle way his fingers absently stroked hers, had a calming, restful effect that somehow encouraged her to tell him the truth.

"That is not quite how it was," she said.

"What do you mean?"

"David and I were as close as two people can be, I suppose. We truly loved each other. But . . ." She was not sure now that she could say it aloud.

His eyebrows lifted. "But?"

She took a deep breath and looked him square in the eye. He needed to know the truth. Marianne sometimes thought Adam's admiration of David a bit too worshipful. Adam often referred to David as the perfect man, the perfect husband. He knew him too well, of course, to truly believe in such perfection. David was only human, after all.

But perhaps if Adam could be forced to acknowledge that there were certain areas in which David was less than perfect, it would be easier to accept her desire to find a lover. She took a deep breath, and plunged forward.

"But there was no physical passion between us."

Adam's mouth fell open in shock. "Good God."

"I didn't realize it at the time. I didn't know there was anything missing in our relationship. It was not until I heard other women tell of the passion they shared with their husbands that I discovered I had never known such passion. And I have decided it is something I want to experience, even if only once in my life."

Chapter 9

Adam released her hand and rose to his feet. He walked to the window overlooking the street and watched the raindrops trickle down the glass. They might have been tears for his shattered illusions.

He could not believe what she'd just said. David Nesbitt had always been the man who had everything. A good man, an excellent man, who deserved every ounce of good fortune in life. Adam had loved him and envied him. For his intellect, his character, his marriage. For his wife. And yet this man who met success at every turn had failed at the one thing Adam could now admit he'd envied the most. God!

"I do not know what to say." He could not look at her. She would see the torment in his eyes. The torment of knowing she had never experienced the full passion of sexual intimacy. The torment of knowing that someone else would be the one to introduce her to it.

If David Nesbitt weren't already dead, Adam would wring his foolish, imperfect neck. The man had wasted a good woman.

"I am sorry if I shocked you," she said, "but I wanted you to know the truth. I am not looking to recapture something I have been missing these last two years. I am looking to experience it for the first time. Just once."

Just once. With someone else.

He took several long breaths before he turned to face her. "You have taken me by surprise, my dear. I always thought you and David had the ideal marriage."

"It was ideal. Except for that one aspect."

"It is not a small thing, Marianne. It saddens me to know what you missed. You cannot imagine how sorry I am to hear it." He began to pace in front of the window. "Dammit, I was always so jealous of him. He had everything—looks, brains, charm." *You.*

"He was not perfect, Adam."

He snorted. "Apparently not."

"He always wished he was more like you."

Adam stopped and stared at her. "What are you talking about? He was a prince among men. There was nothing about him I did not envy. How could he possibly have wanted to be more like me? Oh." He raked agitated fingers through his hair. "Oh. You mean in the bedroom." His tone grew sarcastic, caustic. "The one area in his life that was apparently not as perfect as the rest."

He should not be so surprised. As a very young man, David had never been as voraciously experimental as Adam and many of their friends had been. In fact, he could probably count on one hand the number of women he knew David to have been with, and still have a couple of fingers left over. Even while they'd traveled throughout Europe for most of a year, when Adam had developed a taste for exotic, sensual women, David had been circumspect in his behavior. His excuse was always that he had his fiancée, Marianne, waiting for him and he didn't need other women.

Adam had admired his friend's restraint, but apparently it meant he'd come to Marianne's bed with little skill and no finesse, leaving her wanting. Damn the man.

"That is not at all what I meant," she said, "though I suppose he might have envied you for that, too, for all I know. I do know that he envied your recklessness, your sense of adventure, the way you were always up for any bit of mischief, willing to try anything once. And yes, he envied your amorous exploits as well. Not that he would ever have been unfaithful to me. It was not in his nature. David was too responsible, too serious-minded, too cautious, to be as carefree as you were. Don't you remember how he hung on every word of your escapades, how he made you repeat them over and over?"

"So he could laugh at me and have fun with my name. Casanova, he called me. I was a great source of entertainment, I am sure."

She smiled. "Yes, you were. But he did envy you. He loved to hear of every gamble, every curricle race, every love affair, every risk taken, because he would never do such things. He lived a vicarious life of adventure through you. Did you never realize that?"

"No." He frowned and shook his head. "No. I never imagined there was any aspect of my life David could possibly envy."

"Well, he did. And if you want the whole truth, I will tell you that I, too, secretly wished he was more like you."

What? She had wanted upright and steadfast David to be like Adam had been—anchorless and with no direction, capricious, wayward, impetuous, secretly attracted to a woman he could never have? She had wanted such a man?

"Not all the time, of course," she said with a grin. "That would have been exhausting. But he never did anything that wasn't absolutely proper and upstanding. He never did a single outrageous thing in his life. I used to wish he would, sometimes. I used to wish he could be a bit more adventurous."

She was not speaking of sex—at least he did not think so—but that was what Adam heard just the same. When he'd regaled David with tales of his amorous exploits, Marianne had been listening. She said she hadn't known what she was missing at the time, but perhaps she had.

She rose from her chair and came to stand with him by the window. "I am sorry, Adam. I fear I have tarnished your memory of David. I know you loved him like a brother."

"I did. But I had thought him perfect. It is something of a relief to know he was not. And to know that he might have admired me a little."

"More than a little."

"Thank you for that, Marianne. It is gratifying to realize that we both gained something from our friendship."

He took her hand again and kissed it. He kept it in his and played with her fingers. He tried, as always, to make it seem a casual, friendly, almost unconscious gesture so she would not guess what he had only recently realized: that to touch her now and then was a necessity to him. Like an opium addict, he craved the smallest physical contact with her, knowing it was as much as he would ever have. Especially now, when his marriage loomed between them, and contact, physical and otherwise, would soon be limited.

But he wanted more. Needed more.

He took her other hand. "I must be leaving. It is getting late. Thank you for telling me about David. That cannot have been an easy confession. I am honored that you trust me enough to be that open with me."

"I trust you more than anyone I know," she said. "And besides, I wanted you to understand why I set out to find a lover."

"I do understand now. And I hope Sherwood gives you all you are looking for. Oh, and thank you for telling me about your conversation with Clarissa. It's a good thing I did not sell that confounded house in Dorset."

"She will want to spend a good deal of time there, I suppose."

"Most likely. You may call me Squire Cazenove, if you please."

She smiled. "Shall you become portly and smoke a long-handled pipe?"

"Without a doubt."

A softness gathered in her eyes. "I will miss you when you're in the country," she said. "And even when you're not. I daresay we will not have evenings like this when you are married. No more climbing the balcony."

"What? You will miss my large self sprawled ignobly in your chair and my damp coats hanging by the fire?"

"I will miss these quiet, peaceful evenings. The feeling of comfort and contentment I've always had here with you and David."

"My presence reminds you of him."

"Everything here reminds me of him. But there were three of us, not only two. You have always been a part of my life, and I will miss you when you are married."

"My dear Marianne." Without thought or premeditation, he bent down and kissed her.

The instant their lips touched, a fireball of heat scorched his lungs. She felt it, too, for she uttered a soft moan and kissed him back. His arms enfolded her just as hers twined around his neck. With only a gentle nudging, her lips parted and let him in. He felt her tremble when his tongue met hers. The kiss became lush and deep until the blood was roaring in his head.

He wanted to linger forever, wanted more, but was afraid to ask. She was not his for the taking in any case. No longer because she was married to his closest friend, but because he was promised to someone else.

Forgive me, David.

He lifted his head slowly and grinned, deliberately

making light of a moment that was anything but light. A moment that he seemed to have waited a lifetime to experience. A moment that could never happen again.

"Ah, now, see what you've made me do?" he said, adding a wink to reinforce the grin. "All that sentimentality made me forget myself. Shame on you, Marianne, for taking advantage of me like that."

There was a poignant uncertainty in her eyes for a moment, an unbearably sweet flush of desire on her cheeks. Then she, too, made light of what had happened. She returned a playful smile that emphasized her dimples and made him want to kiss her again. "You, sir, are a rogue. What would your Clarissa think to know you were kissing another woman?"

He released her and stepped back, away from temptation. He held up a finger and said, "Leave it to Marianne to remind me of my obligations. Duly noted, my dear. Blame it on the rain. Or the alignment of the stars. Or that fetching little frock you are wearing. I shall return to my lonely rooms and pen a sonnet to my bride-to-be."

"You had better make it a country elegy. With perhaps a sheep or two."

He gave a theatrical groan. "Wretch!"

"You will call at Doncaster House, Beatrice?" Grace asked as they sat around her dining room table writing out invitations for the next ball.

"Yes," Beatrice said, "I will call on Her Grace Thursday next, when she is at home. Perhaps I will take Emily with me so she can meet the duchess. An introduction to her might afford her with new opportunities. Plus, the duchess's son is said to be in town, and the girl is dying to meet him."

"Excellent," Grace said. "I hope she is amenable to hosting a ball at Doncaster House. I hear it is very grand."

"And it has a real ballroom, I understand," Marianne said, without looking up from the parchment upon which she wrote. "That would make for an excellent grand finale for the Season, would it not?"

"I will be sure to report back with all the details," Beatrice said.

Marianne dusted her parchment to dry the ink, and folded the sheet in thirds. Then she dipped her pen in the well and wrote out the name and direction in careful, elegant script, sanded it, and placed it on the stack in the center of the table for Wilhelmina to seal.

The trustees of the Benevolent Widows Fund prided themselves on handwritten, personalized invitations to their balls. Marianne always enjoyed the days when they wrote out invitations. The meetings were less businesslike, with lots of talk and gossip and laughter. Today, the rather mindless task allowed her to dwell on last night and the kiss she'd shared with Adam. The kiss that had shaken her to the very roots of her soul.

As astonishing and wonderful as it had been, she wished to God it had never happened. First, because he should never have done it while engaged to another woman, and she should not have allowed it. Second, because it could never be repeated, so it was rather cruel to tempt her with something she could never have again. And third, because it had meant nothing to him. Nothing at all. He'd laughed afterward, and continued to tease her. It pained her that what was such a momentous experience for her—because she had never reacted to David's kisses like that, and it had truly and irrevocably opened her eyes to everything else she might have missed—had been the most ordinary, common, everyday event for Adam.

Perhaps she should be glad that he was the one to initiate her into physical passion, someone she knew well and trusted rather than a mere acquaintance. Now she could go to Lord Julian, or any man, and feel less unnerved by what might happen between them. She knew now. Some of it, anyway.

But it still aggravated her that Adam could have been so cavalier about it.

"And how are things with Mr. Tolliver?" Wilhelmina asked Penelope.

"Very well indeed," Penelope said with a bright smile. "The man is extraordinarily inventive. He does this thing with his thumb—"

"Penelope!"

"Oh, don't be so squeamish, Grace. We did agree, did we not, to speak openly and share our experiences? Well, I have something interesting to share. Pay attention, Grace. You might learn a thing or two. If you ever find yourself a man to replace old Marlowe, you will be able to suggest a few moves to him."

And she proceeded to explain exactly, in great detail, what Mr. Tolliver did with his thumb. Grace was struck dumb. Wilhelmina looked amused. Marianne was embarrassed, but definitely intrigued. She had no idea that men ever touched women in that way. Would Lord Julian do such a thing? Would she want him to?

"Well," Beatrice said, "never let it be said that our meetings are not educational."

All but Grace burst into laughter.

"Speaking of education," Beatrice said, "you cannot imagine the things young girls know these days. I cannot guess where they learn it, but Emily, for one, is certainly more informed than I was at her age."

Beatrice went on to relate a story about her niece, but Marianne found her mind wandering again and could not pay attention. Penelope's graphic discussion of sex play with Eustace Tolliver brought images of Adam to mind. She would bet her new diamond earrings that he knew that move with the thumb.

Her thoughts kept returning to that kiss. He had kissed her on the cheek many times, to be sure, but never on the mouth. And this had been no simple kiss. It had the power to—what was it Wilhelmina had said? Make your toes curl up in your slippers? Yes, that was it. And that was precisely how she'd felt. Even now, her toes curled just remembering it.

Why had he done it? Why now, when he had no business doing so, when he had a young fiancée who needed his kisses more than she did?

It was not worth worrying about. She should be thinking of Lord Julian instead. He was a charming young man and she liked him a great deal. Was she ready for him to be the one to teach her about sexual pleasure?

Yes. She was ready. More than ready. If only she could stop thinking about Adam and concentrate on Lord Julian. But she kept remembering Adam's constant teasing, the mock disappointment that he could not be the one to show her the pleasures of lovemaking. Had it truly been teasing?

Ever since that kiss, she had wondered if there was any truth beneath his facetious words. She had always assumed he thought of her as a sister or colleague, that she was not the sort of woman he found desirable. But he had kissed her, and so she was left to wonder.

She began to curse that bad timing he was always teasing her about.

"Marianne?"

She looked up from the blank sheet in front of her. She had not written a word. She turned to Wilhelmina. "Yes?"

The duchess laughed. "I have been speaking to you, but you did not hear a word, did you? You were miles away, my girl, and with a dreamy look in your eyes. What were you thinking about? Or should I say whom?"

"Lord Julian, perhaps?" Penelope said with a grin.

"Was that it, Marianne?" the duchess asked. "Is Lord Julian Sherwood still the man of the hour?"

"Yes, I think so," Marianne replied. Let them think it was Lord Julian who filled her daydreams. "I hope so."

"But he has not yet made a move, or offered a proposition?"

"No, not yet."

"What is taking him so long?" Penelope asked. "Lud, the Season will be half over before you get him in your bed. What a waste of time."

"Perhaps he is simply being cautious," the duchess said as she dripped wax onto a folded invitation. "After all, Marianne is a well-respected patroness of a large charity. He must be certain she wants what he thinks she wants. He will not want to offend so important a member of Society."

She brought the seal down on the hot wax very slowly and deliberately. Wilhelmina liked her seals to be perfectly round. She claimed it was her best contribution, since neither her penmanship nor her spelling could be counted on. Her upbringing had not included the genteel education the others had received at the hands of governesses or at boarding schools. Although Wilhelmina made light of it, Marianne suspected she was often painfully aware of the differences in their backgrounds.

Satisfied with her seal, Wilhelmina looked up and smiled. "Perhaps you ought to give the poor man a clear signal, my dear. Do not keep him guessing."

"I will try," Marianne said, "but this is all very new to me. I cannot just walk up and ask him to make love to me."

"Not in so many words," Wilhelmina said. "And a true gentleman will not require such a blatant invitation. He will lead the conversation in the right direction, and all you need do is to follow."

"I hope you are right," Marianne said. She really did. She wanted to purge all inappropriate thoughts of Adam by having a passionate affair with someone else.

"All this talk about men and . . . and lovemaking is one thing," Grace said, "but do none of you worry about the consequences? What will you do, Penelope, if you find yourself in an interesting condition? Disappear for several months and return with a young ward in your care?"

"Oh, dear," Marianne said, "that is rather a good question, is it not?"

"Had you not given it any thought?" Grace asked her. "Or is the pleasure worth the risk?"

"I have given it thought," Marianne said, "but I do not think I need to worry. I am fairly certain I am barren. I had one or two miscarriages early in my marriage." It had been three, in fact, but there was no need to dwell on that sad fact. "But I did not conceive again during the last five years of my marriage, so I do not believe I have to worry about an unexpected pregnancy."

"You should take precautions, nevertheless," Wilhelmina said. "You can never be sure about these matters. Many women have multiple miscarriages and still manage to conceive again. And again. Look at Mrs. Jordan. The poor woman is constantly pregnant, it seems, but has as many miscarriages as live births. And some women never conceive with one husband, but breed like bunnies with the next husband. So don't assume you cannot become pregnant, Marianne. Take precautions."

Good heavens. Was that true? Marianne had just assumed she could never conceive again. But what if Wilhelmina was right?

"Eustace uses French letters," Penelope said matter-of-factly as she folded an invitation.

"How considerate of him," Wilhelmina said. "Most men loathe the things."

Penelope gave a nonchalant shrug. "He is afraid of disease."

"Good God," Beatrice said. "He thinks you might be carrying a disease?"

"He is just being cautious. And since I have quite

enough children and have no desire to present him with a bye-blow, I am happy to oblige him."

One tended to forget that Penelope had three young sons. She did not give the impression that she was remotely maternal, especially with her boys packed away at school. But in fact, she doted on them, and was forever buying presents to send them, and reading aloud amusing passages from their letters. Marianne did wonder, though, if Penelope would have been quite so cavalier about her love affairs if she had a daughter or two underfoot.

"You are fortunate, Penelope," Wilhelmina said, "that your young man is so cautious. As for the rest of you, if your gentleman does not wish to sheathe himself, there are other steps you should consider. Just in case."

"Like what?" Marianne asked. Just in case.

"Coitus interruptus is the easiest method, of course," the duchess said, "but it relies on the gentleman for its effectiveness. If you wish to take matters into your own hands, there are several methods to be considered. There are herbal infusions and brews that may help prevent conception, but they are not always reliable and I do not recommend them. There are insertions, of course, but quite frankly, I find them rather unpleasant, and the smell can be distracting. But they can be effective and you might want to consider them."

Marianne noted that she was not the only one paying rapt attention. All writing had come to a halt and every woman at the table listened intently as the duchess explained how to make pessaries of lard and flour, and the effectiveness of tansy, pennyroyal, bitter almonds, and willow bark. She described douches made of castor oil and camphor and rue, and the best ways to use them.

These were things a girl's mother never told her. Thank God for Wilhelmina.

"And finally," Wilhelmina continued, "my personal method of choice is a mixture of juniper juice and wine. Drinking it after an evening's pleasure can be most effective. It has never failed me."

The duchess had been experienced with men from a young age, and as far as Marianne knew, she had no children. The juniper juice must have worked.

"Perhaps we should visit an apothecary when we are finished with these invitations," Beatrice said, smiling. "We would not want to find ourselves without a supply of juniper juice."

"But we would give away the game," Marianne said, "if we all marched in there at once."

"Yes, and we might inadvertently start a run on the stuff," Penelope said, "causing a great shortage. And then how merry would we be?"

All five women, including Grace, burst into laughter.

"How about this blue brocade? It would look lovely with the Turkey carpet." Marianne fingered the fabric from one of many bolts arrayed on the display table for Lavinia Nesbitt's inspection. When she heard that her mother-in-law was looking to replace the drawing room curtains in her London house, she decided an expedition to the linendraper's might be more amenable than another afternoon in Lavinia's drawing room. She had no desire to spend another strained afternoon sipping tea, watching Lavinia stitch her late husband's embroidered waistcoats into cushion covers, and listening to all the ways Marianne had done harm to David's memory.

"Oh, no," Lavinia said. "I could never use blue. William hated blue. He insisted on dark red draperies in the drawing room, and that's what we shall have."

"Forgive me, Lavinia, but William has been gone for over fourteen years. I am sure he would not mind if you preferred blue or green draperies."

Lavinia glared at her with contempt. "I will never

do anything that would have displeased William Nesbitt. I am his widow, and unlike some other widows, I honor my husband's memory."

Marianne stifled a groan. She would not allow the woman to get under her skin. Not today, when it would be too easy to make her feel that she was betraying David by pursuing a relationship with Lord Julian. Or by sharing a heated kiss with his best friend.

"Then by all means," she said, "let it be the dark red. How about this beautiful velvet?"

They spent another half hour sorting through dozens of red velvets and silks and brocades before Lavinia found one to her liking. When they left the linendraper, Marianne suggested another stop before returning home.

"The British Institution is only a short walk up the street. Would you like to see the preparations for the Reynolds exhibit? Your painting should be on the premises by now."

"I believe I would enjoy that," Lavinia said. "I know how much it would have pleased David."

She took Marianne's arm and they walked up Pall Mall until they came to the building that once housed Boydell's Shakespeare Gallery, and had been purchased eight years ago by the governors of the British Institution, with a bit of help from the Prince Regent, to become their main gallery. They stepped inside to find the current exhibition and sale of contemporary British art still in progress. Lavinia, who shared something of her late son's taste, turned up her nose at most of the paintings as they strolled through the arched doorways from gallery to gallery. Many of the artists were protégés of Adam and were quite talented.

Finally, Marianne was able to locate the gallery's keeper, Mr. Green, and asked if they might view the preparations for the Reynolds exhibit.

"I would be honored," he said. "The mother and widow of David Nesbitt are always welcome. Your painting arrived last week," he said to Lavinia, "and it's a beauty. And I cannot thank you enough," he said, turning to Marianne and beaming a smile at her, "for convincing so many of your friends and acquaintances to send their paintings. But who could refuse Mrs. David Nesbitt?"

"It was not difficult," Marianne said. "Everyone was willing to contribute."

"This exhibit was David's idea, you know," he said. "He'd been talking about it ever since the Institution was founded. You have done him proud, both of you. I know he would be pleased. Come, let me show you what we've collected so far."

They followed him through a doorway and into a large storeroom, filled from corner to corner with crates and with paintings, some of them enormous, leaning against the walls.

Mr. Green made a sweeping gesture with his hand. "And here is the fruit of your husband's idea, Mrs. Nesbitt. His legacy."

They walked through the storeroom looking at the life's work of one of Britain's greatest artists. It was a stunning collection, and it had all come together because of her husband. Marianne had never felt more proud to be Mrs. David Nesbitt. Her mother-in-law actually took her hand and squeezed it.

"I have concocted a plan," Lord Julian said, "and I am hoping you will approve."

Marianne's arm was tucked in his as they strolled through the park near the Serpentine. She felt quite smart in her new cambric muslin dress with a pleated bodice, a Russian mantle of Pomona green, and a matching cottage bonnet. She had dressed to impress Lord Julian, and she was fairly certain he had dressed to please her. He wore a tight-fitting black coat that showed off his physique to perfection, a red waistcoat with fine silver stripes, gray pantaloons, and gleaming

Hessian boots. Marianne was quite sure they made the handsomest couple in the park.

The sun was shining and the air smelled fresh after the rains—a perfect setting for what she hoped would be the beginning of an understanding between them.

"What sort of plan?" she asked.

"You know of my home at Ossing Park?"

"Yes, of course." It was a famous stately home that had been written up in the guidebooks and featured in *The Beauties of England and Wales*. It was one of many properties that had come to the dukedom of Warminster over several generations, mostly through marriages. Ossing Park had become the favorite home of the dowager duchess, Lord Julian's grandmother. It was not entailed with the other ducal properties, having come from her own mother, and she was free to do with it as she pleased. Lord Julian had apparently been her favorite grandchild, for she had left it to him on her death.

"Ossing is very close to town," he said. "Only a fifteen-mile drive."

"The very best sort of country estate," she said. "Close enough to London that you could pop up for a day of shopping and a night at the theater."

He smiled, and his blue eyes twinkled with amusement. He really was a very attractive man. "Close enough for a short house party, don't you think?"

"A house party?"

"Yes. I have made some small improvements that I am anxious to show off to guests. But mostly, I thought you might enjoy the grounds and the gardens, and I would love to show them to you. It would give us an opportunity to get to know each other better. If that is something you would like, of course." He leaned in closer. "Would you like it? To become better acquainted in a more rustic setting?"

Wilhelmina was right. There was no mistaking what he meant. Oh, dear.

A swarm of butterflies had taken up residence in her stomach. "I would like it very much," she managed to say, amazed that her voice sounded so calm when her pulse was racing. "But I doubt I will find Ossing at all rustic."

He took her free hand and brought it to his lips. "I shall leave that for you to judge. I look forward to showing it to you, Mrs. Nesbitt."

She chuckled. "If we are to tramp about your estate together, my lord, you must call me Marianne."

He smiled, and the look in his eyes was like a caress. "I am honored, Marianne. And you must cease my-lording me and call me Julian."

"Julian. I am very pleased to be invited to Ossing. You said it was to be a party?"

"I would prefer a party of two, but I daresay that would never do. It is a large house. If I fill it up with enough people, you and I can wander off on our own and no one will miss us."

"Is that what you plan to do?"

"It is my fondest wish. But there must be other guests, so I have taken the liberty of sending out a few invitations. I hope you will not be offended that I preferred to invite you in person."

"Not at all." But he must have been very certain of her acceptance if he'd already sent out invitations.

"Excellent. My sister, Lady Presteign, will be my hostess. I do not believe you have met her."

"No, I have not, but I look forward to it."

"I have invited a few friends, but I thought I would ask your help with suggestions for other guests. If you have friends you'd like to invite, please let me know and I will have cards sent around."

It might be a good idea to have the support of a few friends when she took this big step. Someone to share her excitement with if things went well, to commiserate with if they did not.

"I would be delighted if you were to invite my fellow Fund trustees. Lady Somerfield, Lady Gosforth, Mrs. Marlowe, and the Dowager Duchess of Hertford."

"I will send invitations to each of them. Some old family friends will be there as well. Lord and Lady Troutbeck are particular friends of my sister. And the Leighton-Blairs, of course."

"The Leighton-Blairs? Clarissa and her parents?"

"Yes. I have known them all my life. Our estate in Wiltshire, where I grew up, marched up against theirs. I have known Clarissa since she was born. I have also invited her friend Miss Stillman and her parents. And Cazenove, of course. And his friend Rochdale."

Adam was to be there? Oh, dear. She was not sure she liked that idea, having him so close by when she finally took a lover.

On the other hand, it might be a good opportunity to throw more temptation in Clarissa's path. "It sounds as if you might have uneven numbers, with so many ladies in attendance. The younger ladies might appreciate a few gentlemen near their own age."

She suggested a few young men who'd shown an interest in Clarissa, and Julian seemed agreeable. She also hinted that Eustace Tolliver be invited. Why should Marianne be the only widow to be merry?

Now, who might she invite for the other three?

Adam stared again at the invitation from Sherwood while his valet packed his bags. Was there no end to the nightmare of this business of Marianne and her lover? Sherwood would almost certainly begin an affair with her at Ossing. It was no doubt the whole reason for the house party. The last thing Adam wanted to do was to be that close a witness to her initiation into sexual passion. Especially since he'd experienced a hint of that passion when he'd kissed her.

But apparently Clarissa's family and Lord Julian's

had known each other for years, and Clarissa was excited to go. "I look forward to a respite from town life," she had said.

Bloody hell.

Adam hated country house parties, and he did not look forward to being in close proximity to Clarissa's mother, who could be a dragon at the best of times. It might have been tolerable if Clarissa had been allowed to come alone, under the general chaperonage of Lady Presteign. He might have been able to make another attempt or two to break down Clarissa's reserve. But with her parents underfoot, he was unlikely to have a moment alone with her.

Instead, he would have the dubious pleasure of watching Marianne's love affair unfold before his eyes.

He had confronted her about it last night at Lady Durant's rout party.

"What are you up to?" he had said. "You hate country house parties as much as I do."

"It was Julian's idea, not mine." Her demeanor was a bit prickly, as it had been ever since their kiss. "I think it will be great fun."

"Great fun? Is this the same Marianne who not so long ago complained that there was never anything for ladies to do at house parties?"

"I daresay there will be something particular to interest me." She gave him a look that sent a rush of heat through his veins. "I am looking forward to it."

"Yes, I am sure you are," he said, countering her look with a soft stroke of his fingers along the bare skin of her upper arm, just above the top of her long glove. She gave the tiniest of shivers and stepped out of his reach. "All those long walks in the fresh country air," he said, "communing with nature, and any number of rustic pastimes."

"Indeed." She kept her distance but lowered her voice to a sultry whisper. "Any number of pastimes."

The air between them had grown buoyant with unspoken desire. Ever since that damned kiss, things had changed between them, despite his attempt at the time to make light of it. They had each tasted the other's passion and now it stood looming and huge between them, conspicuous yet unacknowledged. For he was bound to Clarissa, and Marianne was about to give herself to Sherwood.

Adam almost wished he'd never kissed her, for all the tension it created between them. But in his heart, he did not regret it.

He was not, though, looking forward to seeing her face the morning after she'd discovered precisely what it was she'd missed in her marriage.

If Clarissa's parents were not to be there, Adam might have been tempted to slake all that repressed desire by taking her to bed—pouncing, as Rochdale had suggested. Instead, he would be stuck in his own bedroom all alone. Alone and brooding over what might have been.

He checked the portmanteaus and saw that all was in order. He was anything but ready, however. Adam had never dreaded anything so much in his life.

Chapter 10

"What a lovely bridge." Marianne strolled on the arm of Julian through the extensive gardens at Ossing Park. The grounds were beautiful, and he was eager to point out every feature and provide its history: the Italian garden, the rose garden, the cascade, the obelisk, the orangery, the deer houses, the conservatory.

They had been walking for hours and Marianne's feet were growing sore, but he was so charmingly proud of it all that she did not mind so very much. He had never looked more handsome and she was enjoying her time with him.

"Is this the bridge you were telling me about?" she asked. "The one you had reconstructed?"

"Yes, it is." His blue eyes were lit with an enthusiastic fire, and had been throughout their walk. She had never seen him so full of life. In town, he wore the same air of fashionable ennui, of superciliousness, that most men of the *ton* seemed obliged to affect. But he was in his element here at Ossing. Clearly he loved the place.

"The old bridge had become too unsafe to use," he said, "and had to be torn down. And though my architects tried to insist on a modern, more sleek design for the new bridge, I wanted to retain the Palladian style of the old one. Anything else just seemed wrong to my eye."

"I am sure you were right. It looks quite perfect to me. In fact, everything here is absolutely beautiful."

He gave her an intense look that sent a tiny shiver across her shoulders. "Yes, everything here *is* beautiful. Come."

He took her by the hand and pulled her into a nearby grove of trees. Thinking there was a folly or statue or some other feature in the grove that he meant to show her, she was surprised when he stopped, leaned up against a large tree trunk, and tugged her into his arms.

"I am so glad to see you here," he said, pitching his voice low and seductive. "You are as beautiful as anything here at Ossing. No, you are more beautiful."

He pulled her tighter against him, and kissed her.

It was more than a kiss. It was a ravishment. With no attempt at gentle persuasion, he forced her mouth open and plunged his tongue inside. Marianne was a bit startled by the violence of his passion, but a little excited, too. This was rougher than Adam's kiss. More purely carnal. This must be how mature lovers behaved. Nothing coy or subtle. Only raw, unbridled passion.

His tongue fenced with hers and she tried to respond as he would expect her to. But there was an odd sensation of being somehow disconnected from her body, and viewing the kiss as a dispassionate observer. She was very much aware of every move he made—of every stroke of his tongue, of his lips and teeth, of his arm around her neck and the other pressing against the small of her back, of his hips grinding suggestively against hers—and yet she did not feel involved. She felt . . . nothing.

It did not make sense. When Adam had kissed her—and it was not nearly as prolonged an embrace

as this one—she had felt a certain heat, a spark of
something, a fluttering low in her insides. And here
was Julian doing much more intimate things, and she
experienced not the tiniest flutter.

What was wrong with her?

"I think the temple is in that direction."

"No, I'm sure it is this way."

The sound of approaching voices put an end to the
kiss. Julian gave a little groan and pulled away.
"Damn." He smiled as he straightened his neckcloth.
"Almost caught in the act. We shall have to resume
this delightful activity later. I am sorry about tonight,
however. But tomorrow . . ."

His gaze held hers for a long moment, then flickered
down to her mouth, and back again. Her body reacted
more strongly to that look in his eye than it had to
his mouth and his tongue. Perhaps she had simply
been too nervous to enjoy the kiss, wound up too tight
from the expectation of it to unbend and enjoy it.

"Tomorrow, Marianne?"

God, he was so handsome. And his gaze was a
naked caress. How could she resist? "Tomorrow,"
she answered.

He flashed a brilliant smile, then took her arm to
lead her toward the path where voices could be heard.

And so it was done. With one word she had just
invited this young man to share her bed. Tomorrow.

Dear God, what had she done?

There was rather a large group assembled on the
path, several talking at once and pointing in different
directions. Adam was among them, standing silently
while his fiancée spoke to Sir George Lowestoft with
uncharacteristic animation. Several other young men
were gathered around her, vying for her attention, and
she positively beamed with pleasure.

Marianne could not help but wonder if her attempt
to throw temptation in the girl's path was working.

She certainly appeared to be enjoying the company of the younger men, while ignoring her betrothed.

Clarissa turned as they approached.

"There you are!" she said. "You must show us the temple, Julian. I am dying to see it. I thought it was this way, but Sir Neville believes it is through that avenue of trees."

Julian released Marianne's arm and walked toward the group. "You are both wrong," he said with a smile. "It is on the other side of the bridge. Follow me." He held out his arm to Clarissa, and the two of them led the way.

Adam caught Marianne's eye and waited for her to join him. "I have been deserted, as you see, so you must take my arm, my dear."

She did and they followed the others, but Adam kept a slow pace so that they were soon lagging far behind.

"You look delightfully flushed," he said. "Almost as though you had just been kissed."

"I have been."

"Ah. Then our host is losing no time." He said nothing for a moment, and then, "Tonight, I daresay, you will finally achieve your goal."

"No, not tonight. There are guests due to arrive quite late and he must be available to welcome them."

"Is that why you look so glum? You are disappointed that you will not have a lover in your bed tonight?"

"No, that is not it."

"Then what? Something is troubling you. I know that look well. What is it, Marianne?"

She gazed up at him and felt her face about to crumble and the mortifying sting of tears behind her eyes. "Oh, Adam, I fear I have made a terrible mistake."

His eyebrows rose in surprise. "Sherwood is the wrong man?"

"No, I am the wrong woman."

"I beg your pardon?"

"Adam, what if the lack of passion in my marriage had nothing to do with David? What if it was all my fault?"

"What the devil are you talking about?"

"I . . . I felt almost nothing when Julian kissed me."

Adam's eyes, clear and steady, remained fixed on hers, and she knew they were both thinking the same thing. She *had* felt something when Adam kissed her.

"He was extremely . . . passionate," she said, "and yet I felt nothing. My mind was aware of every single thing he was doing, but my body couldn't *feel* what he was doing. I felt strangely detached from the whole experience."

Adam smiled. "You think too much. A passionate kiss is not a moment for rational thought." He did not need to say that there had been nothing rational about the kiss they'd shared. "You worked yourself up into a state of such anxiety that you could not enjoy it. Relax! Loosen up. Open yourself to every sensation, and let them wash over you. Lord, I cannot believe I am telling you this." He gave a wry smile, full of self-mockery. "Don't think about it. Just *feel* it."

"But what if I can never feel anything more than I experienced with David?" The words spilled out in an anguished rush. "What if I am one of those women who simply do not respond to physical intimacy? What if it is simply not in my nature to enjoy it? What if I am a disappointment to Lord Julian?"

"My dear girl." He stopped on Julian's beautiful new bridge and turned her to face him. "You will not disappoint him. You are not one of those women. I have felt your body respond, Marianne. Surely you haven't forgotten that. I have not."

No, she had not forgotten it. At the time, the kiss seemed to have meant nothing to him. But perhaps she had been wrong about that. He took her hand, gently pulled back the kid leather glove, and kissed the underside of her wrist. When he flicked his tongue up to the palm of her hand, she gave an involuntary shiver.

"You see," he said. "That little tremor tells me you are not cold and unresponsive."

He lifted her chin with a crooked finger, then traced that finger along the line of her jaw and very slowly down her neck. She uttered a little sigh and trembled again.

"And there it is again," he said, "your body responding even to so simple a touch. Have no fear that you will not please him, my dear. You are a warm, sensuous woman with a great deal to give. All you need to do is relax and let the physical sensations overwhelm you. Put your mind to rest and let your body take over. There isn't a man alive who would not be thrilled to share such a moment with you."

Including himself? Would Adam be thrilled to share her bed? Considering her reaction to his simplest touch, she was quite certain *she* would be thrilled.

She hoped he was right. If his touch could make her tremble with desire, then surely Julian's touch would be able to do the same. If only she could stop worrying about it.

Why, oh, why could it not be Adam instead of Julian, or anyone else? She would have no trouble relaxing into Adam's arms. No trouble at all.

"Hold the bow steady. Now, pull back slowly. That's it. Keep your draw hand against your jaw and let the bowstring touch your chin."

Adam's arms enveloped Clarissa as he guided her in the use of a bow and arrow. It had been Sherwood's suggestion that the men engage in a competition, but the ladies objected and claimed they must have their turns, as well. The gentlemen were happy to oblige, for most of the ladies had never before held a long-bow. The only proper way to teach them, of course, was to stand very, very close.

It was as near to a full embrace as Adam had yet achieved with Clarissa, and he took advantage, using the opportunity to work off some of the tension that had kept his body as taut as a bowstring for the last two days. His chest pressed against her slim back, his left arm encircled her bow arm, and his right arm was cushioned beneath her draw arm to guide it to the proper elevation. His chin rested against her temple. Soft blond curls tickled his jaw and fluttered against his breath when he spoke.

"Push outward on the bow as you pull back on the bowstring." He rested his fingers over her draw hand. "Make sure all three fingers are pulling equally, and do not touch the nock. Leave a bit of space between this finger and this one."

She made tiny adjustments to her stance as he talked, but she seemed much too tense to make a good shot. No doubt his proximity disconcerted her, and having an audience did not help. He stepped back slowly, reluctant to abandon her soft body. "That's perfect, Clarissa. Now, keep your right elbow up. That's it. And relax your shoulders." He placed a hand on each shoulder and said, "Keep them down. Don't let this one creep up to your ear. Just relax." He kept his hands on her shoulders for a moment, caressing her gently in hopes of easing some of her tension. Then he stepped away.

"All right, Clarissa. Get ready to release. You must let go with all three fingers at the same time. Don't be startled if the bowstring hits your arm. That's why you're wearing the guard. And try not to move. Keep your draw arm up and in position until the arrow is in the air. Ready?"

"I think so."

"All right, then. Release."

She did, and the bowstring snapped sharply against her leather arm guard as the arrow took flight with a *whoosh*. She gave a little yelp of surprise, but to her credit, she kept her stance, as he'd instructed. The arrow fell several yards wide of the target.

"Oh, my," she said. "That wasn't very good, was it?" And she burst into giggles.

"Here, let me show you." Lord Havering, one of several irritating young pups among the party guests, stepped forward to take Adam's place, all but pushing him aside.

Adam glared at the fellow's presumption, but his lordship had the arrogance of youth on his side and was unmoved. Adam gave a little snort and moved back into the line of spectators.

He was then forced to watch the insolent puppy wrap his arms around Clarissa to help her find her stance. He was several inches shorter than Adam, so that his chin was at the level of her ear. She giggled as he adjusted her elbows and shoulders, and Adam would swear he had whispered something in that ear.

"You're gripping the bow too tightly," Havering told her. "Let it rest comfortably in the hand." He placed his fingers over hers on the bow and spent longer than Adam thought necessary in adjusting her grip. "And you must rotate the elbow of your bow arm so that it is not pointing downward. Like this. And your other elbow must be held high. Higher. That's right."

Finally, he seemed satisfied enough to move himself away from Clarissa. Which was a good thing. If he had lingered a moment longer, Adam would have been tempted to pick him up by the collar and toss him aside.

Clarissa released her arrow, and again it went wide of the target. "Oh, piffle," she said, and stamped her dainty foot, then giggled again.

"You placed her draw arm too high," Sherwood

said, and stepped forward to replace the puppy. "I will show her how it is done. Come, Clarrie, let's try once more."

Clarrie?

And Adam was obliged to watch yet another young man wrap his arms around his betrothed. At least he did not have to worry about Sherwood, who had another female on his mind this week. He did not drape himself all over Clarissa for long, unnecessary moments, as Havering had done, or even press close against her as Adam had done. He simply touched an elbow, a shoulder, adjusted her fingers, and talked her through it.

"Now," he said, "keep this elbow parallel to the ground, not poking stupidly up into the air like Havering told you."

"Nonsense," Havering called out. "The draw arm must be held as high as possible."

Sherwood laughed. "Don't listen to him, Clarrie. He doesn't know what he's talking about. Keep the elbow level with the ground. Yes, that's right. Perfect." He stepped back. "Now, pretend the three fingers holding the bowstring are sewn together. When you uncurl them to release the bow, they must move as one. Are you ready?"

"Yes."

"Very well. Release."

She let go, the bowstring thwacked against her arm guard, the arrow whistled through the air and hit the target with a thunk. Clarissa gave a squeal of delight and bounced on the balls of her feet. "I did it!"

"Indeed you did," Sherwood said, giving her shoulder a little squeeze. "Well done, Clarrie."

She beamed with delight, and cast a triumphant smile at Lord Havering.

"You had better keep an eye on her."

Rochdale. How long had he been standing there?

"One of those boys is liable to steal her away from

you." He lifted his eyebrows and grinned. "Or are you perhaps hoping one of them actually will?"

Adam ignored him to watch as Miss Stillman and the Dowager Duchess of Hertford took their turns shooting, with help from Sir George Lowestoft and Lord Ingleby. And then it was Marianne's turn. Sherwood lost no time in rushing to her aid. In contrast with the solicitous way he'd instructed Clarissa, he pressed himself up close against Marianne and took his time about aligning her stance. There was more than archery instruction going on between them.

"Let's go back to the house and have a game of billiards." Rochdale tugged on Adam's sleeve. "Come on, old boy, let's go. I do not trust you not to make a fool of yourself if you continue to watch that performance."

He wasn't going to make a fool of himself, but Adam had no desire to see Marianne in that fellow's arms. A man who apparently did not even know how to kiss her properly. God only knew what sort of experience he would give her between the sheets. "A good idea," he said. "Let's go."

The two of them turned away from the archers and trod up the little hill that would take them back to the house.

"So you are forced to watch this love affair at close quarters."

"Closer even than you can imagine," Adam said. "I was given the room next to hers."

"Good God."

"It appears that she was given pride of place. Her room—I am told, I haven't seen it—is quite grand. Fit for a duchess. Mine, I fear, is much smaller. I suspect it was the dressing room, converted to a bedchamber for the house party." There was even a connecting door between their rooms, which was more temptation than Adam liked.

"Marianne is the queen of the party," he continued.

"I am merely a humble servant in the queen's court, sleeping in the dressing room. Still, it is closer than I would wish."

"Are the walls thin? Did you have to listen to her cry out last night?"

"No, Sherwood was occupied with late arrivals and nothing happened between them." It had been the only consolation so far in this wretched gathering. Adam wondered if there might not be some other duty that called Sherwood away tonight, and the night after that, and throughout the rest of the week.

"But tonight?"

Adam groaned. "Yes, I suppose it will happen tonight, damn it all."

"You cannot stop it, Cazenove. Don't do anything foolish. What you need is another woman to distract you. Amelia Forrester is said to be an obliging sort. A bit of sport in her bed would take your mind off Marianne's bed."

"You forget that my bride-to-be and her parents are here. Her father would likely call me out if he discovered I was frolicking with another woman while under the same roof with Clarissa. Her mother would surely do so, and that one would aim to kill."

"Then take the chit to bed. And don't use the dragon mother as an excuse. What could she do about it, anyway? You're already betrothed to the girl."

"I have considered it, believe me." He had thought of little else since his encounter with Marianne the day before had shot a bolt of fire straight through his vitals. He'd been on edge ever since. He would like nothing better than to bury himself in Clarissa's innocent white flesh and forget about Marianne. "I just don't believe Clarissa is ready to anticipate the wedding night. I fear I am doomed to my lonely bed this week."

"Suit yourself," Rochdale said. "It appears you will have your hands full with that bride of yours anyway, even if she doesn't allow you in her bed. She has developed quite a court of admirers."

"She is simply enjoying herself. She would never do anything improper, especially not with her parents here."

They reached the top of the hill and Adam turned back toward the archery field. Lord Julian Sherwood was setting up Marianne for the next shot by wrapping himself around her once again. Adam turned away.

"I hate country house parties," he said.

"What a marvelous activity archery is," Penelope said. "I had no idea how provocative a sport it could be. How clever of Lord Julian to suggest it."

Wilhelmina, Grace, Penelope, and Marianne walked together on their way back to the house. Marianne was glad the guests had not paired off in couples for once. She had had little opportunity to speak with her friends in private since their arrival at Ossing.

"One cannot help but notice his marked attentions, Marianne," the duchess said. "He certainly took every opportunity to put his arms around you."

"Yes, I know," she said. "I confess it was a tad embarrassing. He was so much more circumspect with the other ladies. I fear he is making no secret of his intentions."

"Not to mention," Penelope said, "that you were given the best bedchamber."

"I scolded him about that," Marianne said. "It should have gone to Wilhelmina, as the highest-ranking guest. But he only laughed and said it was his house and he could assign rooms however he wanted."

"My room is perfectly fine," the duchess said. "You need not have scolded on my account."

"But it is an obvious breach of etiquette that will not go unnoticed," Grace said. "Have a care, Marianne. You may find yourself the object of gossip."

"Bosh," Penelope said. "The oh-so-proper Lady Presteign would never allow a scandal on her watch."

Marianne's gaze strayed to the lady in question, who walked arm in arm with her friend, Lady Troutbeck. Julian's sister was indeed a high stickler. She was the daughter of a duke and the widow of a marquess, so it would be more surprising if she was not.

"I must confess," Marianne said, "that her reception of me was cool at best."

"She will know that this party was arranged on your behalf," Wilhelmina said.

"And no doubt she disapproves of the room assignments," Penelope added.

"I suspect she disapproves of the whole party," Grace said. "She will surely be aware that certain bedchambers will not be slept in. Mr. Tolliver's, for instance." She darted a glance at Penelope, who grinned. "Or that horrid Lord Rochdale. I cannot imagine why he was invited."

"I believe Julian knew that Adam, who must be invited on Clarissa's behalf, would have no particular friend among the other gentlemen guests," Marianne said. "His invitation for Lord Rochdale was a kindness to Adam. Lord Julian is an excellent host in that respect. He made sure everyone had at least one friend in attendance so that no one would feel alone or left out. The Troutbecks are particular friends of Lady Presteign, Miss Stillman is Clarissa's bosom bow, and Mrs. Forrester was no doubt included for her sister, Lady Drake."

"I notice Rochdale is already sniffing about Lady Drake's skirts," Penelope said.

"Is it any wonder Lady Presteign disapproves of such a party?" Grace said, her mouth twisted in distaste.

"But my dear," Wilhelmina said, "that is the whole point of a house party. It provides a somewhat less public stage for seduction than a Society ball in London."

"And the best part of all," Penelope said, "is that

Eustace and I get to spend entire nights together without him having to sneak away before dawn. It was perfectly lovely to fall asleep in his arms last night."

She looked so wistful that Marianne wondered if she had fallen in love with Mr. Tolliver after all.

Wilhelmina gave Penelope an indulgent smile. "Quite so," she said. "But you were not so fortunate, I think, Marianne."

"No. Lord Julian had obligations last night."

"Then tonight will be your night," the duchess said. "How exciting for you."

Penelope put an arm around Marianne's shoulder and gave an affectionate squeeze. "It *will* be exciting, I promise you."

"I hope so," Marianne said. "I confess I have been feeling rather anxious about it." Especially after Julian had stolen another kiss that morning. It had been as rough and passionate as the first, and Marianne had done her best to relax and enjoy it. But there had been no shivers, no flutterings in her stomach. She wished he could have been a bit more gentle, but no doubt that only spoke of her lack of sophistication in these matters. She should not expect to be wooed and gently persuaded like a virgin.

"It is your first time, so to speak," Wilhelmina said, "so a bit of nerves is understandable. But you must try to relax when the time comes. I am certain Lord Julian will know how to put you at ease. You will enjoy it more if you are not so tense."

"That is what Adam says, too."

Grace looked aghast. "Surely you do not speak of such things with Mr. Cazenove."

"He is a close friend, Grace."

"It is one thing to speak frankly with other women about such intimate matters, but with a *man*? Heavens, Marianne, that does not seem at all proper."

"I suppose it does sound odd," Marianne said, "but we are really very close, you know. I feel quite comfortable talking to him about anything." There was, however, a slight edge to that comfort of late. She wondered if they would ever be completely comfortable again together after that kiss. It would certainly help matters if he would stop touching her in ways that made her tingle all over.

"And you do not worry he will gossip about you at the clubs?" Grace asked. "In his cups, he could reveal all your secrets, and soon your name would be bandied about town as a woman of indiscretion."

"I trust Adam more than any person on earth," Marianne said. "He would never be so careless with something I'd told him in confidence. He is far too honorable to jeopardize our friendship in such a way. He is the finest man I know."

"My goodness, Marianne," Penelope said, "it sounds as though you have a tendre for him. He is a very attractive man. What a pity he is engaged to that giggling little chit."

"It is indeed a pity," Marianne said. "I cannot imagine anyone more unsuitable for him."

"You *do* have a tendre for him," Penelope exclaimed.

"No, it is nothing like that. We have been friends for years, that is all, and I do have a great affection for him." She gave a rueful laugh. "I remember when I was first introduced to him, when he came down from Oxford with David for a visit. I thought him quite the most dashing man I'd ever met. Handsome, charming, and with a smile that could make a young girl weak in the knees."

"And older girls, too," Penelope said.

"David whispered to me that his friend was a bit wild," Marianne said, "and that only increased his attractiveness to the innocent girl I was. But that was a long time ago. Now when I look at him I see only a good friend, not a dashing hero."

There had been a time, though, when she had been infatuated with those seductive green eyes and that rakish long hair. Even though Marianne had loved David, for a short while before her marriage she had been a bit *in* love with Adam. She never let on, of course. How could she? And over time she had forgotten that foolish infatuation entirely as she fell more deeply in love with David.

But in the last few weeks she had come to realize that her attraction to him had never really disappeared. It had always been there, buried beneath layers of propriety and sensibility, and the everyday reality of a good and happy marriage to someone else. It was still there. She was still a little bit infatuated with Adam. It had taken his betrothal to another woman to unearth those old feelings, and one stolen kiss to set them churning in her heart again.

But he was promised to another, and so once again she must keep her fantasies in check.

"His betrothal is indeed unfortunate," Wilhelmina said. "Cazenove would have been a good lover for you."

"He has never been interested in me in that way," Marianne said, with a dismissive wave that she hoped belied the deep longing she felt at Wilhelmina's words. "I am not his type."

The duchess lifted a skeptical brow.

"Besides, I have Lord Julian now. That is, if I do not drive myself into a state of collapse from anxiety. Were you this nervous, Penelope, the first time with your young Scot?"

Penelope laughed. "Me, nervous? Surely you jest. No, I was so attracted to him, so aroused by the very sight of him, that the only anxiety I felt was over how quickly we could manage an opportunity to act."

"Try not to work yourself up into such a lather," Wilhelmina said to Marianne. "If Lord Julian is half the man I think him, he will have your body singing to his tune in no time, and put you entirely at ease before you know what's happening."

"And the next morning, you must tell us all about it," Penelope said. "Oh, stop groaning, Grace. That was our agreement. *I* have certainly told all."

"Indeed you have," Grace muttered beneath her breath.

"It is too bad Beatrice cannot be here to share in the tale," Penelope said. "By the way, am I the only one who noticed how little it disappointed her to have to decline the invitation to Ossing?"

"She could hardly skip the Wallingford ball," Grace said. "Lady Wallingford is Emily's aunt on her father's side. Emily will be expected to attend, and Beatrice, too, in her sister's stead. Besides, she could not have come here without her two girls, and she would never have left them alone just for the sake of a short house party."

"Even so," Penelope said, "I could swear there was something else distracting her. Do you think Beatrice has found a lover and not told us about it?"

"I don't think so," Marianne said. "She really is too busy with young Emily. I believe that girl is a bit willful and demanding. Poor Beatrice was probably exhausted, not distracted."

"Perhaps. We shall quiz her when we return. In the meantime," Penelope said as she nudged Marianne in the ribs, "we will entertain ourselves with the details of *your* love affair."

Marianne sincerely hoped there would be details worth repeating.

Chapter 11

Sherwood stood behind Marianne's chair and bent his head close to hers to speak in her ear. There was no mistaking the look in the young man's eyes. He was planning their assignation.

Adam stifled a groan and turned away.

The guests had gathered in the main drawing room after supper. Several of the ladies had taken turns on the pianoforte, including Marianne, who had acquitted herself nicely with a Nicolini air. Others had sung, including Clarissa, who had a clear, sweet voice. She was obviously uncomfortable singing before an audience, but Mrs. Leighton-Blair insisted she do so, just as she had done during Adam's visit to their estate in Wiltshire. Clarissa's singing was pretty and enjoyable, even if not particularly accomplished. Her mother no doubt recognized it as her one true talent, and determined to showcase it whenever possible. Though now that Clarissa was betrothed, Adam thought, the woman could have allowed the girl a respite.

She was more composed when her friend Jane Stillman joined her in a duet of "Roses and Wood-bines So Sweetly That Bloom." She was entirely at ease by the time Sherwood, who had a surprisingly fine voice, joined her in "The Moon-Beam Plays on Yonder Grove."

But the entertainment had come to an end, and

Lady Presteign had announced her intention to retire for the evening. Following her lead, the other ladies rose and prepared to quit the room. Marianne smiled up at Sherwood and he stepped around to the front of her chair and offered his arm. Good Lord, was he bold enough to escort her to her bedchamber and follow her inside, for everyone to see? Surely not. His stiff-rumped sister would never countenance such a thing.

Adam wondered how he could legitimately absent himself from his own bedchamber so he would not be tempted to listen to what went on in the one next door. Should he go for a long walk? Should he hole up in the library with a book? A game of cards would be a welcome distraction.

Yes, a game of cards. That's what he wanted. And perhaps a steaming bowl of rum punch.

"I say, Sherwood, since the ladies are leaving us, how about a few hands of cards for the gentlemen?" The words were out before Adam had time to consider them. He had wished for some obligation that kept Sherwood out of Marianne's bed. It just occurred to him that perhaps he could create one.

"Capital idea," Gerald Leighton-Blair said, and rubbed his hands together.

His wife sent him a sharp look, which he ignored. Apparently Clarissa's father was happy for an excuse to stay away from his wife's bed. With so many guests, each of the married couples had been obliged to share a bed, something they probably seldom did in their own homes with their separate chambers and suites of rooms.

Would Adam and Clarissa keep separate rooms? He rather hoped they would not, but suspected she might feel otherwise.

"Yes, Sherwood, let's have some cards," Lord Havering said. "I do hate to make an early night of it. No need to keep country hours so close to town, eh?"

Some of the other gentlemen voiced their approval and Sherwood, who did not look at all pleased, was stuck. As host, he could hardly deny his guests' wishes.

He managed a polite smile. "Then cards it shall be." He signaled to his butler. "Hibbert, have the Green Room set up with tables for cards, and make sure the fire is built up."

The gentlemen bade the ladies good night. Adam kissed Clarissa's ungloved hand and she actually returned a bright smile without flinching at his touch. Perhaps she was becoming accustomed to him at last. He bowed over her mother's hand as well.

"I do hope you will not be up until all hours," she said. "Lord Julian has promised an excursion to Box Hill tomorrow. Mr. Leighton-Blair will need his rest."

"Yes, ma'am," he said.

She nodded and took her daughter by the arm and left the drawing room. She had not noticed, or so Adam hoped, that he had agreed to nothing more than the fact that her husband needed his rest. He made no promises about late hours. In fact, Adam hoped to make it as late an evening as possible.

He watched Sherwood speaking softly to Marianne and then turned to find Rochdale at his side.

"You are a raving idiot, Cazenove, as evidenced by that self-satisfied grin. You cannot hope to postpone the inevitable forever. He's going to have her."

"But perhaps not tonight, if I can help it."

"But tomorrow, or some other night. He *will* have her. Get over it, old boy."

Adam winced. Rochdale, with his no-nonsense attitude, always had the ability to make Adam feel like a fool. "You are right, of course. But I did not plan this, I assure you. It was pure impulse. I saw them whispering, and I simply could not help myself."

"Well I, for one, do not appreciate this deuced impulse of yours. I have a lady waiting, too."

The gentlemen were herded by Sherwood into the

Green Room, an elegant though masculine room with dark green walls and gleaming woodwork. A fire blazed in the grate and candles burned bright on every surface. Three tables had been set up and chairs arranged round them. Several wine decanters and rows of glasses lined a sideboard. It was not nearly enough for what Adam had in mind.

"I have heard," he said, "that you make a very fine punch, Sherwood."

Since most men were proud of their own special punch recipes, it was not too wide a shot, and it hit its mark.

Sherwood puffed up with pride and said, "I am honored to know my punch has found a measure of fame. I do indeed have an excellent recipe. The best you have ever tasted, I promise you."

"Is it your father's recipe, boy?" Leighton-Blair asked.

"Yes, as a matter of fact."

"Then I can testify to its excellence," Leighton-Blair said. "Warminster always served the best rum punch I ever had."

"Then we must have some, Sherwood," Sir Neville Kenyon said. "For until you have proved otherwise, I will have to consider my own recipe superior. I propose we have a taste so we can properly judge."

"Done," Sherwood said. He asked a footman to bring the punch bowl as well as rum, brandy, lemons, sugar, and nutmeg.

"You had better bring enough for several bowls," Lord Havering said. "It will take more than one to determine its superiority."

Bless you, Havering, you silly pup.

There was nothing like a good, strong rum punch to get a man well and truly drunk before he knew what hit him.

Decks of cards were placed on the tables, and the

men began to arrange themselves about the room. Sherwood passed around a box of Spanish cigarillos and poured wine for those who wanted it. By the time the footman returned with a large blue-and-white porcelain punch bowl, the room was thick with sweet smoke and rowdy laughter.

It had all the makings of a very long night.

Adam smiled and took a seat.

It was a good thing she'd been given the largest bedchamber. It gave Marianne lots of room to pace. And wait.

Now that the thing was finally going to happen, she wished they could get on with it. The waiting only made it worse.

Julian had whispered in her ear that he hoped she would allow him to visit her later. She had agreed, and they had shared a warm look of anticipation. Then Adam had spoiled everything by calling for cards. Did he not know how anxious she was for this evening with Julian to happen?

Of course he knew. He was the one who'd told her to relax. How could she relax when she had no idea when, or even if, Julian was coming? How long would their card games last?

Knowing Julian would not be able to come to her right away, Marianne had taken advantage of the added time to prepare for him. She had donned her prettiest pink silk nightgown and matching silk wrapper. She had taken her hair down and brushed it until it shone. She did not braid it. There was nothing seductive about a thick, matronly plait hanging down one's back. She knew that much, at least, and not to wear a cap. Julian would want to see her hair loose, and so she let it fall straight and thick past her shoulders.

She had dabbed a drop of her favorite tuberose fragrance behind each ear and on her wrists. Not too much. She did not want to overpower him with scent. Just enough to be tantalizing. She hoped.

All the steps of preparation had worked to calm her nerves. But then the waiting began, and anxiety returned in full force. Would he find her desirable? Would he love her slowly and tenderly and not so roughly as he'd kissed her? Would she have the courage to ask for gentleness if he did not? Would he touch her in ways David never had? Would his body be different from David's? Would her body respond to his lovemaking as it ought? Would it be as wonderful and exciting as Penelope said?

Her nerves had reached a fevered pitch when a soft knock sounded at the door. She had not expected him so soon. She took a deep breath and opened the door, only to find a maid holding a tray.

"Beg pardon, ma'am. I am Ginny, Her Grace of Hertford's maid. She asked me to bring this to you."

The tray held a small cordial glass filled with a dark liquid and a larger wineglass filled with bright red wine.

"There is a note, too," Ginny said, and held out the tray.

Marianne took the tray, keeping it balanced so as not to slosh the liquid. "Thank Her Grace for me, Ginny."

"Yes, ma'am. Good night, ma'am."

Marianne closed the door and took the tray over to the nightstand, where she could more easily read by the light of the candle. She unfolded the note, written in Wilhelmina's oddly childish scrawl.

Here are too importent items for yor speshel nite. The first is a aprikot cordial that Hertford taught me to make. Drink it all before Lord Julian arrives, and you will be relacts and reddy for him. The claret is laced with juniper juse. Drink it afterwerds to protect yorself from any unexpected developmint.

   Enjoy yorself!

   —W

She was such a dear. How very thoughtful. She knew Marianne was nervous, and wanted to help, bless her kind heart. And she had not, in fact, thought of protection. She still assumed conception was unlikely, but she appreciated the insurance against it nonetheless.

Marianne took a sip of the cordial, and almost lost her footing. It was extremely potent. Good heavens, her insides were on fire! It was a good thing she had not tossed back the entire glassful in one swallow. She would have collapsed in a dead heap on the floor, and wouldn't that have been a nice way for Julian to find her?

She took tiny sips until she grew accustomed to its warm, tingly path down her throat. It was not long before she discovered she enjoyed that fiery tingle. Its warmth spread through her body, making her feel loose and languorous.

Thank you, Wilhelmina.

Marianne thought she might actually be able to relax and enjoy whatever Julian did.

She looked over at the bed, where it would all happen. It was a grand, stately bed with a huge canopy and heavy curtains—a bed meant for something more regal and important than plain Mrs. Nesbitt. It had grown chilly last night and she had pulled the bed-curtains closed, feeling very cozy and warm.

How would it feel to be cocooned in that dark warmth with Julian?

She wandered over to a pier glass and studied herself in the mirror. The pink silk clung to every curve, leaving little to the imagination. What would Julian think of her body? It was not as firm as it once was, but still slender. Her breasts and hips had grown more womanly, more curvaceous. But he was younger than Marianne. Would he think she looked too old? Not fresh enough?

Lord, she was going to work herself up into another frenzy of anxiety. It did not matter what he thought of her body. She could not change it, after all. He would have to accept her as she was, and that was that.

Several hours later, she had ceased to care what Julian thought of her. Damn Adam for keeping him busy and making her wait.

Adam chuckled softly as he surveyed the state of the formerly elegant Green Room. It looked like something Hogarth might have painted, one of those lesson paintings about the evils of excess.

Chairs were scattered about in disarray, two of them overturned. Bits of clothing were draped over various pieces of furniture—a neckcloth here, a waistcoat there—and a fine bottle green coat dangled from a wall sconce. Playing cards were scattered about willy-nilly. The men had ceased playing hours ago, when those remaining had been too foxed to see the spots on the cards. Empty wine and punch glasses littered every table. More than one had tipped over with its contents spilled across the table and onto the floor. One was broken at the stem. Another was shattered in the fire grate. Butts of cigarillos littered tabletops, were strewn about the floor, floated in punch glasses, and even bobbed in the overflowing chamber pots.

The punch bowl sat drained, but for the dregs, on the center table, surrounded by empty rum and brandy bottles, a bowl of crushed lemons, an overturned sugar bowl with its bits and chunks scattered about—the sugar tongs were under the table—and a fine silver nutmeg grater with its nut falling out.

It had been an uproarious evening, especially after the third bowl of punch, by which time Sherwood's precise recipe had been ignored, and anything and everything was flung into the bowl.

Leighton-Blair was sprawled on a sofa, snoring loudly. Young Lord Havering was passed out in a chair, his head on the table. Rochdale and Tolliver had left hours ago, obviously more interested in assignations upstairs than a rowdy drinking party. Adam had a vague memory of Ingleby sneaking off to some lady's room, as well. Had he mentioned the lady's name? Adam could not recall. Stillman, Kenyon, and Troutbeck had also left at some point, though Adam wasn't sure when. He'd been too busy making sure Sherwood imbibed more than his share.

Adam himself had had a great deal to drink, but as often as not had made a pretense of drinking so he could ensure the party continued into the wee hours. His ploy had worked. Sherwood was so drunk he couldn't possibly perform. And he was gentleman enough not to visit a lady when he was so thoroughly foxed.

Sir George Lowestoft, a young man with an amazing capacity for drink, made an effort to rise from his chair.

"Call it a night," he said in a thick slur. "Shleep on m'feet. Well done, Shlerwood. Exshellent punch." He rose with deliberate slowness, then placed one foot carefully in front of the other in an unsteady path to the door. "God'sh teeth, wadda head I'll have t'morrow. 'Night, lads."

Sherwood glared plaintively at Adam, obviously not wanting to desert his last guest still awake. Adam was satisfied that there was no way the man would disturb Marianne at this hour, and in his condition. His work for the night was done.

"Yes, I believe I will call it a night, as well. Egad." He surveyed the room in a sweeping glance. "Had quite a time of it, didn't we? Better get some help for those two, Sherwood." He gestured toward Leighton-Blair and Havering.

"Right y'are." Sherwood rose very carefully. "Good God. F'got how potent th' duke's punch could be. Yesh, better fin' a footman t' help get theshe two t' bed. Wonder where t' find one at thish hour."

He stood for a moment, seeming to gather his bearings, to steady himself before attempting to walk. "All right, then. I'll jus' go—arggh!"

Sherwood's feet became tangled with Adam's outstretched legs, and he went sprawling on the ground. There was a horrible crunching sound, and then a crack as his head hit the brick hearth.

Hell and damnation.

Adam scrambled out of his chair and looked down at his young host, who lay in a heap at Adam's feet, his head bloodied and one leg bent at an unnatural angle.

Adam uttered a moan of horror. Good God, had he killed him?

Sick with worry and chagrin, Adam bent over Sherwood and placed a hand in front of his nose. He was still breathing. Thank God!

"What the devil?" Lowestoft, who'd not quite made his way out the door, turned to see what had happened.

"He tripped," Adam said, neglecting to mention it had been over his own leg. "And he looks to be badly hurt. His head is bleeding and I believe his leg is broken."

"My God." Lowestoft came back in the room and stood beside Adam. "He ain't dead, is he?"

"No, thank heaven. But he needs help. Can you make it downstairs?"

"Yes, of course," he said, suddenly sobered and pale with shock. "What should I do?"

"Find the butler. Hibbert is his name, as I recall. Tell him to send for a doctor at once."

"Are you going to try to move him?"

"No, I don't think we should move that leg. We might do more harm. I'd prefer to wait for the doctor. Now please, go find Hibbert."

The young man hurried out, still not entirely steady on his feet, but considerably more agile, and more sober, than he'd been a few minutes earlier.

"Wha' happened?"

Lord Havering's sleepy voice startled Adam. He'd forgotten about him. Had he seen anything? Had he seen Sherwood trip over Adam's foot?

"Thought I heard a crash. Somethin' fall over?"

"Sherwood tripped and fell. I'm afraid he's badly hurt."

"Good Lord."

The young man rose shakily from his chair and walked on wobbly legs to the hearth. "Egad. That leg don't look right. Damnation if he ain't broken it." He bent down to examine the twisted limb.

"Don't move it," Adam said. "I think we should wait for the doctor. But hand me that neckcloth, will you?" He pointed to one draped over a nearby chair.

Havering retrieved the neckcloth, moving slowly, dropping it twice before he handed it over. Adam carefully examined Sherwood's head. There was a gash above his right ear where he'd hit the sharp edge of the hearth. It did not look deep, but there was a lot of blood. His blond hair was soaked on one side.

Adam used the neckcloth to stanch the bleeding. He removed his own neckcloth and wrapped it about the head as a makeshift bandage. It might not be at all effective, but he had to do something. He felt helpless and plagued with guilt.

He had hoped to keep the fellow away from Marianne, but he hadn't intended to disable him. He had never meant any real harm. But he kept seeing Sherwood's ankle locking with his own. Had he left it stretched out on purpose? Had he wanted the fellow to trip?

Adam did not think so. But he kept seeing his outstretched leg, and thinking how he might have moved it, but didn't.

Hell and the devil. He'd gone too far this time. But no more. Never again. He would never, ever interfere with Marianne's life again. If she wanted a dozen lovers, she could have them. If she wanted to set up a male harem full of her personal love slaves, she could do so.

It took almost killing a man, but Adam had finally realized how utterly ridiculous he'd been as far as Marianne was concerned.

The door opened and Lowestoft entered with the butler, who'd thrown a dress coat over his nightshirt.

"Dear heaven," he said when he saw his employer.

"We did not move the leg," Adam said. "I thought it best to wait for the doctor."

"Yes, yes, that is best," Hibbert said.

"You've sent for him?"

"Yes, I sent one of the grooms who can ride faster than the rest. Dr. Sneed is only about three miles from here, in Richmond. It should not take him long to arrive. Poor Lord Julian. I hope he is not in too much pain."

"Fortunately, he'd had enough drink to dull the pain," Lowestoft said.

Hibbert looked up and took in the room for the first time. His eyes narrowed for the briefest instant before he schooled his features into his usual cool butlerian reserve. "Thomas."

A young, disheveled footman who'd been standing wide-eyed in the doorway came into the room. "Yes, sir?"

"I want you and Charles to tidy up this room."

"Now?"

"Now. Before the doctor arrives. And help Mr. Leighton-Blair to his room. Dr. Sneed may need use of the couch."

In all the commotion, Adam had forgotten about Clarissa's father, who was still asleep on the sofa. Hibbert excused himself so that he could be dressed properly when the doctor arrived. Adam helped the footmen rouse Leighton-Blair. Once fully awake, he was surprisingly alert. He did not return to his room, but stayed behind to offer what help he could.

Dr. Sneed made an appearance some forty-five minutes later. He set the broken leg—during which time Sherwood came awake, howling with pain—and stitched the head wound. Sherwood was given a heavy dose of laudanum, and fell unconscious again. He had to be carried upstairs to his bedchamber, which was an awkward process, with Leighton-Blair, Havering, Lowestoft, and Adam taking turns with the two footmen to lift him.

When they reached the corridor of his bedchamber, several heads popped out of doorways to see what the commotion was all about. Rochdale's dark head appeared in the doorway of a bedchamber that was not his own. Lady Drake's? Adam was not sure.

Rochdale closed his eyes and shook his head in disbelief. "My God, what have you done?" he whispered.

"I'll tell you later," Adam said, keeping his voice low. "But it was not deliberate, I promise you."

Grace Marlowe's startled face peeked out from another doorway, a woolen shawl clutched at her breast. One thick, blond plait hung over her shoulder all the way down to her waist. "Good heavens, what happened to the poor man?"

"An accident," Adam said. "His leg is broken."

"Oh, my." Her eyes darted from the limp form of Sherwood being hauled into his room to the other end of the corridor. She saw Rochdale, pursed her lips in disgust—she likely knew it was not Rochdale's bedchamber, and probably also knew which lady's it was—and closed her door.

Lord Troutbeck's head peered out from another doorway, a long-tailed nightcap on his head, and Miss Stillman's shocked face appeared from another. Mrs. Leighton-Blair, in a voluminous cap, glared daggers at her husband from yet another open door as he helped carry Sherwood into his bedchamber. When Adam walked into the room to help settle Sherwood on his bed, there were a great many hushed whispers behind him.

Marianne's door, he noted, had remained closed.

Chapter 12

The doctor settled his patient, taking care with the splint on his leg and insuring the head wound would not be jarred during sleep. The other gentlemen departed one by one, feeling confident there was nothing more they could do. Adam remained, along with Hibbert and Jarvis, Sherwood's valet, who'd been roused to come to his employer's aid. There was nothing Adam could do, either, but he felt so damned guilty for what had happened, he needed reassurance that the young man was in no danger.

"A clean break," the doctor told him. "It was easily set and should heal without difficulty. And the gash on his head was not deep. I have no fear of infection. He will have a fine goose egg of a lump by the morning, though, and will be in some pain. Thank you for your help, sir. It was very helpful to have that bleeding stanched early."

He turned to the valet. "He should sleep soundly through the night. Give him this dosage of laudanum when he wakes. He will need it. That leg is going to hurt like the very devil for a few days. Don't let him try to get out of bed. He needs to keep the leg still so it can set properly. Keep the dressing on his head dry. I will change it when I return."

After a few more instructions, Hibbert escorted the doctor downstairs. Jarvis thanked Adam profusely for his help, and turned his attention to tucking in the covers around Sherwood's leg. Adam slipped out of the room.

The corridor was quiet now. No one stirred and no lights shone from beneath any doors. The house had settled into a calm peace. It must have been about three in the morning. It had been a very long night.

A candle burned on a hall table, where a small supply of other candles had been set out for guests who might need a light during the night. Adam lit one and headed for his bedchamber.

He stopped at Marianne's door. She must have given up waiting for Sherwood hours ago and fallen asleep. She had been expecting a lover tonight, and damn it all, he had denied her that pleasure. And not only for tonight. Sherwood's leg would keep him out of commission for some time. All because of Adam's bloody selfishness.

But what if she was still waiting? What if she still expected him to come to her? There was no light under her door, but she could be awake, anxiously waiting, tying herself into knots of uneasiness and insecurity and frustrated desire. If she was awake, he really ought to tell her what had happened so she could go to sleep in peace.

Adam scratched softly on her door, but there was no sound from within. He turned the door handle. It was not locked. Of course it was not. She was expecting Sherwood. He very carefully and quietly opened the door.

The room was extremely dark, his small candle offering little light. The fire in the grate had burned out, and the air was cool.

"Marianne?" he whispered.

No response. She must be asleep.

The enormous bed loomed dark in the center of the room. He held up his candle and saw that the bed-curtains were pulled closed. She must have become chilled when the fire burned out. He stepped closer. He wanted to see her. Just to see her. He pulled back one of the draperies and held up his candle.

She lay sound asleep facing away from him. Her dark hair spilled out onto the pale linen of the pillow and over the counterpane. In all the years he'd known her, he'd never seen her hair down. That was a privilege for a husband. Or a lover. He'd no idea it was so long. One hand was curled up against her cheek. He could see part of a pale, shimmery nightgown. Silk, no doubt. She had worn it for Sherwood, for her lover.

He gazed at her for a long moment, drinking in the sight of her. He had never wanted her more than at this moment, when she lay there so peaceful, so beautiful.

It was his fault that Sherwood was not here to see how glorious she looked. But Adam could make it up to her. She wanted a lover.

By God, she would have one.

He dropped the curtain and made his way to the long bench at the foot of the bed. He placed the candle on an nearby candlestand. Adam did not think too closely about what he did. He did not allow his mind to probe, to question his actions. If he considered it rationally, he would never do it. And he wanted to do it, so he turned off his brain and let his body lead the way.

He stripped off his coat and waistcoat and shoes. When he pulled the shirt over his head, the air was stirred enough so that the candle blew out.

Damn. It was pitch-dark. The heavy window draperies were closed and not a hint of light crept in. He couldn't even see the hand he held before his face. It did not matter. He did not need light. He had seen her. Now he would feel her.

He finished disrobing until he stood naked in the

dark room. He felt his way around the bed, found the opening between the curtains, and gently, ever so gently, slipped beneath the covers.

She stirred slightly and made a tiny sound, but did not yet come awake. He eased his body against hers, his chest against her silk-clad back, and curled his arms around her.

For several moments, he just held her. At last. Everything he'd ever wanted, even though he hadn't realized—or admitted—he wanted it, was in his arms. The rightness of it was astounding. He would think of the wrongness of it later. For now, he simply allowed love and desire to overwhelm him.

God, she smelled delicious. It was a scent he always associated with Marianne—a bit floral, a bit spicy. She wore it often, and hints of it clung to the furniture and draperies and carpet in her sitting room. If he were blind, he would still know when she entered a room because of that distinctive fragrance. He'd asked her once what it was. What had she said? Some odd sort of flower. Tuberoses. That was it. She always smelled of tuberoses, but he'd never been close enough to inhale it so completely. It was intoxicating. He brushed her hair aside and put his mouth on the back of her neck. She tasted as sweet as she smelled.

She came awake slowly to the feel of his lips on her neck. It felt nice. So soft. So warm. And suddenly she realized what was happening and came fully awake with a jolt. "Oh!"

He'd come to her. Finally.

"It's me, Marianne." His voice was soft and low and slightly muffled as he nuzzled her.

"Yes." She turned her head toward him, but could not see a thing in the dark. She reached behind her and touched his head as he nibbled her neck. His hair was thick and soft and she ran her fingers through it while he worked magic with his lips.

"Are you disappointed?" he whispered, his breath tickling her ear. "Angry?"

She had been both when he had failed to show up after several hours, even though she knew it was not his fault. She had cursed Adam for his damned card game when she'd finally given up and crawled into bed. But none of that mattered now. He was here, and oh, God, he was loving her and he felt so good.

"No," she replied. "I am not disappointed."

"Oh, thank God," he muttered against her neck. "Thank God."

She gave a little groan as his lips trailed up to her ear, and she arched her neck to give him better access. And it occurred to her that she was not at all nervous. She was letting it happen, and it was lovely.

Adam had been right. All she had to do was relax in order to enjoy it. Having been sound asleep, she'd had no time to become anxious or nervous. Instead, she felt languid and sensuous and . . . sexual. She had never felt more relaxed. She was almost glad it had taken him so long to show up that she had fallen asleep.

His lips planted butterfly-soft kisses on her jaw and cheek, and she turned her head so she could reach his mouth with hers. With a quick movement, he flipped her over to face him. It was then she realized he was naked. Dear God. David had never been completely naked with her. He had always worn a nightshirt.

She reached out a hand to touch him.

"Marianne. My love." He gave a little growl, and covered her mouth with his.

It was nothing like his other kisses. He'd saved the best for now, for the loving. His lips moved against hers, tasting, teasing, exploring. He ran his tongue along the seam of her lips, and she parted them to let him in. A new kind of pleasure unfolded inside her as he drew her tongue deeper into his mouth, caressing it with his own.

He stroked her hair with one hand, twining its length around his fingers. She put her arms around him, loving the feel of skin and muscle, pulling him closer. And suddenly the kiss became torrid and urgent, almost painful in its soul-searing intensity. Ripples of sensation spiraled through her. And she wanted more.

He moved one hand to her waist and slid it up the silk of her gown to her rib cage until he cupped her breast. His thumb circled her nipple and her whole body shuddered at his touch. His mouth left hers and trailed moist kisses down her chin and throat and neck and onto the bodice of her nightgown. He kissed her right through the silk, dipping lower and lower. And then he took her breast into his mouth.

Marianne cried out and arched into his mouth. Dear God. They had not even completed the act yet, and she had already felt more powerful sensations than she'd ever felt with David. But David had never kissed her like this.

"I want all of you," he whispered. "All of you."

He reached down and grabbed the hem of her nightgown and raised it—to her thighs, to her hips, to her waist, and over her breasts. Finally, she lifted her arms and he stripped it away. And she was naked. She had never been completely naked with a man. It felt . . . exciting.

He explored her in the darkness with his hands, soft fingers grazing and kindling little erotic fires here, there, and everywhere. It was as if he was trying to see her with his hands, to discover through his touch how her body looked. She was somehow emboldened to do the same. She ran her hands over his chest, intrigued by the crisp hair that covered it. She discovered smooth places on his sides and along his rib cage, places without hair where the skin was soft as a baby's.

She wished it were not so dark, for she would like to see him, to see the play of skin and hair and firm muscle. But the closed bed-curtains created an inky darkness that was impenetrable.

She pressed her lips to his chest, inhaling the musky masculine scent of him, with just a hint of bay rum. His chest hair tickled her nose. She flicked her tongue over his nipples, eliciting a gasp, while her hands explored the taut muscles around them. Her hands skimmed lower, following a line of hair down his abdomen to his navel, where the hair grew thicker again. Her hand moved lower still, and he groaned.

He put his arms around her and pulled her close. "My love," he whispered, and kissed her again.

The combination of his mouth on hers while her naked breasts pressed to his bare chest was the most extraordinary feeling. Her smooth skin against the crisp hair of his chest—feminine against masculine, hard against soft—was a potent and provocative sensation. She rubbed against him like a cat and kneaded his back and shoulders with restless desire.

If this was all there was, it would be enough. She had already experienced more pleasure than she'd ever known; her body had come alive as never before. If there was nothing more, she would be satisfied.

But she wanted more. She wanted it all.

He turned her onto her back and moved on top of her. The end was near, then. The unbelievably wonderful preliminaries were almost over and the main act was about to begin.

But she was wrong.

He kissed her again, long and hard, while he stroked first one perfect breast, then the other. She arched up into his hand, and he felt her need. His mouth left hers, and marking the trail with his tongue, he made his way to the soft upper curve of her breast, then lower. Finally, inevitably, he took the peaked nipple into his mouth and curled his tongue around it. Her cry of pleasure was one of the sweetest things he'd ever heard. This woman who had never known physical pleasure was writhing with it. He had done this for her, and he was glad.

He circled her nipple with his tongue, then explored the soft underside of her breast. He paid equal homage to her other breast, then slithered down her body as he trailed kisses along her abdomen and belly.

He paused to consider if he should go farther. She might be shocked. But she had said she wanted to experience the full pleasure of physical intimacy. Just once. Since there could only be this once, he would give it all to her.

But not yet. Slowly.

He moved over her and kissed her again. He ravished her mouth with wild, hungry kisses while his hand stroked the fine curve of her hip and her long, elegant thigh. Distracting her with his tongue, he slowly stroked his hand up her inner thigh until he cupped the soft mound of her sex. He felt her tense, but he continued kissing her and let his hand rest on her for a few moments. Then, very slowly, his fingers parted her and began to stroke the intimate flesh of her sex. He swallowed her gasp and continued to touch her. She was already damp with desire when he pushed a finger inside her.

She groaned and ripped her mouth from his. "Oh, my God!" she cried. "Oh, yes."

He pulled her mouth back to his and pleasured it with his tongue while he worked his finger inside her. He removed it at last and gently rubbed the tip of his damp finger against the one spot he knew would give her the most pleasure. She moaned into his mouth, and he continued to touch her. She lifted her hips and opened herself to him. She was ready.

He broke the kiss and made his way again down her body, kissing, licking, and nipping every inch of her while his finger continued its concentrated motion.

He kissed her belly, then down and down until his mouth replaced his finger and his tongue pleasured her.

She uttered an almost painful cry, and then, "What are you doing? Oh, my God, what are you doing?"

Adam lifted his head, replacing his tongue with his finger once again. "I am pleasuring you, my love."

When he brought his mouth back down on her, she thought she would die. She had never felt anything like this in her life. The sensation was so intense it was almost unbearable. Everything was focused on that one spot, the place she had never dreamed was meant to be touched by a man's lips and tongue. It was shocking, but she did not care. She couldn't think. She could only feel. Every muscle tensed as she arched and stretched and rocked her hips in immodest response to the caress of his tongue. The pleasure increased—the tension rose higher and higher—until there was a steady roaring in her ears and she thought she was going to explode.

And suddenly, she did. An explosion of pure sensation shook her body and she cried out in astonishment. She soared on a wave of intense pleasure as the explosion's ripples shimmered over every inch of her body.

Adam savored the incredible shudder of her climax. Her first, he suspected. No other man had given her this. It thrilled him to know that he was the first, and it sent a great surge of passion rolling through him. Before her trembling had subsided, he moved on top of her, spreading her legs with his knees. He pressed his erection against the still-pulsing entrance to her sex. She lifted her hips to receive him, and with one long stroke, he was inside her.

She uttered a low moan that ended in a contented sigh as he entered her. After he allowed her body to adjust, relax, and accept him completely, he stilled. A profound sense of rightness, of home, enveloped him.

He was almost overcome with the poignancy of the moment—the first time inside her body, finally, and the last time.

Her hips shifted beneath him. "Don't stop," she said. "Love me. Please, love me."

He placed his mouth beside her ear. "I am loving you. I will always love you, Marianne." He could no longer deny it. Now that she was in his arms, he knew he loved her. He always had, just as Rochdale claimed.

He began to move inside her, thrusting and withdrawing slowly at first. He wanted to bring her to climax again if he could, deliberately keeping his own at bay in exquisite torment. So he took his time and brought her through several stages of arousal. She lifted her legs to draw him in more deeply. She entwined her body elaborately with his, putting every possible inch in hungry contact with him.

When he felt the tension build in her again, and her moans became quick little pants, he increased the rhythm, driving harder and harder until he felt her muscles close around him like a fist. Only when he felt her stiffen, and then buck and twist, and then press her face against his shoulder to muffle her scream, did he finally allow himself to finish. He buried his face in her sweet hair and drove his love into her.

Her body continued to tremble with reverberations of new sensations that had shaken her to the core, releasing ecstasy from every pore. Even the roots of her hair tingled.

Marianne could not believe what had just happened. Twice he had brought her body to that incredible peak and taken her over the edge. This was what Penelope had meant. Now she understood. And dear God, it was amazing.

How she wished she could see him, could look in his eyes and see if there was a wonder in them such as she felt must be in hers.

His weight was heavy on her, but it was somehow pleasant. And inside, where he was still joined to her, she could feel a pulsing as her body recovered from the powerful climaxes that had rocked it. And after a moment, as her mind and body calmed, an intense lethargy swept over her.

"Marianne, my love."

He kissed her so tenderly it almost made her weep. She wondered why his kisses had been so rough before, and how she could possibly have felt so little when she was now awash in more feelings than she could name.

He moved off her, tucked her close to his side, and pulled the bedcovers up over them. She nestled her head against his shoulder and he wrapped an arm around her. Marianne could not recall ever feeling so contented.

It had been the most gloriously wonderful night of her life.

It was an extraordinary thing he'd given her. He would never know how extraordinary. Whatever happened after tonight, she would always remember him as the man who taught her about physical pleasure, the man who gave her something she'd never experienced before.

And Adam was right. She was not cold or unresponsive. She was sexually alive for the first time.

She wished she could explain how she felt to the man beside her, but she was so drowsy. She would tell him later. Now she just wanted to sleep and could manage only a few words, spoken from the heart.

"Thank you, Julian."

Chapter 13

Thank you, Julian.

The words shook Adam to the marrow of his bones. She had thought he was Sherwood. He'd been so thrilled that he'd given her all that pleasure, that he'd aroused such sweet cries of passion from her, and she had not even known it was him.

Hell and damnation.

Adam cursed the darkness for this unbelievable situation, not sure whether to laugh or cry at the absurdity of it.

She hadn't recognized him in the dark. But he had not pretended to be Sherwood. Devil take it, he had told her it was him, and been thrilled beyond description when she'd said she was not disappointed. A large measure of the joy he'd experienced in making love to her had been the knowledge that she accepted *him*, welcomed *him*, desired *him*.

And all along, she'd thought he was someone else. "It's me," he'd said, but she'd believed he was Sherwood.

Of course, she had been expecting his bloody lordship. She would never have expected Adam to creep naked into her bed. And the damned darkness meant she could not see him. The few words he'd spoken to her had been whispered, so she had not recognized his voice. All her sighs and moans and cries of pleasure had been for Sherwood. Every generous offering of her lush body, every shuddering response, had been for Sherwood.

Damn, damn, damn.

He gazed down at her head nestled against his shoulder. She was dead asleep, drained by the passion of their lovemaking.

Marianne. His love. He had known in his heart that this moment, after the loving, would be painfully bittersweet. The end of a long-unacknowledged dream, briefly come true. For there could never be another night like this. Adam would marry Clarissa, and never hold Marianne in his arms again. They would both have to keep the thrill of this night, this one remarkable night, forever secret in their hearts.

Only her memories would not be of Adam, and so this ending was worse than bittersweet. It was damned near devastating.

Good Lord, now what was he to do? Should he wake her up and confess his true identity? Should he wait for her to awake and, assuming light ever made its way into this blasted room, discover she was not curled up beside Sherwood, but was naked in the arms of her husband's best friend?

She would very likely murder him.

And what good would it do her anyway, to know she and Adam had spent one illicit night together but could never do so again?

Adam half wished he had not crawled into her bed, though he could not have stopped himself if he'd tried. And now he would enter into a marriage with a sweet, innocent girl he barely knew, just when he had finally been allowed, if only by mistake, to hold in his arms the only woman he'd ever loved.

This night had not been fair to either woman, and Adam's gut twisted with a horrible guilt for it. And for finally acknowledging that he was in love with David's wife, and had probably been so even while the man lived. It had been a night steeped in guilt—first Sherwood's accident, and now this. All because Adam had placed his own desires above everyone else's. He'd been selfish enough to deny Marianne a lover, and even more selfish to assume that role himself.

And he'd hurt more than just her. He'd done harm to Marianne, Clarissa, and Sherwood with his damned self-indulgent arrogance.

And yet, he had given Marianne what she wanted. He had shown her the joys of physical love, and she had responded with more passion than he'd ever imagined. It was a memory he would cherish forever, even if he could never admit it had happened. Not even to Marianne. Especially not to Marianne.

He wished he could tell her. He would like her to know that he was the one who'd held her while she'd shuddered beneath him with her first sexual climax. He might have been tempted to wake her and tell her if he believed she would accept the night as a gift, one precious night, a sweet shared memory.

But he did not believe Marianne would see it that way. He rather suspected she would hate him for tricking her, for allowing her to believe he was Sherwood, even though he'd never meant to do so. Even worse, he had introduced her to pleasure, all the while knowing it could be only this one time. She might hate him for that most of all.

Adam realized the nature of their friendship was destined to change once he married Clarissa, but he did not want it to end altogether. He did not want Marianne to hate him.

And so he could not tell her.

He stroked a hand over Marianne's soft hair, ever so gently so as not to wake her. He had to leave before she woke, but he wanted to hold her just a while longer. Just for a few more minutes. How he wished he could see her. Instead, he'd memorized the lines of her body, every curve, every angle—the full breasts, the slender waist, the soft belly, the curve of hip, the round bottom. Every detail was etched in his memory. If he were to meet her in the dark again, he would be able to touch any part of her and recognize it as Marianne.

The darkness heightened other senses as well. He turned his head slightly and inhaled the sweet scent of her. That heady, familiar fragrance would be on his skin now, as a reminder. He was tempted never to bathe again.

But if he was to keep tonight a secret, he would need to erase anything that might identify him as her lover. He could not walk around with Marianne's fragrance on his skin. As much as it would pain him to do so, he would have to wash it off. It would be a punishment, a ritual purging of Marianne from his body and soul.

Would she wake if he kissed her? He wanted to kiss her one last time, just once more, but he could not risk waking her. He could not take the chance. He would have to live on memories of other kisses. Kisses full of tenderness and passion, of gentle exploration and frenzied hunger.

She had not responded to Sherwood's kisses, she'd told him. Yet she had responded to Adam's kisses with wonder and urgency and mutual desire. How could she have thought he was Sherwood?

He pressed his lips to her hair, ever so gently. "Good night, my love." His words were no more than a breath, barely a whisper in the darkness. "I love you, Marianne. I will always love you."

Adam eased himself from the bed and tucked the covers around her. She stirred slightly but did not wake. He let the bed-curtains fall back, enclosing her in darkness.

He stumbled to the window and moved the draperies aside. There was no hint of dawn yet, but the moon was almost full and poured its light into the room. He used the moonlight to locate his clothes and shoes. He began to dress, thinking it would not be a good idea to be seen creeping naked out of Marianne's bedchamber.

And then he noticed the other door. Of course. The connecting door to the former dressing room. He walked over and tried the handle. It was unlocked. Excellent. No one would see him leave Marianne's room after all. No one need ever know he had been there.

Not even Marianne.

He gathered up his clothing, taking care not to leave a single incriminating item behind, walked through to his own pokey little room, and closed the door forever on his dream of love.

After much searching, Marianne found her nightgown bunched up with the covers at the foot of the bed. She slipped it over her head and tugged it down over her hips. There would be too many questions if her maid found her naked in bed.

And she was not ready to leave the bed just yet. She wanted to lie there a bit longer, languorous and lazy, reflecting on the miracle of the previous hours. She rolled to her side and buried her nose in the pillow. She could still smell him there, and everywhere.

It was a shame he was gone when she awoke. But he was being cautious and protective of her reputation, and she silently thanked him for it. She wished only that she hadn't fallen so deeply asleep. She would like to have spoken to him, perhaps make love with him again. She hadn't even heard him leave. Sexual activity was apparently like an opiate to her, drugging her into a sound sleep.

When she had first wakened and found him gone, she remembered Wilhelmina's juniper-laced wine. She'd fumbled around in the dark until she found it, and downed it in a few long swallows. She still was not entirely sure it was needed, but she supposed it was best to be safe. Besides, it tasted good and made her drowsy again. She had fallen asleep, and must have slept for a few more hours.

As she lay there now, very much aware of her bare skin beneath the slippery silk of her gown and savoring the suddenly erotic sensation, Marianne reviewed all that had happened between them, and marveled again that such pleasure was possible. Julian had done things to her she'd never expected, touched her in ways she'd never even imagined. When she thought of that first explosion of sensation—which must have been the climax Penelope had mentioned; it was certainly climactic—and what he had done to make it happen, she pulled the covers over her head and squealed. It was beyond shocking to think about and seemed a horribly indecent thing to do, but it had also been utterly spectacular.

That, and everything else he'd done, had been so thoroughly wonderful that she could not stop smiling. No wonder Penelope and the others—with the exception of Grace, of course—were willing and eager to take lovers. They knew. Even Beatrice, who had not yet taken a lover, at least knew what a lover could give her.

But Marianne had never really known. She really *had* missed something with David, and that realization was a source of great sorrow for her. They had loved each other. They ought to have experienced this sort of sharing, this unbelievable intimacy. And yet, they had never even been fully naked together. He had never touched her as intimately as Julian had done. There had certainly never been a climax with David. There was a world of experience they had never shared, and it saddened her to think of it.

It angered her a little, too. *Why* had they never shared this together?

With David, the sexual act had always been simple

and quick, with his nightshirt and her nightgown bunched around their waists. But he had held her in his arms afterward and she had always loved that best of all. Perhaps some men simply were not as skilled or as knowledgeable about these things, though she was quite sure Adam could have told David what to do if he had asked. How she wished she could have shared this more complete experience with him.

But at least she had shared it with someone. She had chosen wisely, too, as it happened. Julian was a magnificent lover. He took her completely by surprise with his tenderness and generosity, not to mention the incredible magic he worked with his hands and his mouth.

Judging by his previous kisses, she had rather expected him to be somewhat rough and frenzied and overpowering. She had certainly not expected him to spend so much time arousing her. It was as though everything he did was for her, as though he had put her pleasure above his own. He'd had his share of pleasure, too, naturally. His desire for her was obvious and he'd seemed more than satisfied. But she could not help feeling the whole experience had been for her, unlike his previous kisses, which had been all for him.

And then there were the words he'd whispered in her ear. Words of love. All part of the seduction, of course, and not to be taken literally. Just sweet lies. Even so, it was lovely to hear them spoken, and quite unexpected.

Perhaps all that he did for her and said to her was his way of making up for the fact that he made her wait so long. It was strange how completely she had misjudged him.

She heard Rose, her maid, stirring about. Marianne could not, unfortunately, lie in bed all day. She would have to get up and get dressed and go downstairs for breakfast. Would it be awkward to see Julian at the breakfast table? Would everyone be able to tell what had taken place between them last night? She was quite sure the warm glow she felt inside would be reflected in her face. As with Penelope, there would be no disguising it.

Sometime later, she made her way downstairs. She had dressed to suit her mood, wearing a dress of printed muslin in cheerful yellow and white stripes, trimmed with bright yellow ribbon. A passing footman held open the breakfast room door for her. She paused and took a deep breath before entering. She did not wish to embarrass herself by blushing crimson at the sight of Julian. Donning her best composure, she stepped inside.

Her gaze quickly swept the room. He was not there. She was a bit relieved, since she would not have to worry about making a fool of herself, but she was also disappointed. She really was anxious to see him and speak to him. She wanted to make sure he understood that another evening in his arms would be welcome.

The Stillmans were there, as were Mrs. Forrester, Sir George Lowestoft, and Wilhelmina. Marianne caught her friend's eye and flashed a smile. She exchanged greetings with all the guests and made her way to the sideboard. Marianne enjoyed the breakfasts at Ossing. They were the most informal meals of the day, where the guests served themselves. Servants did not hover, but came in only to replenish the plates of food.

Feeling uncharacteristically hungry—is that what a night of passionate sexual activity did for one?— Marianne filled a plate with toasted bread and butter, a French sweet roll, a boiled egg, and a slice of cold ham. She carried her plate to the table and took the empty seat beside Wilhelmina.

She leaned over and pitched her voice low so no one else would hear. "Thank you for sending the cordial and the wine last night. They were very welcome and much appreciated, I assure you. That cordial was extremely potent, I might add. What was in it?"

"I will write out the recipe for you," Wilhelmina said. "I am glad you liked it, though it is rather a shame that it wasn't necessary after all."

Marianne furrowed her brow. "What do you mean?"

"I trust all the noise last night did not keep you awake, Mrs. Nesbitt."

She turned to Sir George and smiled. "Did you gentlemen create a rumpus last evening with your card games? How provoking that you should have so much fun without the ladies. But I assure you, I heard nothing. I slept like the dead."

Which was quite true, of course. Another consequence of strenuous sexual activity. She slanted a glance toward Wilhelmina and smiled.

"Oh, no," Sir George said, "I did not mean that at all. Though, of course, we did have rather a boisterous evening. As I recall." He flashed a grin.

Marianne imagined he and some of the others had likely imbibed somewhat more than they ought. It was only to be expected when a group of men gathered for cards.

"No, I meant the accident," he said. "I'm afraid we made quite a racket getting poor Sherwood up to his bedchamber."

Poor Sherwood? What on earth was he talking about?

"I heard nothing, sir," she said. "There was an accident?"

"I'm afraid so," he said.

"Lord Julian fell and broke his leg," Miss Stillman said.

She gave a start. "What?"

There must be some mistake. Julian was with her and she was quite sure his leg was not broken. In fact, it had been in very good working order. Unless something happened to him after he left her room?

"Yes, isn't it just awful?" Miss Stillman said, her eyes as big as saucers.

"Sir George was just telling us all about it," Wilhelmina said, and shot Marianne an apologetic look. "It appears Lord Julian was quite seriously injured."

He was? Good heavens. Then it had to have been after he left her. The poor, dear man. Marianne experienced a pang of disappointment that he would not be able to come to her bed again that evening. "How dreadful. What happened?"

"I saw the whole thing," Sir George said, puffed up with his own consequence at being able to provide a firsthand account. "It was quite late and—if you will pardon me, ladies, for saying so—we had all had rather too much to drink. Sherwood makes a smashing good rum punch. None of us, I fear, was feeling particularly steady on his feet. We were calling it a night when Sherwood tripped over something—never did see what—and went sprawling onto the floor in a heap. Cracked his head open on the hearth and knocked himself clean out. Broke his leg in the bargain."

"Dear God," Marianne said. How could this be possible? He could not have broken his leg *before* he came to her bed. And yet she was quite sure he'd come *after* the card game was over. It made no sense. "What time did this happen, Sir George?"

"It was deuced late, begging your pardon, ma'am. For the country, anyway. Height of the evening in town, of course. I think it was about two in the morning. I had to rouse the butler from his bed and have him send for a doctor."

Marianne had given up waiting for Julian and gone to bed at one o'clock. She had no idea what time he'd come to her room. Could he have gone back downstairs to the cardroom after he'd left her?

None of this made any sense. A tiny knot of anxiety began to coil and twist in her stomach.

"After the doctor set his leg and stitched his head," Sir George continued, "several of us helped carry poor old Sherwood to his bed—no easy task with the doctor shouting at you every other minute to be careful with the splint on his leg."

"I heard all the noise," Miss Stillman said, obviously still agog with excitement, "and looked into the corridor. I saw the gentlemen carrying Lord Julian. It was quite frightening, I promise you. His head was bandaged and his shirt was covered in blood. It was horrid. I thought he was dead."

"Jane!" her mother said. "What a dreadful thing to say."

The girl gave a petulant shrug. "Well, that *is* what I thought. It was quite a terrifying sight. All that blood." She gave an exaggerated shudder.

"Well, he ain't dead," Sir George said, "nor even close to it. Just a broken leg and a knock on the head. Unpleasant, to be sure, but he will recover soon enough."

Marianne had gone quite still. She heard what was said and felt badly for Lord Julian, but her mind spun with disturbing questions, questions that were creating a serious pain in her stomach.

"Marianne," Wilhelmina said, "are you quite well? You've gone pale as a ghost and haven't touched your breakfast. Lord Julian's accident has upset you, I daresay."

"It is Jane's fault," Mrs. Stillman said, "with all her talk of blood and death. You wretched girl. See how you've upset Mrs. Nesbitt?"

"Tell me one thing, Sir George," Marianne said, making an effort to keep her voice steady. "Was Lord Julian with you in the cardroom the entire time up until his accident?"

"Yes, of course. Excellent host, Sherwood. Makes a devilish good punch."

But he could not possibly have made love to her.

Then who the devil was in my bed last night?

Panic sent a rush of bile into Marianne's mouth and set her body in motion without conscious thought. She jumped up from her chair and fled the room.

Chapter 14

Marianne closed the door behind her and collapsed against the wall. She clamped a hand over her mouth and took several deep breaths, hoping she would not be sick in the hallway.

Last night, she had made passionate love with a stranger. She had been naked with a stranger. A stranger had used his mouth to pleasure the most private part of her body. She had given more of herself to a perfect stranger than she'd ever given to the husband she loved.

Her whole body began to tremble—with shame, anxiety, guilt, and anger.

The door to the breakfast room opened and Wilhelmina came out. She took one look at Marianne and gasped.

"Dear God, whatever is wrong?"

Marianne was shaking too hard to respond. Even her teeth chattered.

"My poor girl," Wilhelmina said, and took Marianne in her arms. "You are trembling like a leaf."

Marianne allowed herself to be enveloped in her friend's warmth. Wilhelmina gently rubbed her back and arms.

"Lord Julian's accident has been a great shock to you," she said. "But you mustn't worry. His life is not in danger. He will be fine. Poor child. Are you very much in love with him?"

"N-no," she managed. Wilhelmina's ministrations were having a calming effect. "No, that's n-not it."

"Then you are devastated that he will not become your lover at this house party. I know it must be disappointing, but there will be other opportunities. With him, after he recovers, or with another man. You must not take it so strongly to heart, my girl. You will find your lover."

Marianne lifted her head from Wilhelmina's shoulder and stepped out of her embrace. The trembling had subsided somewhat, though her stomach was still clenched tight and nausea lurked just below the surface.

She looked into her friend's wise and compassionate eyes. "That's just it, you see. I *did* have a lover in my bed last night."

Wilhelmina's mouth dropped open for a moment in shock. She composed herself quickly and said, "Indeed? Who was he?"

"I don't know." Marianne's voice rose to a plaintive wail. "Dear God, Wilhelmina, I don't know!"

"Good morning, ladies."

Penelope came tripping down the stairs with Grace in tow. The look on her face hinted that she'd had another happy evening in Eustace Tolliver's arms. The look on Grace's face hinted that she'd heard more about that evening than she cared to know.

"Is it not a glorious morning?" Penelope said, then caught sight of Marianne's face. Her smile faded. "Oh, dear." She reached out and touched Marianne's hand. "Are you quite all right? You look pale as death. Has something happened?"

Wilhelmina took Marianne by the arm and signaled that the other two women should follow. She steered them to a little alcove beneath the stairs, partially hidden by a gigantic Grecian urn on a pedestal.

"What has happened?" Grace asked, a look of deep concern on her face. "And what can we do to help?"

"Lord Julian has had an accident," Wilhelmina said. "Last night he apparently fell and broke his leg."

"Yes, I know, poor man," Grace said. "A commotion in the corridor woke me, and I looked out in time to see him being carried into his bedchamber. He looked quite ghastly, I must say. I can understand why you are distressed, Marianne."

"I, too, could see that Marianne was upset," Wilhelmina said, "and I thought it was because she would not now be able to take him into her bed, as expected. But she has quite shocked me. Tell them what you just told me, my girl."

All three women turned expectant faces to Marianne. She was loath to tell them, but they were her friends and she needed advice. She took a deep breath before speaking. "I did have a lover in my bed last night."

Penelope broke into a wide smile. "You sly little vixen! Then you must tell all. Who was he?"

Marianne looked from one to the other and a great wave of shame washed over her. She pressed a hand against her lips and muttered, "I have no idea."

Grace blanched and Penelope's mouth gaped wide as she sucked in a sharp breath.

Wilhelmina frowned. "I think you had better tell us what happened."

Marianne wrung her hands together. How could she tell them? How could she admit to what had happened? How could she bear for anyone to know how wantonly she'd behaved with a perfect stranger? The bile rose to her throat again and she had to take several steadying breaths to insure she did not become ill.

"Marianne?" Grace placed a gentle hand on her arm. "Were you . . . ravished?"

Marianne shook her head. "No. But I am s-so ashamed." She covered her face with her hands and burst into tears.

Wilhelmina put her arms around Marianne again

and let her cry, softly crooning, "It's all right" over and over in her ear. After a few minutes, Marianne lifted her head and looked into the duchess's kind eyes, sending her a silent message of thanks. Wilhelmina nodded and stepped back, out of the embrace.

"I'm all right now," Marianne said softly. "I'm all right."

"Please, tell us what happened," Penelope said, her voice gentle and kind. "You know you can trust us. We are here to help you, if only to provide three sets of shoulders to cry upon. The unwritten creed of the Merry Widows is that we support one another no matter what."

Marianne looked at the friendship and kindness on all three faces. Thank God she had such friends to talk to. Thank God for the Merry Widows. She swallowed, and began her sordid tale.

"Lord Julian had said he would come to my room after the gentlemen were finished playing cards. I waited and waited, but he never came, and so I finally crawled into bed and went to sleep. You have seen my bed, with its high canopy and thick curtains."

"Yes, we have," Penelope said with a smile, obviously trying to lighten the mood. "We all know you were given the best room in the house."

"I only mention it because it is somewhat responsible for what happened."

Penelope's eyebrows lifted in puzzlement. "Your bed is responsible?"

"Let her finish," Grace said.

"The room grows chilly at night," Marianne continued, "and I have found that pulling the heavy bedcurtains closed keeps me warm. It also completely blocks out any light. It is dark as a cave in that bed."

"Oh, dear," Wilhelmina said, and the ghost of a smile crossed her face.

"I was sound asleep when I felt an arm around my waist and lips against my neck. I thought I was dreaming, then realized it was really happening. I thought Julian had finally finished with cards and come to me. But I know now that it could not have been Julian. Someone else crept into my bed and I have no idea who it was because it was too dark to see him."

"Dear heaven," Grace said, her eyes wide with shock.

"And he made love to you?" Penelope asked.

Marianne lowered her eyes in shame. "Yes, he did."

"Oh, my God," Grace said. "A strange man came into your room and forced himself on you? But that is monstrous!"

"He did not force himself on me. Remember, I assumed it was Julian. I allowed him to make love to me. I *wanted* him to make love to me. I had no idea it was not Julian until a few minutes ago when I learned about his accident."

"How extraordinary," Penelope said. "And you have no idea who it might have been? You did not recognize his voice?"

"He spoke in whispers. It was impossible to detect a specific voice. And I wasn't trying to do so, in any case. I naturally assumed it was Julian's whispered voice."

"And there was nothing distinctive about the rest of him?" Penelope asked. "Something about his body that might help identify him?"

"Since I have never seen any of the gentlemen guests without their clothes on," Marianne said in a sarcastic tone, "it is difficult to say who it might have been. But I am convinced it must have been a deliberate ruse. Someone who knew I expected Julian, and decided to take his place."

"Did he actually pretend to be Lord Julian?" Wilhelmina asked. "Did he ever say his name?"

"No. Oh, wait. When I first came awake, he did say, 'It's me.' I naturally assumed he meant 'It's Julian.' Who else could it have been?"

"Perhaps he assumed you knew who he was," Wilhelmina said. " 'It's me' sounds as if he believed you were expecting him, or would at least know who he was."

"But the only man I expected was Julian. And given the marked favor he has shown me here at Ossing, I would guess that almost everyone knew I was expecting him. How could I assume it was anyone else?"

"Well, it has to be one of the guests," Penelope said, "which narrows the field somewhat. Unless it was one of the footmen."

"Dear God in heaven," Grace said. "A footman? Are none of us safe in our beds here?"

"It is unlikely to have been a footman," Wilhelmina said. "Don't work yourself into a lather, Grace. I doubt there is a ravisher on the loose at Ossing. Only one man who specifically sought out Marianne." She lifted an eyebrow. "Or did he? I wonder if it was someone who mistook the room for some other lady's? A lady who was expecting him. Could he have thought *you* were someone else?"

"No," Marianne said. "He called me by name several times. He knew who *I* was. I just don't know who *he* was."

"But you must have some idea who it could have been, my girl. You must."

"I wish I did," Marianne said, her voice rising in exasperation. "Someone gave me the most fantastic sexual experience I've ever known, and I have no idea who he was."

Adam stood still as a stork on the stairs above them. He should not be eavesdropping, of course, but he could not help himself.

The most fantastic sexual experience I've ever known.

That made him smile. And he was curious to hear what else she had to say about his performance. Adam was nothing if not confident of his skills in the bedroom, but it was reassuring to have that confidence confirmed.

"So this stranger was a skillful lover," the duchess said.

"More than skillful," Marianne said. "I hate to give such credit to a man who would do something so vile as to use trickery to get himself into my bed, but he really was the most splendid lover."

Adam could not wipe the smile off his face. He was pumped up with pride that she would heap such praise on him. Or on her secret lover. She wasn't singing Adam's praises, since she had no idea he'd been the one in her bed.

Now that he considered it, the fact that she was speaking of the matter at all was somewhat unsettling. For some reason, he'd always assumed women did not have such frank discussions with one another. Interesting. Shocking, even.

In fact, the very idea that women spoke as openly with one another about sex as men did was enough to strike terror into the heart of any rational man.

"It was not Lord Rochdale," Mrs. Marlowe said. "He was otherwise occupied. I saw him in Lady Drake's bedchamber."

"Well, it was not Tolliver, either," Lady Gosforth said. "You can be sure I kept him well enough occupied that he had no time to be sneaking into other bedchambers."

Aha. He'd had been right about those two.

"There must be *something* about the man that will help you identify him," the duchess said.

"Let me think," Marianne said. "He was well muscled and without an ounce of fat. His stomach was very flat."

"That eliminates Lord Troutbeck."

"And Mr. Leighton-Blair."

Feminine laughter rose up from the alcove below. This was truly one of the most remarkable conversations Adam had ever heard. He just hoped they would not be able to eliminate too many of the guests until he was the only one left.

"He had quite a lot of chest hair," Marianne continued. "And his shoulders seemed quite broad."

"Lord Ingleby?" Mrs. Marlowe suggested.

"It was not Ingleby," the duchess said.

There was a moment of silence, then more laughter.

"Wilhelmina, you sly puss," Lady Gosforth said. "You never said a word. You're supposed to tell all, you know. We made a pact."

These women had a pact to share the secrets of their love lives? Marianne, too? Good God.

"I wasn't certain about it," the duchess said. "Besides, my history is practically a public record. You don't need to hear any more tales from me."

"Yes, we do," Lady Gosforth said. "And when we return to town, you must be prepared with a full confession. But we have to deal with this ticklish situation of Marianne's first. So, who else has shoulders broad enough? Lord Havering? Sir Neville Kenyon?"

"Sir Neville is an interesting possibility," the duchess said. "I wonder if there is a well-muscled hairy chest beneath his fancy waistcoats and frilled shirts."

"Yes, and he often has that charmingly seductive look in his eye," Lady Gosforth said. "It makes one think he might be an intriguing bed partner. He could be your man, Marianne."

"Do you think so?"

Kenyon? Damnation, did she really think he could have been the one to take her to such heights of ecstasy? That he'd been the one to hold her close as she shuddered with the first climax of her life? God's teeth!

"I cannot believe you are all calmly listing gentlemen who might have crept into Marianne's bed." Mrs. Marlowe's voice was filled with outrage. She turned to Marianne and said, "Yes, you enjoyed it, but trick-

ing you was loathsome. If there is a man here who is
capable of that, what else might he do?"

"What are you saying, Grace?" Marianne asked.

"Have you considered that he might be tittering
with the other men about your encounter? What if he
were to make it known that you are available to any
man willing to creep into your bed? What if he ban-
dies your name about town as a loose, adventurous
woman? Have you thought of that?"

"Oh, my God," Marianne said.

"And you have no idea which man did this," Mrs.
Marlowe continued. "How can you bear to stay here
with that uncertainty? Wondering if all the men know,
or only one? And if only one, which one? It is a mon-
strously intolerable situation."

Marianne uttered a mournful little cry. "Dear God,
Grace, you are right. Dear God. How can I face them?
How can I look any of them in the eye, not knowing,
always wondering, is he the one? That is bad enough,
but I had not considered the possibility of him spreading tales." She choked on a sob. "I could not bear it.
I have to leave."

"I think that is best," Mrs. Marlowe said. "If you
stay, he will think you do not mind what he did. And
then he might think he can do it to someone else."

"Oh, no." Marianne's voice was a plaintive wail that
tore at Adam's heart.

"Wise counsel, Grace," the duchess said. "I completely agree with you. Marianne must not allow this
man to believe his cruel prank was of no significance."

"Then I must leave at once."

The words were barely out of her mouth when she
rounded the enormous urn, hiked up her skirts, and
began to climb the stairs. She saw him standing half-
way up the flight, and stopped. She studied his face
for a moment.

"You heard, didn't you?"

"Some of it. I heard that you intend to leave."

"I have no choice, Adam. I must go at once."

"Of course, my dear. Allow me to make the arrangements for your carriage while you pack your things."

"That is very kind. Thank you, Adam." She dashed up the stairs past him. "I'll be ready in twenty minutes."

He watched her go, then turned to find the other ladies at the foot of the stairs with their heads together, talking softly. The duchess looked up and caught his eye. Her lips curled up in an enigmatic smile.

Adam stood on the front steps of the main entrance and watched as Marianne's bags were loaded into the carriage. He waited for her to appear so he could say good-bye.

And it was going to be a true good-bye. He had botched things terribly, and decided it was best to put as much distance between him and Marianne as possible. For her sake and for Clarissa's. He was finished with causing so much harm to others. It was time, at long last, to put someone else's needs above his own. It was time he behaved like a man of honor.

He had spent what remained of the night considering what he'd done and what he should do next. For the near future, at least, and possibly longer, Adam needed to remove himself from Marianne's life. It was the only solution.

After the Ossing party broke up, Adam was going to travel down to Dorset, to the estate he'd once thought to sell. He was going to start putting it to rights, making it ready to receive his bride. Then he would invite the Leighton-Blairs for an extended visit, and make plans for the wedding to be celebrated in the parish church. On this point, he would remain steadfast. He would not return to London for a Society wedding at St. George's. He would not return to the house on Bruton Street with its adjoining balconies.

In fact, he would have his man of affairs put the Bruton Street house up for sale. His staff could pack up the furnishings and his personal belongings and send them to Dorset. There was no need for him ever to return to that house and its memories and its tempting proximity to Marianne.

It would be a clean break. He would give up the town life he'd always preferred and set up life in the country, where his bride would be happiest. He would become a country squire and raise a brood of country children. He would devote the rest of his days to making Clarissa happy. He would try to make something meaningful of his life.

And perhaps one day, years from now, when he had carved out this new life for himself and settled comfortably into it, when his affections for Clarissa had developed into something deeper, when his roots in Dorset had grown so deep, his life so entrenched, that he could never leave—perhaps then he would visit London again and Marianne. They would greet each other as old friends and reminisce of their days together with David. Their one special night together at Ossing Park would be little more than a sweet, faded memory. And even less for her, since she would never know she had shared it with him.

It was a fitting punishment for what he'd done. For hurting her. For deceiving her. For loving her.

The guilt that he had betrayed his best friend with that love was almost more overwhelming than the possibility of losing Marianne forever. His remorse was not so much about what had happened last night or for loving her now, but for all those years when David was still alive and Adam had been secretly in love with his wife, even if he'd never admitted it.

Forgive me, David. I never meant for this to happen.
Never to see her again, though, never to touch her

or hear her laughter again—it would be the worst sort of torture. He would endure it, though, to atone for his sins. And because it was the only possible solution.

But dear God, it would be painful. Adam had known Marianne forever, it seemed, and enjoyed her friendship. He liked her immensely, and now loved her, as well. But he knew her body now, too, and her passion. He'd had more of her than he'd ever expected, and that would have to be enough to last him a lifetime.

He turned at the sound of footsteps. Marianne's maid appeared, dressed for travel and carrying a hatbox and what looked to be Marianne's jewel case. She nodded at Adam as she passed, and handed the hatbox to a footman who was strapping boxes to the roof of the traveling chariot. She kept the jewel case with her when she stepped up into the carriage.

Marianne came next. She wore a green velvet spencer jacket over the pretty yellow-striped dress he'd noticed earlier, and had donned a straw bonnet with an upturned brim. It was a fetching outfit, cheerfully bright, but her pale, grim face dispelled any hint of gaiety. She stopped and looked up at him. There were clear signs of strain in those soft brown eyes.

"Thank you for seeing me to the carriage," she said.

"It was nothing."

"You do understand it is impossible for me to stay. You heard enough of what happened."

"Yes."

She closed her eyes, and there was a sudden flush of color in her cheeks. Shame? Embarrassment? Misery? That look was like a knife plunged into his chest, to know that he had done this to her.

"I am so confused, Adam. I don't know what to do. But I have to get away from here."

"I understand."

"Oh, Adam. You are so good to me. What will I ever do without you?"

The knife twisted.

He held out his arm. She smiled—thank God he got to see one more smile—and took it as he led her down the entrance steps to the carriage. He studied her closely as they approached the carriage, and memorized every inch of her face—the elegant curve of her jaw; the straight nose that was just a shade shy of being too long; the fine-pored porcelain skin that had felt so smooth against his rough beard; the soft down on her cheek, more like the skin of a peach, that caught the light of the sun; the big brown eyes with long lashes that curled up and made them look even bigger; the soft mouth with its bottom lip slightly fuller than the top, ripe and succulent as a fig. The dimples were not on display, of course, but he could see the hint of indentations where they would appear when she smiled.

He surveyed it all with the intensity of a portrait artist, for he might never see it again.

She turned to face him when they reached the open carriage door. "Good-bye, Adam. And thank you."

He took her hand and pressed it to his lips. Her glove held the faint fragrance of tuberoses. "Good-bye, my dear."

He handed her up the steps and into the carriage. She settled herself on the squabs, arranging her skirts about her legs. She looked up and said, "Oh, Adam, I forgot. Will you do me a great favor?"

"Anything."

"I took my leave of Lady Presteign, but I could not, of course, speak with Lord Julian. When he is able to receive visitors, would you tell him how dreadfully sorry I am about his accident? And offer my apologies for this precipitate departure?"

"Yes, of course."

"Do not, I beg you, give any hint about why I left. Just tell him . . . tell him something personal came up and I had to return to town. That is more or less what I told his sister."

"Do not worry, my dear. I will simply give him your apology with no further explanation."

"Thank you again, Adam. You are, as ever, a dear friend."

He forced a smile and nodded.

"Enjoy the rest of the party. I will see you when you return to Bruton Street."

No, she would not.

Without conscious thought, he reached in and took her arm, pulled her toward him, and kissed her. Softly and sweetly and with all the poignancy of farewell. He lingered slightly longer than he ought, savoring one last intimacy, unwilling for it to end.

But it had to end, before he was tempted to snatch her out of the carriage and into his embrace. He pulled away and released her arm. She sat back and stared at him, wide-eyed.

Adam closed the door of the carriage, turned, and walked away.

Chapter 15

He had stunned her again with a kiss. Her body still tingled in its aftermath as the carriage rolled through the gates of Ossing Park. Why had he done it? She was already in a state of emotional turmoil over all that had happened. He must have known that. Marianne was quite sure he had overheard a great deal more than he let on. So why had he done something that would only add to her misery?

Rose, her maid, sat beside her in the carriage and pretended she had seen nothing. Or perhaps she assumed it had been nothing, just a brief kiss between friends. Marianne would be tempted to believe the same if she had not sensed something deeper at work. There had been a disturbing note of finality in that kiss, which she found most unsettling. And something else. Something tickling the back of her mind, but she could not grasp it.

It did not matter. She could not worry about Adam right now. Under other circumstances, she would turn her mind to how his kiss had felt and what it had meant, but she had bigger problems to consider.

Who was the stranger in her bed?

Rose could sometimes be a chatterbox when it was only the two of them together, but Marianne did not want to engage in idle conversation. She had to think.

She leaned against the window frame and closed her eyes, pretending sleep.

Every time she thought about the things that man had done, her stomach roiled with nausea. When she had awoken, naked in her bed—was it really less than two hours ago? it seemed an eternity—she had been flooded with recollections of every intimate detail. She had savored each remembered touch and kiss and stroke and movement. When she'd closed her eyes she'd almost still been able to feel his touch, and her traitorous body had reacted even to the memory.

But now, as she recalled the same details, they only made her sick. Who had he been? And why had he done it? Could it truly have been Sir Neville Kenyon? She barely knew the man. She conjured up an image of him in her mind, and compared it with what she recalled of her secret lover.

Her lover's arms had been strong and firm and well muscled. They were covered with soft hair, just like his chest. Never having seen Sir Neville without a coat, she could not say whether they could have been his arms. Her lover's shoulders were broad. So were Sir Neville's. Her lover's hair had seemed longish when she ran her fingers through it. Sir Neville's hair was neither particularly short nor particularly long. It might have been his hair, but she could not be certain.

And she vividly recalled her lover's smell, the one that had lingered on the bed linens, and on her skin, long after he'd gone. It had been a seductively musky and masculine scent laced with a hint of bay rum. She remembered it distinctly.

Her eyes flew open. *Oh, my God.* She knew that scent. She knew it. She had just inhaled it again not five minutes ago.

Adam!

He had broad shoulders and longish hair. She'd seen a hint of chest hair whenever he'd removed his cravat in her sitting room. His stomach was flat. And the scent was unmistakable.

Adam! Adam was her secret lover.

She closed her eyes and sighed. Adam. The lover she'd always dreamed about. The man with whom she'd had a platonic friendship for years, but whose touch had recently sent her senses reeling. The one man above all others who she had secretly wished could be her lover.

Adam. Adam. Adam.

She clasped a hand to her breast and stifled a little cry.

It had been Adam, not some stranger, who'd taken her to such heights of passion. Adam who had touched her in ways she'd never imagined. Adam who had made sure it was all about her, all *for* her, who had taken time to insure she experienced the full extent of physical intimacy.

Because Adam knew the truth. He'd known what she'd never had, and he made sure to give it to her.

Oh, Adam. Thank God it was he and no other. The man she most trusted. Her dearest friend.

The bloody scoundrel!

The cad!

The blackguard!

How could he! How could he have done such a thing to her? He was soon to be married to Clarissa. He and Marianne could never be lovers. He knew that. Why had he done it, then? Despite the tension that had lately charged the very air between them, he had known it could never be. Is that why he'd crept into her bed in the dark and pretended to be someone else? Because he knew she would never have accepted him any other way?

She recalled all his teasing about how he would have been glad to be her lover if he hadn't become engaged to Clarissa. Had it never really been teasing at all? Had he wanted her all along? If so, then why the devil hadn't he told her? She would have opened her arms to him in an instant if she'd ever thought he wanted her.

It was all beginning to make sense now. From the beginning, he had made clear his disapproval of her plan to find a lover. Was it because he wanted her for himself? Even though he could not have her? With the exception of Julian, every other potential lover had been eliminated for one reason or another. Had Adam been behind it all? Good Lord, had he even been responsible for Julian's accident?

How dare he! What made him think he could interfere with her life like that? What gave him the right to deny her the opportunity to explore physical passion with another man?

And worse. Rather than allow another man to make love to her, he disabled the poor fellow and took his place. Pretended to be someone else.

He must have known she would discover the truth as soon as she learned about Lord Julian's accident. And then what? Was she to thank him for giving her such pleasure? Even knowing she would never be able to experience it with him again? Was she to thank him for breaking her heart and betraying Clarissa?

A wave of sheer fury swept over her. Marianne was half tempted to tell the driver to turn the carriage around and return to Ossing. She wanted to take Adam out to the archery range and make him stand there like Saint Sebastian while she shot him full of arrows. Or maybe she would push him down the stairs where he had stood and listened to her confession to the Merry Widows, no doubt gloating every time she mentioned how wonderful his lovemaking had been. Or maybe she would wait until he returned to London, leap over the damned balcony, and wring his interfering neck.

Clearly, she was too enraged to face him now. She had to consider what to do.

Marianne stared out the window, too angry and confused to appreciate the scenery. She simply could not believe what Adam had done. And she remembered *everything* he'd done. She closed her eyes and relived every touch, every kiss. He'd given her such glorious pleasure. Perhaps she *should* thank him for that. And despite her anger, it was a huge relief to know it had been Adam and not some stranger to witness her total abandon. When all was said and done, she was glad it had been Adam and none other.

When she considered the efforts he'd made to keep other men from her bed, she had to admit it was rather sweet. In an irritating sort of way.

Blast the man. Her head was spinning with conflicting emotions. Anger at his deception. Relief that it had been Adam and not Sir Neville or anyone else. Aggravation at his interference in her life. Gratitude that he had shown her such pleasure. Wicked delight that he had gone to such trouble to eliminate all those other men as potential lovers. And heartbreaking regret that he had given her one night that could never be repeated.

It had been a good decision to leave Ossing. Assuming the house party continued without Julian, she would not see Adam again for several days. She needed that time alone. She had to think.

She wiped away a tear as she stared out the carriage window.

Oh, Adam. What have you done to me?

Adam did not return to the house. His heart was crumbling into bits and he could not be sure he would not burst into unmanly tears. He wandered off into the gardens instead. Not the formally planted ones with paths and such, where he might run into one of the guests out for an early stroll. He headed for the thickest grove of trees, where no one else was likely to be found.

He should not have kissed her. It only made everything worse. But she had said good-bye and was about
to leave his life forever. He had reached for her des-
perately, without thinking.

Last night, when he'd held her naked in his arms,
he had known, finally and without a doubt, that he
was in love with Marianne. Everything in his life had
fallen into place with blinding clarity in the darkness
of that curtained bed. He knew now that the envy
he'd felt for David all those years was not only for
his seemingly perfect marriage. It was for his wife.
Adam knew that he had never had a serious relationship with a woman because he'd compared them all
with Marianne and they had come up short. He'd continued climbing that balcony not to conjure up memories of David, but because he wanted to be with
Marianne.

How could he have denied such an obvious truth
for so long?

And now she was gone. He would not see her again
for a very, very long time. If ever. Punishment, indeed.

Adam walked through the trees for a long while,
girding himself for the new life ahead with Clarissa,
locking away a bit of Marianne with each step. She
was firmly in the past and must be packed away and
put aside, like toys in the attic. Clarissa was his future.
And Dorset.

He could do it. He could. He conjured up images
of Clarissa's beautiful face and the way her body had
felt when nuzzled up against his when he'd taught her
how to use the bow and arrow. He thought of her
sweet innocence and her biddable nature. They would
forge a life together, and he would do everything in
his power to make her happy.

He walked and walked, thinking of fair Clarissa and
banishing Marianne forever to a hidden, forgotten corner of his heart. He did not head back toward the
house until he was confident that he could face Cla-

rissa and the other guests with reasonable sangfroid. He had no idea where he was and it took some time before he found a familiar path and made his way back.

There was no footman at the entrance and he let himself in. The grand entry hall with its high ceiling and marble floors picked up sound from all over the house and amplified it. Just now, the room was filled with the echo of raised voices. He could not tell whose voices they were or where they came from. A door slammed. Running footsteps sounded somewhere above.

What the devil was going on?

Adam climbed the main staircase to the first floor. He caught sight of Lady Troutbeck as she walked from the drawing room into one of the small salons with a comforting arm around a distraught Lady Presteign. Miss Jane Stillman, her eyes red from crying, came bounding down the stairs from the second floor and continued past him to the ground floor. Adam heard the echo of her slippers on the marble tile of the entry hall below as she ran through, then the sound of the front door opening and closing.

Good Lord. Had Sherwood taken a turn for the worse? Is that why the ladies were so upset? Oh, please, not that. Adam was weighed down with more than enough guilt already, for Sherwood and Marianne and Clarissa. If it turned out that he'd actually killed Sherwood, he did not know what he would do.

Mrs. Forrester and Mrs. Marlowe came out of the drawing room together. Both gave him a queer look, then rushed past him. Lord Ingleby was the next one to exit the drawing room. His eyes widened when he saw Adam. He cleared his throat nervously.

"Bad doings, old chap," he said. "Devilish bad." He gave Adam a sympathetic clap on the shoulder and walked on.

Oh, God. It *must* be Sherwood. The poor fellow must have died.

He headed for the drawing room, where all the activity seemed to be, in hopes of discovering what had happened. A buzz of conversation grew louder as he approached. When he entered the room, all talk ceased and a heavy silence fell. A dozen pairs of eyes studied him—some with interest, some with sympathy, some with suppressed excitement.

"Good afternoon," he said to the room at large.

Several muttered greetings were returned.

"I am wondering," he said, "if someone can—*oomph*!"

Rochdale had grabbed him by the arm and was literally pulling him to the door. "What the—"

"Quiet," Rochdale said. "Just follow me and don't say a word."

He pulled him into a smaller salon where Lady Presteign and Lady Troutbeck sat together on a settee. Lady Presteign held a cloth to her forehead with one hand and a vinaigrette in the other. Rochdale tugged him along past them into the next room. Even though it was empty, Rochdale did not stop until they reached the third salon. He closed the doors at both ends, then flung himself into a delicate-looking French armchair. He stretched out his long legs and wrapped his hands behind his head, elbows akimbo.

"What the devil is going on?" Adam asked. He was too concerned about the answer to be seated. He stood in front of the fireplace and glared at his friend. "Has . . . has something happened to Sherwood?"

Rochdale eyed him quizzically. "And where have you been that you don't know?"

"Out walking. I've just returned." He glanced at the mantel clock and realized he'd been gone for hours. He steeled himself for some wretched piece of news that would add to his troubles. "Now, please tell me what has happened."

Rochdale leaned back, supremely at ease, and flashed one of his devilish grins. "I would have to say that all hell has broken loose, that's what."

The look on his friend's face did not signal a tragedy. Adam breathed a quiet sigh of relief. "What are you talking about?"

"My dear fellow, it seems your fiancée has betrayed you."

"What? Clarissa?" It was the last thing he'd expected to hear.

"Sit down, old boy. It's quite a story. I think you might enjoy it."

"I don't want to sit down. Just tell me what happened, for God's sake."

"It seems, my friend, that your bride-to-be has created something of a scandal. Our stiff-rumped hostess actually fell into a swoon."

"A scandal?"

"Yes. It seems the fair Clarissa has long harbored a secret tendre for our host. They grew up in each other's pockets, or some such thing. Anyway, she's apparently been in love with the fellow for years."

"Dear God. She's in love with Sherwood?"

"So I am told. Bit of a wound to your pride, eh, Cazenove?"

"Damnation," Adam said, and sank into the nearest chair. This was too much to take in while standing. "Go on."

"Yes, well, it appears Miss Stillman knew of Clarissa's affection for Sherwood. Last night, the commotion of getting the chap to his room roused her, and she poked her inquisitive head out her door to see what the noise was all about. Saw Sherwood with his bandaged head and bloody shirt and thought he'd been killed. Good friend that she is, she rushed to your fiancée's room to tell her the sad news. And I am sorry to report that your Clarissa lost all sense of propriety."

"Oh, no. Don't tell me she—"

"She did, by Jove." The wicked grin widened.

"Rushed to his bedside and kept vigil all night, her dainty hand clasping his the whole time."

Adam heaved a sigh. The silly little chit. "And I suppose she fell asleep there."

"How ever did you guess?" Rochdale chuckled gleefully. "Our esteemed hostess decided to look in on her poor injured brother this morning, and was shocked—nay, scandalized—to find your Clarissa sound asleep with her head resting on the bed and her hand still clasping that of her one true love. Sorry, old chap, but that would be Sherwood's hand, not yours. Shocking, ain't it? But I have a sneaking suspicion your own hand was busy clasping someone else's, anyway."

Adam refused to rise to that bait. Neither Rochdale nor anyone else would pry that secret out of him. "And I suppose the scandalized Lady Presteign let her outrage be known to all and sundry."

"Screeched like a banshee. Must have been tough on poor old Sherwood with that great pounding lump on his head. Egad, that woman has lungs."

"So. Everyone knows." Adam shook his head in dismay. "That is why they all glared at me."

"Naturally. Anxious to see the reaction of the jilted bridegroom."

Adam raised his eyebrows. "*Have* I been jilted?"

"Ah, that is something you will have to ask the lady herself, I daresay. It is generally assumed, however, that she has transferred her affections to another. A sad story, but there you have it."

It was an incredible story. He could hardly believe it. He would never have imagined Clarissa was in love with someone else. Not that he expected her to be in love with *him*. He was actually rather glad she was not. But to know that all along she had loved Sherwood was quite a shock. And rather irritating. Why had the girl agreed to the betrothal to Adam when her affections were otherwise engaged? Why hadn't the wretched girl said something?

"Damn. I suppose I'd better find her and talk to her." He rose slowly to his feet, feeling suddenly stiff and old.

"Don't look so glum, Cazenove. This could be the perfect opportunity to remove yourself from a betrothal that was idiotic to begin with. That girl would have made your life a misery and you know it."

"I rather suspect it would have been the other way around," Adam said. "But I'm not out of it yet. Clarissa may still want to go through with the marriage." Though he could not imagine why if she was truly in love with Sherwood. And her parents would surely prefer his bloody lordship as a son-in-law. He was the son of a duke and the owner of this grand estate. Adam's fortune could not begin to match Sherwood's.

Rochdale snorted. "Wouldn't that be a happy prospect? Each of you in love with someone else. No, my boy, you must let her go to Sherwood and then you will be free to woo the beautiful Marianne."

That possibility had been spinning around in his brain the whole time. However, Adam was not ready to latch on to that glimmer of hope just yet. Everything was in Clarissa's hands. It would be her choice. If she wanted out of the betrothal, then he would step aside. But if she, and her parents, decided it was best to proceed with the wedding, so be it. He had committed to it, and he would honor that commitment.

But if she wanted out . . . no, he would not consider it yet. He would not set himself up for disappointment. He had braced himself for the worst sort of punishment, and he was still prepared to face it.

On his way back to the drawing room, a footman approached Adam.

"Mr. Leighton-Blair asks if you would meet with him in the library, if you please."

"Yes, of course."

"Follow me, sir."

Adam steeled himself for the interview. Would he

be asked to overlook Clarissa's behavior and follow through with the wedding? Is that what Leighton-Blair wanted? To convince him to honor his commitment? Would he sweeten the dowry if Adam agreed? God, he hoped it would not be such a vulgar scene as that.

The footman opened the door to the library and Adam stepped inside. Mr. Leighton-Blair leaned back against a large desk. Mrs. Leighton-Blair, scowling furiously, was seated nearby. Clarissa, looking red-eyed and miserable, sat in a window seat.

"Ah, Cazenove," Mr. Leighton-Blair said. "Come in. Have a seat." He gestured toward a chair beside his wife's.

Adam would have preferred to stand, but it would be rude to refuse Leighton-Blair's offer, so he took the chair instead. He glanced at Clarissa. She kept her head down and twisted a ribbon that hung from the high waist of her dress.

"I presume," Leighton-Blair said, "you have heard what happened."

"I have heard about Clarissa's vigil at Sherwood's bedside."

Mrs. Leighton-Blair gave a disgusted snort. She looked about to say something, but her husband's glare stopped her.

"I am afraid," Leighton-Blair said, "she reacted rather hysterically when Jane Stillman told her that Lord Julian had been killed. Foolish girl! That is no excuse, however, for such wanton disregard of propriety. I fear that my daughter's disgraceful behavior will make a marriage between you two somewhat difficult. Awkward at best. If you wish it, Cazenove, I am prepared to call off the betrothal."

That glimmer of hope began to glow brighter, but with a supreme effort, Adam kept it in check. He looked at his fiancée. "Is that what you want, Clarissa?"

"I don't know," she said in a small voice. She still

had not looked up, but kept her eyes on the ribbon she was tying into knots. "It is up to you, sir."

Adam rose and went to her. He leaned down on his haunches and took her hands in his. They were cold, and he gently rubbed his thumbs against them to make them warm. For once, she did not seem to mind. "Are you in love with Lord Julian?"

She said nothing, but after a moment she nodded her head.

"And you are not in love with me?"

She shook her head. "I'm sorry."

"Well, then, I do not think you should be forced to marry someone you do not love. Do you?"

"I don't know, sir. I will do whatever you want."

"What I want is for you to be happy, Clarissa. And I suspect you will not be happy with me." He studied her for a long moment, but she would not lift her head. "Shall we call it off?" he asked. "Shall we end our betrothal?"

She looked up for the first time. Her big blue eyes were swimming in unshed tears and she chewed on her lower lip. And then, in the tiniest of voices, she spoke the two words that would change his life. "Yes, please."

Hope finally did burst into dazzling light, bathing him in the brilliance of promise. Marianne! Adam made an effort not to show his overwhelming relief. "So be it," he said, and kissed both her hands. "Be happy, Clarissa."

"Thank you, sir. You are very kind."

He rose to his feet and turned to her parents. Her mother looked ready to have an apoplexy. Her father merely frowned.

"I commend you, Cazenove," he said, "for behaving in such a gentlemanly manner when my daughter deserves no such condescension. We knew of her infatuation with Lord Julian, of course. Considering his position and our friendship with his family, we had welcomed a match between them. But Clarissa told us she no longer cared for the young man and wanted nothing more to do with him. I am sorry we had to learn in so publicly embarrassing a manner that she had deceived us. You can be certain we will make it known that you were the perfect gentleman throughout this business. No blame will attach itself to you."

"Thank you, sir, but you must not worry about me. Look to Clarissa's happiness."

Adam turned to look at her once more, and she smiled. He bowed to her, and took his leave of the library, closing the door behind him.

He paused in the passage outside the library and gave in to the full force of his relief. Afraid he might be seen with a ridiculous grin on his face, he bent his head and placed a finger and thumb at his temples to shade his eyes. He heard someone approaching but did not look up. From the corner of his eye he saw two women coming toward him. As they got closer, he recognized Lady Troutbeck and Lady Presteign. He massaged his temples briefly, then looked up to acknowledge them as they walked by.

"Poor man," one of them whispered as they passed.

And so now he was the object of pity, a jilted bridegroom. But he did not care what any of them thought. He'd never felt so elated in his life.

He was free!

Chapter 16

Adam knew what he had to do. Now that he was free of the commitment to Clarissa, he could go to Marianne and confess all. There would be no more secrets. No more pretending he did not love her. No more using David's memory as an excuse not to act on his love. He would bare his soul to her, beg her forgiveness, and ask her to marry him.

Yes, he wanted to marry her. It was ironic that it had taken a betrothal to the wrong sort of woman to make very clear to him what, and who, would be the right sort of wife for him. He wanted what he always thought David and Marianne had. He wanted a friend as well as a lover. He wanted someone whose mind he admired as much as her body. What was it Marianne has said to him?

Why would you not want someone who excites you, who challenges you, who makes you a better person?

Why not, indeed? And she was all those things, and more. So he would grovel at her feet in apology for deceiving her, and beg her to marry him.

It all sounded so simple, but he did not fool himself. It would be a difficult and painful confession. She would be angry with him for what he'd done. She might even despise him for it, and send him packing. But he had to try. He had to tell her the truth.

And so, for the second time that day, Adam began

to map out a new future. A different one this time, in London with Marianne. If she would have him.

Would she have him? He had no reason to believe she would. She had wanted a lover and not a husband. She had been very clear on that point. She enjoyed her independence, and was determined to remain true to David's memory.

Or had she in fact scorned another marriage simply because she assumed it would be the same as with David, an affectionate union without physical passion? If that was the case, might she reconsider, now that she knew there was more to be shared between a man and woman than friendship and affection? Surely she would know he could give her more than that.

Wouldn't she?

He must remember, though, that he had got himself into this mess through selfishness. He saw now that he could not always have what he wanted, and that if he insisted on it, he only caused harm. If Marianne did not want him, as a husband or as a lover, he would accept her decision. And maybe he would leave town and go down to Dorset after all.

But first, he had to square up one other piece of business. He climbed the stairs to the second floor and knocked on Sherwood's door. Jarvis, the valet, opened it.

"Good afternoon, sir," he said.

"How is the patient?"

Jarvis lowered his voice. "Awake and alert, but in a great deal of pain, I fear."

"Is that you, Cazenove?" Sherwood called from his bed. "Come on in."

Jarvis stepped aside and Adam entered the room. Sherwood was propped up on a mountain of pillows. The bandage around his head, with his blond hair falling over it, gave him a rakish look. His left leg was uncovered, the splint still in place.

"How are you feeling?" Adam asked.

"Like I'd been run over by a mail coach," Sherwood said with a grimace. "Dashed stupid thing to have done, tripping over my own feet like that. Must have been the punch, eh?"

"I'm afraid it was my feet you tripped over."

"Did I, by Jove? Well, it was still deuced clumsy of me."

"I ought to have moved my legs out of your way," Adam said, feeling in a confessional mood. He wanted to get everything off his chest—the lies, the secrets, the guilt—and start his new future, whatever it would be, with a clean slate. "If I had made the effort," he said, "you might not have fallen."

"We were both more than a bit castaway, as I recall. Can't be blamed for bosky legs, old chap. Nobody's fault."

"That's good of you to say, Sherwood, but I still feel responsible."

"Well, you weren't responsible, and that's that. It's a clean break, I'm told. Bothersome, to be sure, but it will heal. Nothing to raise a breeze about."

"I am glad to hear it. But I hope you will accept my apology nonetheless."

"If you insist, apology accepted."

"Thank you. Now, if I might have a word in private."

Sherwood signaled to Jarvis that he should leave. The valet made sure the splinted leg was properly situated, straightened the covers a bit, fluffed the pillows, then took his leave through the dressing room door.

"Bit of a fusspot, old Jarvis," Sherwood said. "Excellent valet, though." A sheepish expression crossed his face. "I daresay I know what it is you wish to talk about."

"Clarissa."

"Yes. Don't know what to say, Cazenove. Had no idea she'd been here all night. Had no idea she'd been here at all, in fact. I imagine Sneed gave me a prodigious amount of laudanum. That and all the punch I'd had . . . well, I was out cold the whole night. Never stirred. Too painful to move in any case, with this damned splint. I didn't know anything until my sister walked in and shrieked loud enough to pull the house down. No amount of laudanum is a match for Marjorie's screams. It was only then that I opened my eyes and saw Clarrie beside me, her hand holding mine."

"We have ended our betrothal."

Sherwood frowned. "Damn. I'm dreadfully sorry, Cazenove. I had hoped it would not come to that."

"She claims to be in love with you."

"Yes, I know. The silly goose."

Adam lifted an eyebrow. "Quite a little scandal has been created here, Sherwood. Everyone here knows that Clarissa was found in a compromising situation. Now that she is no longer betrothed to me, the field is clear for you to make her an offer." Adam narrowed his eyes and glared at the young man. "And I trust you will do so. It would not go easy with me to know that her reputation was in jeopardy."

"I know my duty, Cazenove. No need to lecture. She will have her offer."

"Duty?" Adam said. "Then her affections are not returned?"

Sherwood chuckled. "I've been crazy in love with the chit since she turned sixteen and was suddenly no longer a skinny, big-eyed nuisance. I thought she loved me, too, but she took offense to what she called my 'wild behavior' in town. I was always trying to impress her with how worldly I'd become, what a man-about-town I was. But she was not impressed. One day she announced I was too young and frivolous to be taken seriously. She wanted nothing more to do with me. Claimed that when she went up to town for her Season, she would only accept the addresses of 'true gentlemen' and not young popinjays."

Had she thought Adam a "true gentleman"? Or had she only wanted to make Sherwood jealous?

"So I stepped aside," he said, "and watched her blossom into a diamond of the first water, with a constant court of swains dangling after her. She treated me as a friend whenever she saw me, never giving me the slightest hope of anything more. I figured I had been a youthful fancy, and she was finished with me. I confess, though, that I was surprised when I heard of her betrothal to you. I was devilish disappointed, but I assumed I never had a chance."

"So you have no objection to marrying her?"

"Objection?" He crowed with laughter. "By heaven, it's all I've ever wanted."

"Well, then."

Sherwood sobered. "I am sorry, old chap. Are you in love with her, too?"

"No, I am not," Adam said. But he was feeling a bit of the fool. Had Clarissa really only used him? Had she never intended to go through with the marriage? Is that why she had been reluctant to set a wedding date?

"I suppose we must be thankful for that broken leg of yours," Adam said. "Otherwise she would have been stuck with me and none of us would have been happy."

Sherwood smiled. "Then you must take back your apology and accept my gratitude for allowing me to trip over your feet."

Adam nodded. "Done. There is one more thing, Sherwood." He narrowed his eyes as he studied the man. "Mrs. Nesbitt."

Sherwood's smile faded. "I understand she has gone home."

"She has, and asked me to tell you how sorry she is about your accident. But tell me, Sherwood. Were you planning on seducing Mrs. Nesbitt while at the same time trying to woo Clarissa away from me? That is why you invited the Leighton-Blairs, is it not? To try to win her back?"

Sherwood pulled a face. "I never had any hope of

winning Clarrie. I just wanted to spend time with her in the country. She had never seen Ossing and I thought she might enjoy it."

"You thought to tempt her with it."

Sherwood shrugged. "Perhaps."

"And Mrs. Nesbitt?"

"I only hoped for a bit of sport with her, since Clarrie was not available to me."

Adam winced. Marianne, a bit of sport?

"And now that Clarissa *is* available? Will you still try for a bit of sport on the side? You will forgive the question, I hope, but I feel somewhat responsible for the girl. I want her to be happy."

"Can't imagine why you care a fig about a young chit who threw you over. But not to worry. Clarrie's all I ever wanted. If I can have her, I won't need anyone else."

"Good man. I shall not, then, fret over Clarissa's future happiness."

Sherwood reached out a hand. Adam clasped it and they shook in confirmation that all was well between them.

"You're a great gun, Cazenove. A real gentleman. I promise to try my best to make Clarrie happy. I only hope you won't suffer publicly from this dustup. And I trust that you will someday find another lady, one who will truly make you happy."

He had found the lady. Now he had to find out if she was ready to make him happy. And there was something he had to do first, just in case she was.

Marianne had brooded over the situation with Adam for three days. Her mood had swung from anger to euphoria and back again. She had cried and laughed and stormed about in a rage. She hated that he had shown her such pleasure when he knew he could never be with her again. She wished and wished he had not done it.

And yet she'd had one glorious night of love that she would remember for the rest of her life.

Over and over in her mind she had relived every aspect of Adam's lovemaking. Every scandalous detail. She had come to believe that it had been so wonderful *because* it had been Adam. She was quite sure it would not have been at all the same with Julian or any other man. Adam was certainly a skilled lover, but there had been more than just skill involved. There had been tenderness and affection and generosity that only Adam could have given her. She had even begun to suspect that he had not actually set out to dupe her. She kept recalling his words.

It's me.

He must have assumed she would recognize his voice or his body or something else about him. Now that she knew it had been Adam, she remembered lots of little things that she ought to have recognized. His long hair. The shape of his hands. The way he smelled. The strong line of his jaw.

But she had been expecting Julian and so none of those things had come to mind to suggest it was anyone else.

Are you disappointed?

She thought the question had been because he had made her wait so long. But now she believed he had been asking if she was disappointed that he was not Julian. And he had been so pleased when she'd said she was not.

She was, therefore, willing to concede that he may not have set out to pretend he was Julian. But if so, then why the devil had he acted the next morning as though nothing had happened between them? Marianne wondered if overhearing her panicked confession to the Merry Widows had made him realize she had *not* known it was him, and then for some reason he decided to leave it that way and not tell her the truth.

But why?

There was one more thing she'd remembered about that night. Adam had whispered words of love to her. He had called her "my love" over and over, and told her he would always love her. Believing it was Julian, she had not taken the words seriously. It had just been a part of the seduction, she'd thought. Lovely to hear, but not real.

However, Adam, not Julian, had said those words to her, and so they had taken on a whole new meaning. Adam would not use words of love in such a cavalier manner. Not to her.

It thrilled her to think that he might indeed love her. Her heart soared to imagine it. But if he did love her, then why on earth was he marrying that young twit of a girl? How could he tell Marianne he loved her, make beautiful love to her, and then blithely walk off and marry Clarissa?

It was probably best that he did so. If he was in love with Marianne and had been free, she did not quite know what she would do about it. It was exhilarating, but it also frightened her to consider another man's love. How could she? David was her one True Love and always would be.

So as cruel as it was for Adam to love her for one night and leave her, it was probably for the best.

And there was that kiss in the carriage. She was almost certain it was meant as a kiss of farewell. Without ever admitting he'd been her secret lover, he was telling her it would never happen again, that they could never be together again. He was telling her good-bye. Marianne had the horrible suspicion that she might never see him again. And that would be the cruelest blow of all.

Damn him for turning her life upside down.

"You must repeat your story for the benefit of Beatrice," Penelope said. "She missed all the excitement."

The Merry Widows had gathered at Grace's house for their regular Fund meeting, but it did not look as though any business would be conducted that afternoon. All the ladies, including Grace, were agog with Marianne's predicament.

She related a brief version of the story for Beatrice, who expressed her shock and disbelief. "Who could have done such a thing?" she asked.

Marianne had considered whether or not to tell them the truth. She finally decided to do so because she wanted their advice. "As it happens," she said, "I know who it was."

"You do?" Penelope's voice rose to a squeak and she stared at Marianne wide-eyed. "Well, for heaven's sake, tell us. Who was it? Was it Sir Neville Kenyon after all?"

Four anxious faces were turned to Marianne. The clink of teacups, the rhythmic pinging of stirring spoons, the dainty crunching of tea biscuits—all stopped in the expectant silence.

She drew in a deep breath and let it out slowly. "It was Adam Cazenove."

"No!"

"I don't believe it!"

"Cazenove?"

They all spoke at once. The only one who did not look completely aghast was Wilhelmina, who merely smiled.

"How do you know it was Cazenove?" Beatrice asked. "Did he tell you?"

"No, in fact he pretended nothing had happened. It was only after I'd left that I began to put together all the clues. But there is no question about it. Adam was my secret lover."

"Dear heaven," Grace said, shaking her head.

"You did say it was an extraordinary performance, did you not?" Penelope said. "Cazenove is well-known for his skill in the bedroom. Lucky you!"

"On the contrary," Marianne said, "I am not at all lucky. In fact, I am feeling quite distressed about the whole thing. I really do not know what to do. I'm so confused!"

"I am sure you must be," Beatrice said. "What an interesting development, to be sure."

"I am hoping for your advice, ladies," Marianne said. "Should I tell him I know? Or should I simply forget about it and never mention it again? He is soon to be married, after all, and so it is not as though the experience can be repeated. So there is really no point in discussing it with him. Is there?"

Every time she thought of his marriage, a vivid image came to mind of him pleasuring Clarissa in their bed. She knew now exactly how it would be between them. She wished she did not know, but she did, and it would make it more difficult whenever she saw them together.

"Oh, my goodness," Grace said. "You don't know."

"Know what?"

"It certainly puts a different spin on the situation, does it not?" Penelope said.

"What does?" Marianne asked, her gaze darting between Grace and Penelope. "What are you talking about?"

"There was quite a little scandal at Ossing Park just after you left," Wilhelmina said.

"And now there is to be no marriage at all," Penelope said.

What? No marriage?

"Miss Leighton-Blair behaved most improperly with Lord Julian," Grace said, "spending the night in his room after his accident."

"It turns out she was in love with Lord Julian the whole time," Penelope said, "and when she heard of his injury, she flew to his side. The silly girl fell asleep on his bed, if you can believe it."

She almost could not. It was too incredible. Marianne brought a hand to her forehead in hopes her head would stop spinning. Little Clarissa was in love with the man who was to have been Marianne's lover? And Adam was not to be married? Dear God.

Wilhelmina gave a disgusted snort. "Lady Presteign raised such a fuss that the whole party knew what happened. Everyone was agog with the tale. Poor Miss Leighton-Blair became the center of a scandal."

"And I heard," Grace said in a conspiratorial tone, "that her father insisted she call off the betrothal, so that Mr. Cazenove would not be forced to take on a bride with a ruined reputation."

"I have no doubt Leighton-Blair pressed to end the engagement," Wilhelmina said, "when he can marry his daughter to the son of a duke instead."

"And Cazenove quietly took himself off," Grace said. "He left Ossing that afternoon, and the house party began to fall apart. Lady Presteign put on a good face and tried to convince everyone to stay, but too much had happened. The three of us left the next day, and the rest soon after, I presume."

"Good heavens," Marianne said, quite abashed at the news, and the tiniest bit excited, as well. Adam was free now. Free from that silly girl, thank heaven. But what did it mean? Those words of love came back to mind. Now that he was free, would he repeat them? Would he become the lover she had been seeking all Season? And if he'd left Ossing that same day, where was he? "What am I to do now?"

"About Cazenove?" Beatrice asked.

"What do I say to him? How do I face him?"

"With open arms, you foolish woman," Penelope said. "The man is free to be your lover now. And after that first performance, I'd imagine you would be thrilled to repeat it. With his betrothal no longer an obstacle, what is stopping you?"

"He still deceived me," Marianne said, not quite ready to confess her biggest fear, that he was in love with her. "He had not ended his betrothal when he crept into my bed. He was still committed to someone else, and must have assumed the marriage would proceed as planned. I cannot ignore that."

"Perhaps he deserves a bit of punishment," Wilhelmina said with a smile. "If he comes to you now and confesses what he did, I do believe you ought to exact the tiniest bit of revenge."

"Excellent idea," Penelope said with a sly grin. "He must be punished for deceiving you."

"I do believe," Wilhelmina said, "that you must not make it easy for him when he comes to you and confesses, even if he declares his love for you."

Dear God, what would she do if he told her he was in love with her? Was there any hope he'd been expressing only the love of a good friend and not . . . something more?

Wilhelmina studied her closely. "Oh, he *will* make a declaration, my girl, mark my words."

"What makes you think so?"

"One need only watch the way he looks at you to know he loves you. I have suspected it for some time. When I realized he'd made love to you, I was certain of it."

"You knew it was Adam?" Marianne asked.

"I suspected as much. The man is head over ears in love with you, and I cannot for the life of me imagine why he tied himself to that foolish Leighton-Blair girl. The only reason that comes to mind is that you had given him the impression you were not available to him."

"I did tell him in no uncertain terms that I never wished to marry again."

"And until recently, you were not looking for a lover, either. There. You see? And so he engaged himself to that little twit, but before the deed was done he decided to steal one night in your bed by pretending to be someone else. The sneaky devil."

"Oh, yes," Penelope said with a gleeful grin. "He most definitely should be punished."

With much laughter and creative enthusiasm, Wilhelmina and the others proceeded to tell Marianne just exactly how she might punish Adam for playing such games with her.

"But remember, my girl," Penelope said, "not to be too hasty if he tries to entangle himself in another betrothal—with *you* this time. We pledged ourselves to find lovers, you know. Not husbands."

"Don't worry," Marianne said. "I still have no intention of marrying again. But once I ring a peal over Adam's head, I just might need a supply of juniper juice."

The laughter of all five ladies echoed in the room.

"And what about you, Beatrice?" Penelope asked a few minutes later. "What have you been up to while we were enjoying all the interesting happenings at Ossing? I don't suppose you have found yourself a lover, have you?"

Beatrice smiled enigmatically. "It is quite possible I have."

"I knew it!" Penelope exclaimed, slapping a hand on the tea table, rattling cups and saucers precariously. "I told the others you were up to something."

"I wasn't up to anything before you left," Beatrice said, "but something quite extraordinary happened while you were gone."

"Well, don't just sit there grinning about it," Penelope said. "Tell us. Who is he?"

And while Beatrice told them about the exciting evening she'd spent with a mysterious young man, Marianne's thoughts wandered to her own situation. She was too full of the news about Adam to concentrate on anything Beatrice was saying.

Marianne's stomach lurched at the thought that Wilhelmina might be right about Adam's feelings toward her. Was he truly head over ears in love with her?

She wasn't sure what answer she wanted to that question. To know he was in love with her would be a thrill beyond imagining. But could she accept his love without betraying David? And what of her own feelings? She was more than attracted to him, and always a bit infatuated by his seductive charm. She had loved him as a friend for years. But was she *in* love with him?

She did not know what to think. She needed to see him again to decide how to go on.

But where was he? It was almost a week since she'd left Ossing, and Grace said Adam had departed that same day. Where the devil had he gone? He was not at the house on Bruton Street. She had been watching for signs of his return, but the house remained dark.

Was he avoiding her? Now that his betrothal had ended, was he reluctant to face her after all? Was he regretting that glorious night and his words of love? Damn the man for making her crazy. If he ever did return and come to her, she was determined to make him suffer. The Merry Widows were right about that.

And afterward? When he'd been properly punished? Marianne knew exactly what she wanted to happen. She wanted him in her bed again.

Chapter 17

It had taken him almost a week, but he'd done it. It was difficult to obtain a special license when one was an ordinary mister with no title and did not have any special connection to the Archbishop of Canterbury. It meant long, tedious days of waiting around Doctors' Commons and plowing through endless bureaucratic nonsense. One would think he was trying to obtain permission to commit some heinous offense to human nature rather than to marry the woman he loved.

But he'd done it. Adam now held in his hand the special license with both their names on it. It was good for three months. Hopefully it would not take that long to persuade Marianne to accept his offer.

He had taken a room in a nearby inn while he waited for the license to be issued. He had not wanted her to see him at Bruton Street until he was prepared. If she knew he was at home, she might try to contact him, might even come to his front door. And he did not want that. Not yet. Instead, he had decided to stay away until he could present himself to her complete with a confession, a declaration, an offer of marriage, and a marriage license. As an added incentive, he'd also purchased a huge bouquet of her favorite pink lilies. He was ready now to make his case.

He had been practicing his speech for days. He

wanted it to be just right. He wanted her to know how much he loved and honored her, how sorry he was for deceiving her, even though he had not meant to do so, and how he wanted to repeat that one night of love every night for the rest of their lives.

Adam had always been confident in his dealings with women. But he'd never bared his soul to the woman he loved. He was as apprehensive as a schoolboy with his first infatuation. His stomach churned with nerves. What if she sent him packing?

For the first time in years, Adam knocked on the front door of number 7 Bruton Street. This interview was too important for a clandestine scramble over the balcony. He wanted this to be formal and proper and honorable.

The butler, Fyffe, opened the door. Only a slight lift of his eyebrows, quickly schooled, indicated his surprise at seeing Adam at the front door.

"Good afternoon, Fyffe. I've come to see Mrs. Nesbitt, if you please."

"I will see if she is at home, sir. Follow me to the drawing room, where you may wait."

Adam knew she was at home. But Fyffe was required to pretend she might not be, just in case she refused to see him. Marianne would never refuse to see him, though. Would she?

She had not expected him to come to the front door, but she was especially glad he had done so. It gave her time to prepare. When the footman came to announce that Adam waited in the drawing room, Marianne sent him to have the carriage made ready. He was given instructions to let her know as soon as it arrived at the front door. And with the help of Rose, she quickly changed her clothes.

She wondered what it meant that Adam had made a formal visit and hadn't climbed over the balcony. The only reason she could imagine was that he had something important to say. Or that he was feeling extraordinarily contrite. She rather hoped both things were true, but quelled her excitement. She could not let him see her feelings if her plan was to work.

Part of that plan was to look her best. She donned a new white cambric dress she'd never worn that she thought was especially pretty. It had a pleated fanlike frill at the neck that looked smart and stylish. The hemline was decorated in a beautiful design of tucks and white needlework. It was a lovely dress, but even better was the Prussian hussar cloak of Sardinian blue velvet, lined and edged with pink satin and trimmed with pink and blue knotted fringe. She fastened it at her throat with pink ribbons tied beneath the fan-pleated cambric frill of the dress. The entire effect was elegant and exceedingly fashionable, the cloak being the very latest mode. The finishing touch was a Moorish turban hat of the same blue velvet and pink trim.

Marianne could face anything wearing such a costume. She did not believe it was an exaggeration to say that she looked fabulous, which was precisely what she wanted for the role she was about to play in Adam's punishment.

She was dabbing a bit of tuberose scent at her ears when the footman returned to tell her the carriage was ready. Excellent. The stage was set. Now, if she could only be strong enough to play the role she had assigned herself. She could have used some of Wilhelmina's cordial just now.

She checked herself in the pier glass once more, grabbed her gloves and reticule, took a deep calming breath, and headed downstairs to the drawing room.

Adam's nerves were stretched to their limit. She had kept him waiting for over twenty minutes. He supposed he should be glad she had agreed to see him at all, but the wait was excruciating. Too jittery to sit, he had worn a path in her carpet as he paced back and forth.

He heard the sound of a carriage outside. Damn. Was she expecting another visitor? He sincerely hoped not. He would have to postpone his declaration and his offer until another time, and he was very anxious to get on with it. He wanted to know where he stood, and would not be happy to have to wait to find out.

He looked out the window to the street below and saw Marianne's own carriage at the door. Confound it all, she must be on her way out. That was likely why he'd been kept waiting—she was getting herself ready to go somewhere. But surely she would spare him a few minutes to pour his heart out to her.

He resumed pacing and mentally rehearsed his speech.

He heard footsteps in the hall and a moment later Marianne burst in. She beamed at the sight of him, looking so stunning she quite took his breath away.

"Adam! How lovely to see you. And in the drawing room, for once. How very singular. I am afraid I am on my way out, however, and cannot spare you the time just now. What beautiful lilies. Did you bring those for me? How exceedingly thoughtful of you."

She reached out to take the flowers from him, buried her face in them for a moment, then looked up and smiled. Her dimples were on full display, and he could not remember seeing her look so happy. Or so beautiful.

"You look positively delicious, my dear. That cloak is dazzling."

She smiled coquettishly. "It is rather cunning, is it not? I confess I am quite pleased with it. I wanted to look my best today. But really, Adam, I must run."

"I hope you can spare me a moment, my dear. There is something important I wish to say to you."

"Oh? Well, be quick if you will—I really am in

quite a hurry. Why don't I just put these lilies in a vase and you can tell me whatever it is you have to tell me? And then I simply must dash."

She glowed with some sort of excitement as she went to a marble-topped commode and placed the lilies on top, opened the doors in its base, and retrieved a Chinese porcelain vase. She kept her back to him as she held it up for consideration.

"And so what is it, Adam? If you are here to tell me that your betrothal has ended, you may be sure I already know. It was quite the on-dit for several days. I trust your heart is not broken."

He wished she would turn around. But she had apparently decided the Chinese vase would not do, and was now examining what appeared to be a Sevres vase decorated in shades of pink and pale turquoise.

"No, my heart was never involved, as you know."

She looked over her shoulder and smiled. "Then no great harm was done." She turned back to the lilies and began arranging them in the vase one by one.

"Marianne, would you mind turning around, please? I would prefer not to say what I have to say to your back."

"Oh? Well, all right." She shrugged and carried the vase and flowers to a tea table. She faced him and smiled, then proceeded to arrange the lilies.

It was not what he hoped for. He wanted her full attention, her eyes on his. No doubt when she heard what he had to say, she would stop fussing with the flowers and look at him.

"Marianne, I want you to know how glad I am that my betrothal has ended."

"Oh? Well, of course that girl was all wrong for you, as I told you from the start." She looked displeased with the arrangement of flowers, removed most of them, and began again.

This wasn't going as he'd planned. Her distraction

with the flowers was disconcerting, but he had not got to the main point yet.

"She was not the right woman, that is true. I am in love with someone else."

She continued to place flowers in the vase and did not look up. Or react. Damn. "You see, I have been in love with someone else for years, only I didn't realize it until it was almost too late." Suddenly, the practiced speech flew out of his head and the words spilled out in a jumbled rush while she continued to arrange the lilies.

"Don't you see, Marianne? It's you, it's always been you. Even when David was alive. I can't say for sure when it happened, but I probably fell in love with you the first moment we met. But I kept it hidden, of course. I would never have betrayed David's friendship. And so I buried my feelings for you. So deep and for so long, in fact, that I forgot about them, and convinced myself you were a close friend and nothing more. And since his death, I kept my love for you a secret, even from myself. It was only when I became engaged to Clarissa and you set out to find a lover that those long-buried feelings came alive again. When I realized I'd rather be with you than the woman I was to marry, I knew I'd made a huge mistake. But now that it's over, I don't want to keep my love a secret anymore. I want you to know how I feel. I love you. I don't think I can live without you, Marianne. You are the most important thing in my life, and I was a fool not to realize it. I have spent so many years making excuses for hiding my love—fearing rejection, feeling guilt for betraying the memory of David, feeling unworthy. None of those things matter anymore. Only the truth matters. And the truth is that I love you more than life, and I want to spend the rest of my days with you, if you will have me."

He stopped the rush of words to take a breath. Marianne had not looked up from her flowers. She removed one from the arrangement and replaced it on the other side, then picked up another and studied where to place it. She had not said a word.

"Marianne?"

No response.

"Marianne?"

She looked up and gave a sheepish giggle. "Oh, dear. Were you speaking to me? You must forgive me—my mind was wandering."

Her mind was wandering?

She looked at the arrangement again, gave a nod of approval, and took the vase to a small table in the window.

"You will think me the rudest creature on earth," she said as she pulled on her gloves, "but I am afraid I haven't heard a word you said. I am so distracted this afternoon."

"I was asking you to marry me, dammit," he said, his voice filled with frustration.

She tilted her head and gave him an indulgent smile. "Were you? How terribly sweet, Adam. You must be very disappointed that your betrothal was canceled. I am honored that you would ask me to take Clarissa's place. But quite frankly, even were I interested, I cannot marry anyone just now. I am too preoccupied with discovering the identity of the man who crept into my bed at Ossing."

"But, Marianne—"

"You see, he gave me such incredible pleasure, I really must seek him out and let him know I would be more than willing to be his mistress."

"But, Marianne—"

"I have not been able to stop thinking about him, you see. He was a fantastic lover."

"But, Marianne—"

"And between you and me, I am fairly confident it was Sir Neville Kenyon. In fact, I am hoping I can persuade him to admit it today. That is why I must dash. I am all aflutter with excitement."

"But, Marianne—"

"I am sure you will forgive my, my friend, but I really do not want to keep him waiting another moment."

Like quicksilver, she was at the door and out before he could take a breath. "I know you can show yourself out," she called as she descended the stairs. "Goodbye. Wish me luck!"

And she was gone.

Adam stood in stunned silence in the middle of the drawing room. He could not believe what had just happened. She hadn't even heard his declaration of love, and she had not taken his marriage proposal at all seriously.

Or had she?

Even were I interested, I cannot marry anyone just now.

Even were she interested. Which could only mean that she was not. Perhaps by her flippant response she had hoped to soften the blow of rejection by pretending not to take him seriously.

And damn it all to hell, she still thought it had been Kenyon in her bed.

He had to tell her the truth about that. He had meant to, but she had not let him get a word in. It had been the wrong time. He should never have tried to make a serious declaration of love when she was in a hurry and so obviously distracted. He would simply have to come back and try again.

"Dear God, Grace, it was the most difficult thing I've ever done."

Marianne had told the coachman to take her to Grace Marlowe's house. She had not known where else to go. Every time she needed a friend to talk to, a friend who was not Adam, she came to Grace's house. The other Merry Widows were usually there, too, but today Marianne had simply arrived unexpected and fretful and in need of commiseration. Grace had welcomed her warmly and was gently forcing her to drink a restorative cup of tea.

"The poor man must be brokenhearted," she said.

"Well, I did want to teach him a lesson, you know. But listening to his beautiful words of love and pretending not to hear them was painful, Grace. I wanted to weep. He said he loved me more than life. He said he could not live without me."

"Oh." Grace gave a sigh. "How terribly romantic. I do not know how you refrained from throwing yourself into his arms."

"It was an effort, I assure you." And it had taken an even more valiant effort not to burst into tears. What was she to do about a man who declared his love so beautifully? "And he said he's always loved me, Grace. For years. I had no idea. Even when David was still alive I had harbored a tiny infatuation for Adam. But I never, ever dreamed he cared that way about me. It is quite a revelation. And I don't know what to do about it."

"Do you love him, too?"

"Yes, I think so, but . . ."

"But?"

"But what about David? I don't want to replace David in my heart."

"You don't have to, you know. David will always be your first love. That will never change."

"No, it will not." But could Marianne accept a second love?

"Then there is nothing to keep you apart."

"Except that he wants to marry me."

Grace groaned. "Please do not tell me you feel bound to keep to that agreement among the Trustees not to marry again. The intent was that we should not allow one another to be forced into marriage by our families. But if Adam loves you and you love him—"

"It doesn't matter," Marianne said. "I cannot marry again, Grace. It has nothing to do with the Merry Widows. It is just . . . I cannot."

"Why?"

"I am Mrs. David Nesbitt. It is who I am and who I want to be. It is all I ever wanted to be. I do not want another husband."

"Are you certain?"

"Absolutely. But I still want a lover. I want that. I want Adam."

Grace gave her a look of disapproval. She still did not believe in this business of taking a lover. But, bless her heart, she did not scold. "I trust you are not going to keep him dangling for long," she said. "A man who loves you like that deserves better."

"I know. I won't keep him guessing for much longer, I promise. Just another day or two. Just long enough for him to know how it feels to have one's emotions tangled into knots."

Adam called upon Marianne again late that afternoon. He'd seen the carriage return and knew she was at home. But the inscrutable Fyffe left him standing at the door while he checked on his mistress's availability. When he returned, he told Adam that Mrs. Nesbitt was busy getting ready for the Benevolent Widows Fund ball at Hengston House and could not see him at this time.

It was a dismissal, pure and simple, and obviously at Marianne's instructions. The ball was not for several hours. She did not want to see him.

Adam was shaken by this unexpected attitude. He had tried to steel himself for rejection, but he never thought he would be dismissed so cavalierly. It hurt, dammit.

He was not, however, ready to give up. She still did

not know that he'd been the one in her bed at Ossing. If nothing else, he wanted to set her straight on that matter. He could not bear to think that she believed it was Sir Neville Kenyon. Kenyon, for God's sake! Even if she rejected Adam's love and his offer of marriage, he wanted her to know that he was the one who taught her the joys of sexual intimacy. By God, he wanted her to know that.

He met her in the receiving line at Hengston House, along with all the other patronesses as well as Lord and Lady Hengston. She was determined to dazzle him with her beauty yet again. She was dressed in a peach-colored silky dress that shimmered in the candlelight. Over it was a long sleeveless robe of net so fine it looked like gossamer. She smiled and offered her hand.

"May I hope for a dance this evening?" he asked. He would persuade her to take a walk during the set instead, and he would use the opportunity to tell her the truth.

"I am terribly sorry, Adam. I am afraid every dance is promised. Perhaps some other time."

Other guests waiting to move through the receiving line pressed him ahead and he had no chance to respond. But he definitely heard the sound of laughter from several of the patronesses. Had she told them of his offer? Were they laughing at him?

Damnation.

Several times during the night he sought her out between sets, but she was always with a group of people and never seemed willing to be steered away for a private conversation. He saw Kenyon approach at one point. She leaned over and whispered to Adam from behind her fan, "Here is Sir Neville to claim his dance. Perhaps I will yet be able to coax the truth out of him." Her eyes danced with merriment.

Adam could take no more. "It was not Kenyon in your bed at Ossing, dammit. It was me."

Her eyes twinkled over the edge of her fan and she laughed. "Oh, Adam, you are such a tease."

And off she went with Kenyon, flashing her dimples at the young man.

This was maddening. She did not seem ready to believe anything he said anymore. What was wrong with her?

Adam was stymied. He'd never expected it would be this difficult or this painful. He'd figured either she would reject him outright and ask him to remove himself from her life, or she would accept him and make him the happiest of men. But she had done neither. She had placed him in this monstrous limbo where he didn't know what she truly thought of him. She had not taken either his proposal or his confession about Ossing seriously.

He simply did not know what to do. But he was not quite ready to give up.

The next day he tracked down a florist who carried tuberoses. He sent her a small bouquet with a note.

It really was me at Ossing. And it was wonderful. You smelled as sweet as these flowers. I love you.

Later that day, he called upon her again. Fyffe looked ready to roll his eyes heavenward at the sight of Adam on the doorstep yet again, but he maintained his usual reserve. Once again, however, he kept Adam waiting at the door rather than inviting him inside. It was not a good sign.

"I am sorry, sir," Fyffe said when he returned, "but Mrs. Nesbitt is not at home."

Adam's heart sank. She was not at home to *him*.

"You may leave a card if you like."

Damned if he'd leave a card. He'd already left her a note that told her everything she needed to know. What more clear rejection did he need? He stormed away and heard Fyffe close the door behind him.

And so it was over. He'd done his best. There was nothing more to say. His declaration had put an awkward end to their friendship. She was embarrassed by his ardor and did not want to see him anymore. Once again, Adam had ruined everything. He ought to have kept his mouth shut, kept his wretched secrets to himself.

He'd meant it when he told her he did not think he could live without her. But he would have to learn to do so. That damned estate in Dorset was beckoning again. It might have to be his escape from the pain of watching their friendship slide into a polite acquaintance.

Damn her for making him feel like such a fool. And damn her for not wanting him.

Chapter 18

He was wearing a hole in his carpet, pacing the length of his sitting room. He was trying to decide what to do with his miserable life when he was distracted by the sound of something pinging against the glass of the balcony doors. It sounded like hail, but the skies were clear. How odd. He went to the doors, opened them, and stepped out onto the balcony.

"It's about time." Marianne stood on her balcony, hands on her hips, arms akimbo. She was smiling, thank God. "I've been flinging bits of gravel for a quarter hour. I was just about to hurl a large rock in hopes of breaking the glass to get your attention."

He smiled so broadly he felt sure his face would crack. She still wanted to see him, praise heaven. "Hullo, my dear. No need for such violence, I assure you."

"We'll see about that. You and I have some talking to do, Mr. Cazenove. If you know what's good for you, you'll jump over that damned railing and get over here."

"Ah, but I see no orchid on your balcony," he teased. "Are you certain I am welcome?"

She left the balcony, and returned a moment later with the potted plant in her hands.

"Here's the blasted orchid. Now haul yourself over

here before I lift my skirts and make the climb myself."

He grinned. "All right. Stand aside, my dear. Here I come."

He swung himself over the railing, and followed her into the sitting room. She stood before the fireplace, arms crossed over her chest.

He moved to touch her, but she stepped back.

"Explain yourself," she said in a tight voice. "I wish to know what made you do such a hateful thing. You must have known I'd learn it was you."

"I told you as much, more than once. In words and in writing."

"I already knew. I've known since the next day, in fact."

His eyes widened. "You knew? I thought you believed it was Kenyon."

She gave a sheepish smile. "That was punishment."

"Punishment?"

"Yes. My revenge for what you did to me. But I have decided you've been punished enough."

He heaved an audible sigh. "Thank God. So you were not ignoring all my declarations."

She smiled. "Not entirely."

"My love," he said, and reached out for her. But she brushed his hands away.

"First, I want an explanation," she said. "Why did you come to me that night? You were still committed to Clarissa. You knew it was wrong."

"Yes, I did. But I hadn't intended to make love to you when I came to your bedchamber."

"What *did* you intend, then? To have a cozy chat?"

He grinned. "Something like that. I came to tell you about Sherwood. I knew you were expecting him and I thought you should know what had happened. But you were asleep and you looked so beautiful—"

"Liar. You could not have seen how I looked. It was pitch-dark in that bed."

"I had a candle. But it was accidentally snuffed out as I undressed. I had not anticipated that inky darkness. And I thought all along you knew it was me. I had no idea you did not until at the end when you cut me to the quick by saying, 'Thank you, Julian.' "

Marianne laughed. "Did I say that?"

"Yes, and proceeded to fall dead asleep. I didn't know what to do, and finally decided to skulk away and never tell you. I thought you would hate me."

"I almost did. I was *so* angry with you. But I could never hate you, Adam."

"My love." He would not be stopped this time. He went to her and took her in his arms, and she allowed it, wrapping her own arms around his neck. "My love." He bent his head and kissed her.

Passion flared between them instantly. He devoured her mouth in a kiss to end all kisses. The most important kiss of a lifetime, marking the end of one phase of his life and the beginning of another. A kiss filled with undiluted passion and love and sheer joy at the rightness of it. He set up a frantic dance with her tongue while his hands found the curves of her buttocks and pressed her hard against his sex, so she would know how much he wanted her. She gave a little moan, and he pulled away.

"Adam, I—oh!"

He swept her up in his arms and headed toward her bedchamber. "You set out this Season to find a lover, my dear. I am determined you shall have him. Right now."

"Oh, yes, Adam. Yes!"

He entered the room, all the while kissing her neck and throat. He was about to place her on the bed, but decided to undress her first. And so he put her down and took her in his arms again, ravishing her mouth with his kiss.

"Thank God there are candles burning," he murmured against her neck. "I want to see you this time."

He put her away from him, turned her around, and began to untie the straps of her dress.

And then stopped. They both went still at the same moment. They were facing a large portrait of David, who smiled benevolently down upon them through the exquisite brushwork of Thomas Lawrence.

"Damn. I can't do this with him watching."

"Neither can I," she said. "Even though I do not think he would entirely disapprove. He loved us both, after all."

"Even so, this will not do." Adam pulled a chair in front of the portrait and stood upon it. The painting was large and with a heavy frame, but he somehow managed to remove it from the wall. He stepped down from the chair, hoisted the picture by its frame and carried it into the sitting room. He placed it against the wainscoting, with David's face turned to the wall. "Sorry, old chap. But I really do not want you as an audience for this, or any other performance."

He returned to the bedchamber to find Marianne staring at the blank space on the wall, a frown marking her brow. "Are we betraying him, Adam?"

"No. We loved him, but he is gone. Let us stop worrying about what he would have thought. We can never know, and it doesn't matter anyway." He turned her into his arms again. "This is all that matters."

He kissed her, and they were soon lost in each other again. But Adam wanted more. He spun her around and began to unfasten her dress.

Finally, when she was wearing no more than her chemise and corset, she began to undress him. When they were both naked, he held her apart and they drank their fill of each other, admiring and touching and exploring with their eyes only, uninhibited, unafraid, unashamed.

She was every bit as beautiful in the light as she'd felt in the dark. Slender, but curved and soft in all the right places.

"I never thought you could want me like this," she said. "I am not like all those other women you've had. I don't have the sort of voluptuous body you always seemed to admire."

He cupped her face in his hands. "I never wanted your body." He felt her stiffen and knew he'd wounded her vanity. "I wanted *all* of you. Not only your beautiful body, but your heart and soul as well."

"Oh, Adam."

"I love you, Marianne. Let me show you how much."

He laid her gently on the bed and began a full exploration of her body with his lips and tongue and hands. And Marianne was not passive. She made her own explorations and discoveries.

He loved her breasts and loved the way she cried out when he kissed them. His lips made a slow path down her abdomen to her belly and lower.

"I seem to recall," he whispered hoarsely, "that you particularly enjoyed this."

"Oh, God, yes!" she cried as his tongue stroked the most sensitive nub of her sex. He held on to her hips as she arched and bucked and finally shuddered beneath him.

And at the precise moment of her breaking point, he slid up her body and pressed his erection against her throbbing sex. He waited a moment, until she opened her eyes and looked into his.

"I love you, Marianne." He braced up on his forearms on either side of her, but before he could move, she reached down, found him, and guided him sweetly home.

After relishing their joining for a long moment, he set up a strong rhythm of deep, slow strokes. Then faster and faster until they both cried out, one after the other, in a wave of shared ecstasy.

Afterward, they lay quietly in each other's arms, sharing tender kisses and lingering looks.

"Will you ever forgive me?" he asked.

"Since you have introduced me to such pleasure, I am tempted to forgive you."

"I have been very selfish. I never wanted anyone else to have you."

She propped herself up on an elbow and looked down at him. "Are you to blame for all those other men who disappointed me in one way or another?"

He gave a shamefaced grin. "None of them would have suited you."

"Was Lord Hopwood's estate truly threatened by flooding?"

"I have no idea. It might have been. I only mentioned the possibility to him. Anything is possible during heavy rains."

"And Mr. Fitzwilliam with his wretched gardenias?"

"Did he send gardenias? How odd. I could have sworn I recommended lilies."

"And Sir Arthur Denney's gruesome cockfighting tales? Was that your doing?"

"I might have mentioned that David and I enjoyed a good sporting event. He must have thought I said *Mrs.* Nesbitt, the fool."

"And Sidney Gilchrist? What did you do to him? He was attentive one day, then avoiding me like the pox the next."

"Let's just say he did not feel he could measure up to the task."

Marianne burst into laughter. "Oh, Adam, how could you?"

"I was made crazy by my love for you. I was driven quite mad with visions of you naked like this with some other man."

"And what of Lord Julian? Did you engineer that accident?"

Adam sobered and frowned. "I am more sorry for that than you will ever know. I only meant to keep him up late and away from your bed as long as possible. I promise you I never meant to hurt him."

"I was told he tripped and fell."

"Over my leg."

"Adam!"

"It was an accident. Truly it was. I never set out to cause him any physical harm. I was devastated by what happened."

Even so, they laughed together over poor Lord Julian's plight, and blessed the serendipity of that fall, for it brought Adam and Marianne together at last.

"You truly are incorrigible," she said. "But how could a woman not be impressed by a man who goes to such lengths to keep other men away from her? Such a man would have to be either completely mad or in love."

"And I am both. Madly in love with you. When I came to you that day, bearing my pile of lilies, I had a wonderful speech I'd rehearsed, but you pretended not to hear."

"I heard every word."

"You said you could not marry anyone until you discovered the identity of your secret lover. Well, you know who it was. You knew all along, you wretch. Does that mean you are now ready to consider marriage? I procured a special license."

She gave a little start. "You have a license?"

"Shall I get down on one knee, my love?"

She grew silent, and a sudden pang of uncertainty gripped his insides.

"I thought you understood," she said, sitting up against a pile of pillows, the sheet covering her breasts. "I do not wish to marry again. I only wanted . . . this."

Adam flung off the covers and walked to the end of the bed. "Only this?" His arm swept over the bed. His voice rose in anger. "But you cannot have 'only this' from me."

"What do you mean? You've known all along that I don't mean to marry again."

"That was before . . . *this*." He made a sweeping gesture over the bed again.

"It doesn't change anything," she said in a small voice. "I wanted a lover, that's all. And you said you wanted to be that lover. I thought you understood. I don't want another husband. I never have."

His heart dropped all the way down into his gut, where it twisted and coiled into a knot of cold anger. "Because I can never replace your precious David."

She did not answer, but she did not have to.

"Even though he never gave you what I just gave you? Even though he was never able to make you cry out in pleasure like I can? Even though I love you as much as he ever did? Still, I am not good enough to replace him?"

"It has nothing to do with being good enough. It's just . . . I can't. I'm sorry, Adam."

Hot anger seared the back of his throat so he could barely swallow. His voice came out coarse and raspy. "And so this is all you'll ever want from me? To be your lover?"

"Well . . . yes. And my friend, too, of course."

"Damn it all to hell." Adam rooted about for his clothes and began to dress. "You haven't figured it out yet, have you, Marianne? You can't just have a lover. You will never be the sort of woman who has a simple affair."

"Why do you keep saying that? Of course I am that sort of woman. It would not be precisely simple with you, of course, but—"

"But you want the freedom to take other lovers if you want. You want your damned independence."

"It's not about other lovers. Or independence. I just don't want another marriage."

He tugged on his breeches, not bothering with the

small clothes underneath. "Damn you, Marianne. I don't want a simple affair with you. *I* want more."

"Just because you're determined to get married? To please your father?"

"No, dammit, because I love you."

"And I love you, Adam. So why can't we love each other and enjoy each other without the yoke of marriage?"

"Yoke? Is that what you think it means? Is that how you thought of your marriage to David?"

"No, of course not."

"But marriage to *me* would be a yoke?"

She heaved a sigh and it only made him angrier.

"You are deliberately misunderstanding me," she said. "It's nothing to do with you, Adam. I don't wish to marry anyone. Ever. I am Mrs. David Nesbitt and always will be. It's who I am. I don't want to be married to anyone else. And remember, too, that I am most likely unable to have children. I would not burden you, or any other man, with my inability to produce an heir."

"You think that matters to me?"

"Isn't that why you became engaged to Clarissa? So you would have a fertile young wife to give you a family?"

He went silent at that. It had indeed been one of the primary reasons for his betrothal. "That would not matter to me, as long as I had you." His throat had grown tight with emotion, and his words were spoken so low, he was not even sure she heard them.

"I am barely out of black, Adam, but I am still David's widow. That's who I want to be."

"David. Always David. I never could compete with the man and now I can't compete with his ghost." There was a fury inside him such as he'd never known. He shoved his bare feet into his shoes. "Enjoy your freedom, Mrs. Nesbitt. I will not be your lover. Find someone else who can contend with David's ghost."

Adam walked into the sitting room and retrieved the portrait of David and brought it back into the bedchamber. He didn't have the energy, or the desire, to rehang it. He propped it against the wall facing the bed.

"Here's your beloved husband to watch over you again. For I shall not be doing it for him any longer. Good-bye, Marianne."

He slung the rest of his clothing over his shoulder and strode out of the room, and out of her life.

Marianne spent the rest of the afternoon and evening curled up in the bed that still held Adam's unique smell. She did not eat or drink. She cried and cried until there were no tears left to her.

She was sure she had done the right thing, but did it have to hurt so much? She wished Adam could understand. She could shake off her mourning clothes, enjoy Society events, and even take a lover. But she could not remove David from her life. He *was* her life. And always had been. She'd known him and loved him since she was a girl. Their fathers had arranged a betrothal when she and David were still children. And his family had taken her in and made her one of their own after her father died. She was a Nesbitt now. She could not think of herself in any other way.

She did love Adam, though, and it pained her that she had hurt him. But he had been there, right beside her and David, all those years. Surely he understood how much her identity was tied to her husband.

Yes, Adam gave her something David never had, something wonderful. But could she sacrifice her identity for it? It was too painful a decision to contemplate.

She brooded for several lonely days before venturing out into Society again. Marianne was still feeling unsteady and fragile when she attended a rout party given by Lady Morpeth. She'd hoped the lively conversation and varied company would make her feel more like herself again, but they did not. She felt sullen and moody and was sorry she'd come. She was approached by several gentlemen who seemed keen to win her attention, but she was no longer interested. She wanted none of them. There was only one man she'd ever want as a lover, but he would not have her without a marriage license.

She was moping over Adam's intransigence when she saw Viola Cazenove making her way through the crowd toward her. Damn. The last person she wanted to chat with was Adam's mother.

"Ah, Marianne," she said in a breathless voice when she finally broke through the teeming crowd of people. "I am so glad to have found you."

"How nice to see you again, Mrs. Cazenove."

Viola waved a hand in a fluttery dismissal. "Tell me, my dear, have you seen Adam?"

"Not in several days."

"Blast the boy, I fear he is in hiding over that Leighton-Blair business. I will tell you frankly, my dear, that I was never so glad to hear of a broken betrothal in all my life. Adam's father was thrilled because Clarissa is such a beauty. Men can be so shallow that way, can't they? But the girl was as wrong for Adam as she could be. You agree with me on that, I believe."

"Actually, I do. And I told him so, too."

Viola laughed. "Good for you! He needs someone who will speak plainly with him. But now I am concerned. He hasn't shown his face anywhere, and it makes him look like a lovesick brokenhearted fool. He needs to get back into Society and prove that he is not a beaten man. But he's never home when I call. I don't know what he's up to. I was hoping you knew."

Marianne frowned. Had he disappeared on her account? Was he hiding from her? "I'm sorry. I haven't seen him."

"Well, if you do, tell him his mother wants him to buck up and get back in the game."

"Yes, ma'am. I will tell him." If she ever saw him again.

Viola placed a hand on Marianne's arm and leaned in close. "May I confess something to you? Since your David passed on, I have been rather hoping Adam would court you."

"Me?"

"I have always had a hunch that he was in love with you."

"Oh." Dear God, how had she known?

"But I think he feels it would be a betrayal of his friendship for David to act on it." Viola looked at her intently, then said, "But David is dead, so it would not be a betrayal, would it? One cannot hold on to the past forever, after all."

Marianne's throat went dry and she could not find her voice.

"I beg your pardon, my dear, I have embarrassed you. I should let my son speak for himself. And if he ever does, you may be sure that his mother will welcome you with open arms."

Marianne did not know what to say. Turbulent emotions raged inside her. Was she truly beginning to wish she had not rejected Adam's offer? And why was she suddenly comparing Viola Cazenove's warmth with Lavinia Nesbitt's chilly disapproval?

She said a few awkward words to Viola and made her slow exit from the party. She could not think clearly. Her head was spinning. She had to leave.

When she returned home, she found herself standing at her sitting room window, watching the house next door. Adam's windows were dark. Had he left London? Was he out carousing with Lord Rochdale? Or was he perhaps sitting alone in the dark, brooding just as she was?

She loved Adam. She wanted him, wanted his body

and his lovemaking. She wanted his friendship, but even that had been denied her.

Marianne was grateful he had shown her the pleasures of sexual love. In fact, now that she had sampled it, she did not know how long she could go without it. But she could not imagine giving herself to another man.

She walked to the desk, where she found her old list with the names of potential lovers lined up in two neat rows. Not a single gentleman on the list interested her anymore. It was as she studied that list that she realized Adam was right. She did not want a casual affair now and then with one of them. She *did* want more. She wanted her best friend back. And her lover. She wanted them both, and maybe a bit more as well.

Chapter 19

Marianne stood in the entry hall of her mother-in-law's town house, prepared to endure her weekly visit despite her prickly mood. She was still unsettled by a torrent of conflicting emotions. A housemaid stood waiting as Marianne untied the ribbons of her bonnet to hang on one of the wooden pegs lined up in a row above an umbrella stand.

Her hands froze. She stared at the slightly battered and worn tricorne hat that had always hung there. It had belonged to William Nesbitt, David's father. Lavinia insisted that it remain there, where William had last placed it before he died. It had hung on the same peg for fourteen years.

All at once, the sight of that hat sent a wave of emotion washing over Marianne, a wave so strong it had her mind whirling in drunken circles and caused her to sway unsteadily on her feet.

"Mrs. Nesbitt? Are you all right?"

Marianne made an effort to compose herself. "Yes, Patsy, I'm fine. Just . . . a bit of the headache."

William's hat. She could not take her eyes from the hat. Its presence in the hall represented only one of a thousand little ways in which Lavinia Nesbitt had held on to her husband's memory. Held on to the past with a tenacious grip and wouldn't let go.

Marianne had been determined to be a different

sort of widow from her mother-in-law, a modern open-minded widow who lived in the present. Who wore bright colors and had lovers.

But who could not let go of David.

Staring at William's hat was like looking into a mirror. She was no different from Lavinia, after all. She held on to David's name and her identity as David's widow just as Lavinia had held on to that old hat. Marianne had not been able to let go of the past.

But what was she holding on to? A memory of love? An illusion of perfect love that had lacked physical element she now knew to be so important? And what had made her think a memory of love was somehow superior to a living, breathing, here-and-now love? What a fool she'd been. She had always believed she *could* not love again, when the truth was she *would* not allow herself to love again.

Dear God. She was going to end up just as bitter and lonely as David's mother. She was going to sacrifice her life to the memory of a dead man.

She gave her head a shake. No. No, she would not. She would *not* end up like Lavinia Nesbitt. There was no need to. She had a man who loved her, a man she loved—really loved—who wanted to make a new life with her. And yet she had turned him down in order to become a human shrine, something she had sworn never to do.

One cannot hold on to the past forever, after all.

Marianne sent up a silent prayer of thanks to Viola Cazenove for helping her to see the light. She pulled the bonnet ribbons beneath her chin and tied them into a fresh bow.

"Are you leaving, ma'am? You're not staying for tea with the mistress?"

"No, Patsy, I'm not staying after all. Please give my regrets to my mother-in-law. Tell her . . . tell her a light was held up to my eyes and I have become blinded by it."

"Ma'am?" The maid looked thoroughly confused.

Marianne laughed. "Just tell her I could not stay. I will see her next week."

And she bounded down the front steps feeling as though she'd been reborn.

It was several hours past midnight. She watched from the window as the hackney coach dropped Adam off. He was a bit unsteady on his feet when he alighted. He must be drunk. Was that how he'd been spending his time? Drinking and carousing and God only knew what else? Because of her?

Poor Adam. She hoped it was not too late to save him, to save them both. Now that she had freed herself from martyrdom and allowed herself to love Adam, the strength of that love took her breath away. He was everything to her that David had been, and more. She never felt as vital, as unguarded, as real, with anyone else she knew. Certainly not with any of the men who'd been on her dratted list. No matter which other men might come into her life, none would ever be able to give her what Adam could. None would be her best friend *and* her lover. Not even David had managed both. Only Adam gave her everything. She had been wrong all along, wrong about both men.

She waited a long while before moving from her position in the sitting room window, until all the lights in his windows had gone dark, and until she was confident that he would be asleep. Only then did she let herself out onto the balcony.

She hoped to God no one saw her, standing in a nightdress and wrapper, about to climb into a man's window in the middle of the night. But she did not let that worry her. She was determined on her course.

It was a difficult maneuver in a nightdress. It would have been difficult in any sort of dress. Climbing balconies was most definitely a man's job, unless a woman could be allowed to wear trousers. Perhaps she ought to have done that—found an old pair of David's trousers. It would have made the climb easier.

When she managed to get her legs over the spearlike finials of the railing, she almost fell onto the other side. She hoped the sound had not awakened him.

She turned the handle of the glass door and blessedly found it unlatched. She would have felt rather foolish if it had been locked and she had to climb back over the railing. Very slowly and very quietly, she opened the door.

Adam's house was a twin to her own. The balcony led to a sitting room, beyond which was a bedchamber. She approached the door to that room, which was slightly ajar. The drone of soft snoring told her Adam was sound asleep, just as she hoped.

She closed the door to the sitting room and drew the draperies across the windows in the bedchamber. Then she loosened the bed curtains and pulled them closed on both sides of the bed. When she was convinced it was as dark as it could possibly be, she untied her wrapper, dropped her nightdress to the floor, and crawled into Adam's bed.

It was a wonderful dream. Marianne was lying practically on top of him, naked, and smelling of tuberoses. He reached up and touched soft, real flesh and came awake.

My God.

He wrapped his arms around her. "Marianne, my love."

She wriggled against him. "How do you know it's me? It's too dark to be certain. I might be anyone, some stranger who sneaks uninvited into your bed, hiding behind a cloak of darkness. Such things have been known to happen, you know."

"I do not care how dark you make it in here, my dear. I would know you anywhere." He rubbed a hand against her bare bottom. "I came to know you very well in the darkness. And what, may I ask, are you doing here?"

"I have come to ask a favor."

"A favor? At this hour? And may I assume that you came over the balcony?"

"I did. You should try it sometime in a nightdress, catching on those blasted finials every minute. It's not easy, I tell you."

"But you did it anyway. For the first time ever."

"It was important. I have that favor to ask."

"Ah, yes, your favor. I suppose you wish me to do you a favor of making love to you."

"Well, now that you mention it, I would like that very much." She caught his hand as it stroked her breast. "But first . . . remember that list of potential lovers you helped me review?"

He groaned. "How could I forget it?"

"I have created a new list."

"Oh, God." He maneuvered himself out from under her and sat up on the edge of the bed. "Do not tell me you want me to help evaluate another set of candidates."

"Actually, that is precisely what I was hoping."

"Dammit, Marianne. You go too far." He stood up and walked naked to the sitting room door and opened it. "I think it best that you leave."

"Oh, don't be such an old poop, Adam. I need your help."

"And so you came to offer your body in exchange for more advice on how to secure another lover?"

"I think you should see the list."

"Dammit, I don't want to see the bloody list." He went to the bedroom window and tugged on the draperies to let in a bit more moonlight.

Marianne came up behind him and pressed her naked body against his. His own treacherous body reacted instantly. He tried to move away, but she kept an arm about his waist, and her hand slowly crept lower. With her other hand, she thrust a folded piece of parchment at him.

"Read the list, Adam. It shows only those gentlemen whom I would ever consider for a lover. Read it."

Damnation. She was going to be the death of him, seducing him with one hand and killing him with the other. He unfolded the parchment.

There was only one name on it. His.

He grabbed the hand that had crept down too far for his peace of mind, and swung her around. "What does this mean?"

"Isn't it obvious? You are the only one, Adam."

"Wonderful. But you still only want a lover, and I have said that I will not oblige you in this. It's all or nothing with me."

"But you see, Adam, here's my dilemma. If there is only one name worthy of my list, then what is the point of the list?"

"I beg your pardon?"

"If I can only ever accept one man in all the world as my lover, and never anyone else as long as I live, and if I happen to love that man to distraction anyway, then why not just marry the fellow and be done with it?"

His heart did a little flip-flop in his chest. Did she mean what he thought she meant? His arms came around her and his erection pressed against her stomach. "Do I understand that you are ready to entertain an offer of marriage?"

"Are you offering?"

"The offer stands, my love. There is nothing I want more." He released his hold on her and went down on one knee.

"Oh, Adam. It's a lovely gesture, but we're both naked as the day we were born. I do not think this is quite necessary."

"It is absolutely necessary." He buried his face against her belly and ran his tongue in circles around her navel.

"Oh, dear. I think you're right."

He lifted his mouth just long enough to ask, "Will you do me the very great honor of marrying me, Mrs. Nesbitt?"

"Oh, my. I think I had better. I suspect you will not finish this otherwise."

"Quite so. Consider it blackmail." His tongue dipped lower.

"Oh, dear God. Consider it successful blackmail. Yes, I will marry you, Adam. I am sorry it took me a whole week to figure out that you were right. But please, *please,* will you take me to your bed so we can do this properly?"

"We are doing it properly."

His tongue parted the folds of her sex, and her knees buckled until she collapsed on the floor. They never made it to the bed. Instead, they both expressed their love and the joy in their new commitment in a bout of lovemaking that began tenderly and sweetly, grew more urgent, then frenzied, and finally was mutually explosive as they reached the peak of pleasure together on the Aubusson carpet.

Afterward, he scooped up her limp body, took her to his bed, and tucked her up snugly against him. Though she felt drowsy and languorous, she did not fall asleep. She lay in his arms, enjoying the gentle stroke of his hand against her hip.

"Marianne, I want you to know that I will try to be the very best husband I can be to you. I will love you and cherish you and keep you close all my life, even though I may not be the most perfect man in the world. I can never hope to be the man David Nesbitt was—"

She pressed a finger to his lips. "Stop. No more comparisons with David. Remember when I said one of the reasons I never wanted to marry again was because he had been the love of my life? Well, I have discovered something in the last week. Each day without you, I grew more miserable. Yes, I had the freedom to do whatever I wanted, to flirt with other men, to seek out another lover. But I found I wanted none of that. I didn't need that freedom after all. I needed you."

"My love." He put his arms around her and pulled her close.

"And it finally dawned on me," she said, "that I had everything all turned around in my mind. I had always thought David was the love of my life and you were my best friend. But that's not true. David was my best friend and *you* are the love of my life."

He buried his face in her hair and held her tight while he waited for the swell of emotion inside him to subside. Finally, he lifted his lips and whispered into her ear. "And you are both to me. And everything. Friend and lover. Soul mate. Partner. Love of my life. Everything."

He kissed her tenderly, with all the joy of the moment and promise of the future.

When they pulled apart at last and looked into each other's eyes, Adam's heart soared as it never had before. His life seemed to fall into place in that moment. All the years of reckless living and womanizing had simply been restless compensation for the one thing he could never have. His best friend's wife.

Thank you, David, for leaving her to me. Did you always know? Did you know she was all I needed to make my life complete?

"And so," he said, "I will honor my promise to David to look after you. For the rest of our lives. And we'll be happy, Marianne. We'll tear down those damned balconies—by God, we'll tear down the adjoining walls. We'll make a new, grander house, one out of two. Big enough to raise a family, if we're lucky.

Maybe we'll have children and maybe we won't. But we'll always have each other, and that's more important. You will always be first with me, if we have a dozen children or none. And I will always love you. I promise to love you as much as David ever did."

She reached down and touched him. "If you please, Adam, could you love me more?"

And he did.

Read on for an excerpt from

Just One of Those Flings

Next in the Merry Widows series by
Candice Hern,
Coming August 2006

Beatrice Campion, the Countess of Somerfield, adjusted the gilt girdle around her waist and fluffed the blouson that fell over it. She felt positively naked in this dratted costume. She didn't know what had possessed her to wear something so revealing—even her toes were bare in the gold sandals that laced up her feet—but, then, that was the fun of a masquerade, was it not? To be a little bold, a little shocking. Her niece, Emily, had certainly been shocked, but only because she feared Beatrice would draw attention away from her. But it had taken only a moment before Emily realized that no one would take note of an elderly, widowed chaperone, no matter how provocatively dressed.

"After all," she had said, "you will be gathered along the wall with the other chaperones and dowagers, and no one is likely to take note of you. Indeed, I cannot imagine why you bothered to wear a costume at all when a simple domino would have sufficed."

"My dressmaker insisted it was just the thing," Beatrice had said in her own defense, "that classical garb was exceedingly fashionable."

"And it would be," Emily said, "on someone not so . . ."

She appeared to have literally bitten her tongue.

Beatrice laughed and then finished the thought. "So old?"

Emily shook her head, cheeks flushing prettily, and then changed the subject to the advantages of her own frothy costume.

Beatrice did not care what her niece thought. She did not feel at all elderly tonight. Not in such a costume. In fact, even at the advanced age of thirty-five, something about the way the tiny pleats of yellow silk felt against her body made her feel quite . . . womanly. Sensual, even. Especially when a certain gentleman kept staring at her.

She wondered who he was. There was no clue to his identity beneath the exotic costume, which she presumed to be Indian. Did she know him? Is that why she so often found him staring at her? Even when her back was turned, she could feel his gaze on her, like a naked caress that sent a tingling through the fine hairs at the back of her neck.

What sort of man could make a woman's body react so, simply by looking at her? And what sort of brazen woman felt the urge to display that body to him with subtle movements she knew made the dress cling more closely?

Beatrice shook her head to clear it. This awareness of her body and how a man might perceive it was something entirely new. She had become acutely aware in recent weeks of how men looked at her, and even more aware of her own reaction to them. She had been a widow for three years and missed the physical intimacy she'd shared with her husband. Though she had no wish to marry again, she had lately begun to feel a longing for that intimacy. And when a man looked at her in a way that left no question as to what he was thinking, Beatrice did not feel shock or outrage, as a respectable widow should. In fact, shameful as it was to admit, she found she rather liked it.

She blamed it on her friends, with all their frank

talk of late about lovers and lovemaking. They called themselves the Merry Widows in private, though in public they maintained very proper respectability. When Penelope, Lady Gosforth, had confessed to taking a lover, she somehow managed to convince the rest of them to do the same. Or at least to make an effort to do so. None of them, so far, had actually succeeded. Except, perhaps, for Marianne Nesbitt, who was even at that moment attending a house party at the estate of Lord Julian Sherwood, whom she was likely to take to her bed. That had certainly been her plan.

Beatrice was rather glad her dressmaker had convinced her to wear the Greek chiton. She had not deliberately worn the clingy silk dress in order to capture a man's attention—or had she?—but it had certainly done the job. She wondered if the unknown gentleman was going to ogle her from afar all night, or if he would ever actually speak to her, or even ask her to dance.

She watched a couple leave the room arm in arm— for a private tryst?—and thought again of her friends. Marianne would very likely return from the party full of the details of her own romantic encounter. That had been part of their Merry Widows' agreement, to be candid among themselves about their sexual activities. Penelope, who had wasted no time in finding a new lover in town, had certainly been candid. As Beatrice felt the eyes of the intriguing stranger on her again, all that frank speech came back to mind.

"He's coming!"

Beatrice pretended nonchalance at Lady Wallingford's urgent whisper, though her stomach muscles twitched in anticipation. "Who?" she asked in a disinterested tone.

Lady Wallingford uttered a mocking little snort. "You know who. That striking-looking man dressed as a maharaja, the one's been staring at you all night.

The one you've been pretending not to notice. But I've seen your glance stray in his direction more than once."

Beatrice glared at her friend as if to deny that she'd done any such thing, but was undone by the knowing twinkle in the eyes behind the jeweled Elizabethan mask. She returned a sheepish grin and asked, "Who is he, Mary? Do you know?"

"I have no idea. We did not have a receiving line, as you know, so that everyone could keep their identities secret, if they desired. But he had to have an invitation to get past our majordomo. So I must have invited him."

"Unless he used someone else's invitation."

"He could have done that, I suppose," Mary said. "I certainly do not recognize him. But with the mask and the turban, he could be Wallingford, for all I know."

"I doubt your husband would look at me the way this maharaja has done."

"If he does," Mary said, "he'd better not let me catch him doing it."

Beatrice looked at her friend, and they each burst into laughter at the thought of the portly, reserved Wallingford flirting with another woman.

"Dance with me."

Beatrice gave a start at the deep voice, then turned to find the unknown maharaja standing before her with a hand outstretched. He was even more intriguing up close. Mary was right about the mask and turban being an effective disguise. There were only a few hints of his true identity: dark eyes behind the mask, a well-shaped mouth below, a firm jaw, and a very slight cleft in the chin. He was above average in height, though not overly tall, and had a powerful build set off by broad shoulders. Beatrice had the impression that he was about her own age or perhaps slightly older. And extremely virile. Every inch of her skin, even to the very roots of her hair, tingled to be so close to him. *Who was he?*

"Dance with me," he repeated in that rich, deep voice, pitched low and mellow.

It was not a request. It was a demand. Or more like a fait accompli, as though he'd known she wanted to dance with him, as if she'd willed him to her side somehow.

Beatrice wanted nothing more than to take that proffered hand, but her gaze was inevitably drawn to the dance floor, where Emily danced with young Lord Ealing. She was charged with chaperoning her niece while her mother, Beatrice's sister Ophelia, was indisposed with a broken leg. At an event such as this, where the rules of propriety were loosened a bit, one really had to keep an eye on the headstrong girl. Beatrice wasn't here for her own enjoyment.

But those smoldering dark eyes beneath the mask beckoned.

"Go ahead," Mary said, giving her a discreet nudge. "I'll look after her."

Beatrice looked again at the tempting hand, then at her friend. "You don't mind?"

"Of course not. She's my niece, too, after all." Mary was the sister of Emily's father. But as she was a mere viscountess, Ophelia, always with an eye to the best advantage, had chosen her higher-ranking sister to act as Emily's chaperone. "Go on and dance. Enjoy yourself."

"Thank you, Mary." Beatrice took a deep breath, and placed her hand in the maharaja's.

Since neither of them was wearing gloves—another impropriety one could risk at a masquerade, for the sake of the costume—the shock of skin against skin was momentarily disconcerting. He softly caressed her fingers in a manner that caused her breath to catch. Hearing that tiny gasp, he smiled, then brought her fingers to his lips. Instead of a chaste salute, however, he flicked the tip of his tongue over her knuckles, very discreetly, so that not even Mary would realize what he'd done. Unless she noted the sudden stiffening of Beatrice's spine and the involuntary shiver that danced along her shoulder blades.

Before she could entirely compose herself, the maharaja had placed her still-tingling fingers on his arm and led her toward the dance floor.

Beatrice mentally ticked off all the dark-haired, dark-eyed gentleman of her acquaintance, but could reconcile none of them to the man at her side. "Do I know you, sir?"

"I doubt it."

Though she, too, was masked, Beatrice was quite certain her costume was no disguise. Most of her friends had recognized her. "Do you know me?"

"You are Artemis, the Huntress. A most beautiful huntress."

"Thank you, sir. But do you not recall what vengeance Artemis has been known to wreak against men who stare at her?"

He smiled. "Ah, yes. The unfortunate Actaeon. But you were not bathing in private, so you must forgive me. I was overcome by your beauty."

"You are not afraid, then? I do have a weapon, you know." She grinned and gestured at the quiver and bow on her shoulder.

"As do I." He indicated a large jeweled dagger in his belt. "But mine is quite real, I assure you, whereas yours is merely decorative, I think."

"Then perhaps I am the one who should be afraid."

He turned to look at her, an intense expression in those dark eyes. "Perhaps."

Lord, who was this man?

"We have not met before?" she asked again.

"Unlikely. I've been away from London for several years. Away from England, in fact."

"Oh." He obviously was not going to be forthcoming with his identity. It was an unspoken rule at masquerades that one was not required to reveal oneself until the unmasking at midnight, so Beatrice did not press him.

He took his place opposite her and let his gaze slide over her as they waited for the music to begin. She felt more naked than ever beneath that warm gaze as he studied the pleated silk that fell sensuously along her hips and thighs. She stood up taller under his scrutiny, stretching her spine and thrusting her breasts forward.

What was wrong with her? She'd never behaved in such a wanton manner in her life. When his eyes returned to hers, she was so enveloped in that warm, dark gaze that they might have been alone rather than in a crowded ballroom. She hadn't been so affected by a man's presence since Somerfield passed away. Her husband had sometimes had that same look in his eyes. A look of raw desire.

The music started and brought Beatrice back to earth. She loved to dance and tried to concentrate on the figures being set by the lead couple. But she was so thoroughly distracted by the exotic stranger that she tripped once or twice. His hand steadied her each time, distracting her even more.

When the dance called for their bare hands to join, it was nearly electric. Skin against skin, sending unspoken messages. Beatrice felt awash in pure unfettered desire, the air around her heavy with it, so that every move was tinged with sensual promise. She had almost forgotten how potent such feelings could be.

When they weren't touching, Beatrice took pleasure simply in watching him. He moved with a powerful grace, like a large tiger she'd once seen at Polito's Menagerie, arrogant, full of masculine confidence. His costume was unlike any garment she'd ever seen, consisting of a long skirted coat richly and elaborately embroidered with gold, worn over trousers that fell in loose folds around his feet, which were shod in slippers that curled up at the toe. There were jewels around his neck and on his turban. The total effect was surprisingly masculine. Perhaps it was the dagger. Or perhaps it was the man himself.

Beatrice thought once again about her friends, the Merry Widows. She had told them she had no time for lovers this year, not with Emily's Season to oversee and her own two young daughters underfoot. But this man, this stranger, made her feel that she could make time.

When the dance, at long last, came to an end, the maharaja took her by the hand and led her from the dance floor.

"Come, Artemis" he said. "Neither of us is interested in dancing. At least, not this sort of public dancing."

His words sent a rush of heat through her veins, for she did not misunderstand their meaning. Her throat went hot and dry so that she feared she could not speak.

He asked for no words, however, but simply led her out of the ballroom—and through the doors that opened onto a terrace. He drew her outside. There were a dozen or so people standing about the terrace, ladies fanning themselves, couples in quiet conversation. The maharaja took quick note of it all, then captured her hand again and conducted her down the curving stone staircase that led to the formal garden below.

Chinese paper lanterns had been placed throughout the garden, and several couples could be seen strolling along the gravel paths. The maharaja guided her down a pathway, then doubled back and went down another, and then another, apparently seeking privacy. Finally, he turned away from the formal pathways and plantings, and pulled her around to the side of the house.

It was quiet, save for the soft strains of the music

inside, and thoroughly deserted. And very dark. The moon was hidden behind a thick bank of clouds and there were no lanterns nearby.

The exotic stranger positioned himself with his back against the wall, then pulled Beatrice against him with a single rough jerk, wrapping one arm tightly around her waist. With his other hand, he stroked her arm. The brush of his knuckles against the bare flesh sent a shiver of desire in its path. All her awareness followed his touch, every sensation enhanced by the darkness and the mystery of the man. She could not see his face, even the parts left uncovered by the mask. But she felt his firm body pressed to hers, and the unique scent of him—a masculine musk tinged with something else—sandalwood?—sprang sharp in her nostrils. She did not need to see him to be thoroughly aware of every part of him.

"I want you, Artemis."

"I know." Her voice came out raspy, breathless.

"And you want me."

"Yes." There was no denying it.

"Then let us have each other." He smiled, then lowered his head and kissed her.

All your favorite romance writers
in one place

SIGNET ECLIPSE

Dakota Dreams by Madeline Baker

Sworn to avenge the death of his wife, Nathan Chasing Elk sets
off on a perilous journey of danger, destiny,
and unexpected passion.
0-451-21686-5

All's Fair in Love and War by Alicia Fields

The *Goddesses* series continues with the story of Athena,
the wild and free goddess of the hunt.
0-451-21735-7

Lady Anne's Dangerous Man by Jeane Weston

Lady Anne was eager to marry until her fiancé conspired
to have her virtue stolen. Now she must trust a
notorious rake with her life—and her heart.
0-451-21736-5

Sweet Water by Anna Jeffrey

When Terry Ledger buys a Texas town on eBay, he never
plans to fall in love with it—or its unofficial leader, the
fiery Marisa Rutherford.
0-451-21737-3

penguin.com